KILL COUNT

A DETECTIVE MARCY KENDRICK THRILLER

THEO BAXTER

INKUBATOR
BOOKS

Published by Inkubator Books
www.inkubatorbooks.com

Copyright © 2024 by Theo Baxter

Theo Baxter has asserted his right to be identified as the author of this work.

ISBN (eBook): 978-1-83756-410-1
ISBN (Paperback): 978-1-83756-411-8
ISBN (Hardback): 978-1-83756-412-5

1

THE DANCING QUEEN

EL VIBORA

The bright flashing lights rotated on the ceiling, vibing with the music in the club. It wasn't my scene, but then I wasn't there for a good time.

I headed for the bar and ordered a Hornitos Tequila on the rocks. Then turned and leaned back against the bar counter as I scanned the room. Young, nubile bodies writhed against each other on the dance floor. The party atmosphere was electric, and it seemed everyone in Los Angeles wanted to partake. However, I was only interested in one of those bodies.

"That'll be fifteen, man," the bartender said, grabbing my attention.

I tossed him a twenty and grabbed my drink. "Keep it."

I turned back to the dance floor to track the woman I was after. I found her in the middle of the floor surrounded by sycophants. Ruby Gold. That wasn't her real name of course, but her porn name. When she'd first arrived in LA, she'd been plain Brenda Sheller, a young woman from Lansing, Michigan, with blonde hair and brown eyes that held the warmth of a warm summer day. Nobody would look twice at her. Not until she turned herself into a Kardashian clone and changed her name. Now she had curves in all the right places thanks to implants, and dyed black hair that seemed dull and lackluster to go along with her now vacant brown eyes. It was a shame, really.

I watched her, trying to see if she was here with anyone, but the way she changed partners, it didn't seem so. That worked in my favor. As I sipped my drink, I delayed— procrastinated, if you will—what I came here to do. This was a part of the job that I didn't care for. I swallowed the rest of my drink and slammed the glass on the counter, then headed for her.

Approaching her, I slid my hands about her waist and pulled her flush against me. "Dance?" I murmured huskily into her ear.

She giggled and looked up at me, her eyes glazed over. I could tell she'd already partaken of something earlier that evening. "Sure," she agreed.

We moved together to the beat of some nineties boy-band song I didn't know the name of, nor did I actually care. It served its purpose. Running my hands over her body, I could tell she was into it, enjoying the way our bodies fit together. Had to admit, I enjoyed it as well.

It was getting late though, and I needed to move this along. "I've got a room and some dope; wanna take this party somewhere private?" I whispered in her ear as I caressed her body through the slamming red dress she wore.

"Is it the good stuff?" she asked, practically begging.

"Only the best, baby."

A slow grin crossed her red lips. "Let's get out of here, then."

Taking her hand, I led her out of the club. "My hotel is just down the street."

"What's your name?" she asked as we walked along. "I'm Ruby Gold."

I smiled. "I know. I've seen your films."

"You have? Am I better than Mia Khalif?" she questioned, staring up at me as she hung on my arm, trying not to trip over her heels.

"You're exquisite."

She seemed to like that answer. She glanced up as we reached my hotel. "Oh wow, the Bradford. I've only stayed here once."

"Then you'll enjoy this immensely. I've got a great view." I pushed the button for the fourteenth floor.

"Oh?" She leaned into me, wrapping her hands around my waist.

As we got in the elevator, I said, "I've got a premium view of the rooftop pool."

"And we're going to party, just the two of us?" Her smile was lascivious.

"Absolutely."

The elevator hummed as it climbed, and when it opened on my floor, I led her down the corridor to the room I'd reserved under a false name. I'd have to burn this alias when I was finished here, but I figured it was worth it. I used the keycard to get into the room and watched her stumble in. She really was a beautiful woman. It was too bad she had loose lips.

"So? Where is it?" She sank down on the plush mattress of the king-sized bed and tossed her purse on the table.

"Impatient, aren't you?" I smirked. "One minute, princess." I headed for my case and opened it. Inside lay a couple of needles, a few glassine packages of fentanyl, as well as a few vials of heroin. The only question was, how much should I administer? I didn't want her to suffer; she didn't deserve that. I glanced over my shoulder at her. "Get undressed and scoot up to the headboard. I'm going to make you fly."

She squealed and did as I asked.

As I turned back to my case and looked once more at the needles, her dress fell next to my feet, a puddle of red that reminded me of a pool of blood. That wouldn't be happening here this evening. There would be no blood.

I picked up one of the fentanyl packages and poured it into the vial of heroin and shook it slightly to mix it. I filled one of the syringes with the heroin now laced with a lethal dose of fentanyl. I regretted having to do this, but the hit was ordered, and I didn't have a choice. Still, I could give her one last amazing night before she passed.

I held up the syringe and rubber tube I would use to find her vein, as I turned back to her. "Any special spot you want it?" I asked, then set them on the table next to the bed as I admired her naked body on display for me.

"Nowhere noticeable. I usually do it between my toes," she answered.

I nodded as I took off my shoes and stripped out of the jeans and shirt. Climbing onto the bed, I moved over her, drawing her in for a passionate kiss. The way her body felt curved into mine was a luxury I didn't often get to enjoy. Skimming my hands over her, I got her hot and bothered. I moved down her body, planting kisses along the way.

She writhed beneath me as I continued down her leg, kissing all the way down to her foot. I held it in my hand. I wouldn't need the tubing for this, only if I was going to inject it into a vein. I smiled as I picked up the syringe and uncapped it.

She squirmed, clearly anticipating the high I was about to give her.

"Hold still," I murmured as I spread her toes. I held her foot firmly as I injected the poison into her. A wave of regret passed through me, but I let it go. This was the job I was paid to do, and no matter how much I disliked murdering women, it wasn't my call.

"Mmmm, so good," she murmured, sinking back onto the bed.

I made love to her as she flew, making sure she enjoyed every last breath she took. It didn't take long, but I did manage to finish before she breathed her last.

When she was gone, I pulled on a pair of latex gloves from my case and then headed into the bathroom and turned on the water in the raised tub, then added bubbles and bleach.

Picking her up, I carried her into the bathroom and set her comfortably in the water. She looked peaceful. It was the least I could do for her.

Glancing in the mirror, I noticed the dark, wavy wig I was wearing was coming loose, so I adjusted it and resealed it. Moving back to the bedroom, I cleaned up, putting the syringe back in the case, then stripped the bed and stuffed the bedding into one of the garbage bags I pulled from my suitcase. I'd toss it in the laundry room on my way out of the hotel. The other bag I had, with the empty bottle of bleach and garbage from the room, I'd throw in a dumpster outside the hotel. Picking up her dress and panties, I laid them out on the bed next to her purse and arranged her shoes on the floor just beneath.

I got dressed, then reached into the pocket in the lid of my drug case and pulled out a card. It was the queen of hearts from a Black Cat playing deck. I set it on the dress. I wiped down the room, her shoes and anything else I'd touched, making sure no one's fingerprints would be found.

After taking a few pictures and giving Ruby Gold one last look, I gathered my things and left the room.

2

HOMICIDE OF A HOLLYWOOD STARLET

MARCY

An annoying rattle drew me out of sleep, but I didn't know what it was. When it stopped, I snuggled closer to Frank. I'd stayed the night at his place. It was one of those rare occasions when we not only had an evening free together, but today as well, once we both officially woke up.

My thoughts drifted to the evening before. Frank had taken me to a restaurant on the beach, the Water Grill. We'd tried their wild Spanish octopus appetizer and then had their smoked hamachi nachos. It had been delicious. Afterwards, we'd caught the latest Keanu Reeves action movie. From the theater we'd gone for drinks, then come back to his place and spent hours wearing ourselves out under the covers. It had been well after two in the morning when we'd finally fallen asleep.

Last night had been great, and I was looking forward to relaxing with him and unwinding today after the past month of chasing down suspects. That was one thing about LA, crime didn't sleep, and homicides were plentiful. Frank had it easier out here on the coast, not that I'd say that to him. I knew he worked just as hard as I did, but it wasn't exactly the same. He dealt with more domestics and armed robberies and things like that, whereas I dealt with serial killers and high-profile murder cases. Both were exhausting, of course, and we deserved some time off together, so I was grateful to have it.

I shifted closer to Frank, enjoying his strong arms wrapped around me as I used his chest as my pillow. He was surprisingly comfortable, and his rhythmic breathing soon began lulling me back to sleep. My eyes drifted closed again in the dim morning light that was peeking through the curtains. I was nearly asleep once more when the sound I'd heard before started up again.

What the heck was it? Had a mosquito or fly gotten into the house? I wondered. I lifted a hand and swatted at the air, trying to make it go away.

"Babe, I think that's your phone," Frank murmured into my hair.

"Ugh." I rolled over and grabbed the offensive object from the night table. It had stopped, but as I picked it up, it started vibrating again. "Angel, why the hell are you calling me so early?" I glanced at the digital clock on the table. "It's not even six a.m."

"Good morning to you too." He chuckled. "Captain called; we've got a suspicious death at the Bradford."

"So? Why are we on it? It's our day off," I complained as I flopped back on the bed.

"Yeah, I know, but apparently the vic is some actress, and the mayor wants us on it."

"You've got to be kidding me. Does he not realize we

aren't superhuman? We need breaks occasionally," I grumbled.

"Come on, Supergirl, this is what we get for solving so many high-profile homicides. Now, get your butt in gear. I'll meet you at the Bradford in twenty."

"Yeah, gonna be longer than that. I'm in Santa Monica." I sighed.

"You're where?" He paused. "You stayed at Frank's?" He sounded irked. "He there with you?"

I sat up and moved to the edge of the bed, letting my feet dangle. "Yeah, we were asleep. Need I remind you? It. Is. My. Day. Off."

"Whatever. I'll hold the scene." He clicked off.

I felt Frank move behind me, and then his lips were on my shoulder. I turned and slipped into his arms. "I'm sorry. I'm being called in. An actress is dead, and the mayor has decided Angel and I are his favorite flavors of the week as far as detectives go."

Frank chuckled. "Well, you're definitely my favorite flavor, TT."

I laughed and kissed him. "I need to get moving. Angel is already on his way there."

"You get dressed. I'll go make the coffee."

"Shower with me first?" I suggested. I knew I was procrastinating, pushing back because, as I might have mentioned, this was supposed to be my day off.

"You don't have to ask me twice." He stood up, grabbed me around the waist, tossed me over his shoulder in a fireman's carry, and moved to the bathroom while I laughed. He continued to hold me as he turned the water on and let it get warm before setting me on my feet under the spray of water.

It felt good being with Frank. I loved all our time

together, and I was kind of pissed that I was going to now miss out on spending the day with him.

After the shower, I dried my hair and got dressed while Frank, dressed only in a towel around his hips, made coffee. I hadn't planned on being called into work, so all I'd packed in my overnight bag was a pair of dark blue jeans and a bright red V-neck T-shirt. It would have to do.

Once I was dressed, I headed back into the bathroom and brushed my hair, which was getting longer than I normally liked. It was past my shoulders now, almost hitting the middle of my back. Maybe I'd go see Callie, Angel's girlfriend, and have her give me a cute bob. In the meantime, I pulled my hair tight and twisted it into a low bun at the base of my neck.

I laced my tennis shoes, packed up my bag, put on my holster and secured my weapon, then headed to the kitchen, depositing my bag and purse on the couch in the living room as I passed through. Frank handed me a travel mug of coffee. "Thanks," I said, taking a sip and savoring it.

Just as I was about to head into the living room to grab my things and leave, my phone buzzed again. Pulling it out of my pocket, I looked at the screen.

"Who is it?" Frank asked.

I held up a finger and answered, "Captain?" I glanced at Frank, and his brow furrowed.

"Turn on the news, Channel 5," Captain Robinson said.

"What's going on?"

"Hurry, Kendrick—"

I clicked on the TV in the kitchen and hit Channel 5.

"—found dead in a bubble bath at the Bradford. Again, Hollywood starlet Ruby Gold, age twenty-six, has been found dead of an apparent drug overdose at the Bradford here in Los Angeles early this morning. Sources at the hotel have informed me that LAPD are on the scene."

"I have a feeling this is going to be a bad one," Frank murmured, gathering my things for me.

"How in the hell did they get that information, sir?" I asked.

"I don't know," the captain answered, "but I want you to find out. I want that leak shut up."

"Yes, sir. I'll get on it. I'm leaving now, but I'm coming from Santa Monica. Angel is already on his way."

"Get there ASAP, Kendrick, but keep it safe," he replied.

"Yes, sir." I hung up and turned to see Frank at the door with my bag and purse. I gave him a rueful smile as I shouldered the bag and took my purse with my free hand. "I'm sorry."

"It's fine. Go be the supercop we both know you are," he said, pulling me into him and kissing me as I tried not to splash coffee on him from the travel mug. "I'll call you; maybe we can set something up for later?"

"Maybe, have to see how this goes." I kissed him once more and then jogged out to my car. Setting my coffee on the hood, I pulled my keys from my purse and opened the door, then clicked to open the trunk and dropped my overnight bag in before shutting it. I pulled the driver's door open and tossed my purse in, then started to get in myself.

"Coffee!" Frank yelled.

My brow furrowed as I looked at him, and he pointed. I glanced up and recalled my mug was on the roof. "Thanks!" I called back with a grin as I stood back up and grabbed the cup.

I pulled the siren from the floorboard of the passenger seat and put it on the dashboard. I wouldn't turn it on until I was out of the neighborhood, but I didn't want to have to pull over to grab it once I was on Santa Monica Boulevard. With a wave I backed out of his drive.

It took me a good forty minutes to make it back to LA and to the hotel, even with the siren going. As I found a place to park, I noticed that patrol had a decent perimeter set up around the hotel. There were several news vans and reporters gathered, along with various looky-loos. I had to steel my spine, as I knew they'd be shouting at me once I reached the entrance. It didn't help that I was dressed so casually. My normal work attire was like my armor, and today I was without it. It couldn't be helped.

As I climbed out of the car, my phone buzzed, and then it buzzed again a second later, indicating I had multiple incoming texts. Frowning, I pulled it out and looked at the screen. The messages were from Jordan. He'd been sending me nasty messages for months now, ever since he'd been fired. He blamed me for his drinking, his being fired, the fact he couldn't get another job—you name it. I couldn't deal with him right then, so to the trash those messages went. It was probably best I didn't even look at them.

"Where are we, Garcia?" I asked, approaching the officer standing behind the yellow police tape.

"Did they call you in on your day off?" Garcia asked, raking his eyes over me and arching a brow.

I sighed. "Yeah, now where are we?"

"Oh"—he nodded and lowered his voice—"on fourteen, ma'am. Can't miss it."

"Thanks, and I want to know who leaked the vic's identity to the press and where they got those pictures."

"As soon as more officers arrive, Braun and I will get on that, ma'am."

"Good." I passed him and entered the hotel, heading straight for the elevators. When I reached the fourteenth floor, I ran into a situation.

A tall, blonde woman was attempting to get past Officer Min-Ji Kim and his partner, Officer Julie Desmond. The woman was flashing a badge, but at the moment I couldn't tell why they weren't letting her through, not that I wanted her to be let through, but she was obviously a cop, I just didn't know where from. I thought maybe she knew the victim and had information on the case, but that was pure speculation on my part, and I hated making assumptions, so I decided to ask what was going on.

"Kim? Desmond? What's this?" I asked.

"Detective, this—" Kim started as he gestured to the woman. I could see the frustration on his face.

"This is my case," the woman said, spinning around to stare at me with a scowl on her otherwise pretty face.

I recognized her from Vice. Detective Valerie Burnett. I'd never really met her before, but I'd heard the rumors. She had climbed the ranks in Vice pretty quickly, only to stall about two years ago. I had originally figured it was politics, it usually was when it came to women in uniform, but then I'd heard how difficult she was to work with, and I thought maybe that had something to do with it. Seeing her now, I knew there was something to those rumors.

I crossed my arms and narrowed my gaze on her. "Excuse me? Why would this be a Vice case?"

She huffed. "It just is."

"I'm afraid I'm going to need more than that, considering I was called in specifically for this case, given this is some Hollywood starlet's homicide that the mayor feels my partner and I need to solve."

"I don't care what the mayor wants. This is my case."

I was getting impatient. I was already behind the eight ball, and now she was making me later than I'd imagined. Angel was going to be even more pissed off than he'd sounded when I told him I was in Santa Monica. "Okay, I'll bite. Why do you think this case should be yours?"

"Because I saw it on Channel 5. The playing card."

"What are you talking about?" I asked.

Valerie's eye twitched, and she looked ready to explode. "The fucking playing card! It was right there on the dress. The queen of hearts from a Black Cat playing deck. It's his calling card. That makes this my case."

I had no clue what she was talking about. If there was a calling card, it sounded to me like I might be dealing with a serial killer, which was obviously not a Vice case. It was a Homicide Special Section case, which made it mine. Still I figured I had better ask. "Whose calling card?"

"El Gato."

The name rang a bell, but I wasn't sure if that was just because it was Spanish for cat, or because I actually knew who she was talking about. I raised my eyebrow and waited for her to elaborate. If this guy had a calling card that identified him, why would he leave it at the scene unless he was taunting us? In my experience, that didn't seem like a sane person's idea. Then again, what murderer was actually sane and not a homicidal maniac? None that I knew of.

She blew out an annoyed breath. "El Gato. The drug lord? He's responsible for bringing in millions of dollars' worth of heroin, fentanyl, and cocaine to LA from all over Central and South America. I've been trying to pin a case on him for years, but he always gets away."

"And you think this case is yours because his calling card was left behind here at my crime scene?"

"It is mine!" she insisted.

I pinched the bridge of my nose. It was too dang early in the morning for this. "I'll call the captain. This is his call."

Valerie folded her arms across her chest like she was about to win. Part of me hoped she would, but somehow, I knew it was just wishful thinking.

I hadn't even gotten in there yet, and I could already tell this murder was going to bring me nothing but trouble.

3

CASE SHARING WITH VICE
MARCY

I pulled out my phone and noticed I had left it on vibrate and missed six calls. I didn't recognize any of the numbers, so I ignored them and dialed the precinct.

"LAPD, you've reached the HSS department; this is Jason; how may I direct your call?"

"Jason, it's Kendrick; is the captain available? I've got a situation."

"Let me check." He paused, but didn't put me on hold, thankfully. I could hear him murmuring to someone, and then he came back on the line. "One moment, and I'll patch you through."

A second later, Captain Robinson was on the line. "Kendrick, what's going on over there?"

"Sir, Detective Burnett is here, and she—"

"Tell him it's my case," Valerie interjected.

I turned my back to her and quickly explained the situation. "She's demanding to be let into the crime scene, sir."

"If there is a connection to an open case she's running,

then it might be a good idea to run this as a joint operation; if it proves not to be connected, then neither of you are at a disadvantage. If she's right and it is connected, then you can help take down one of the biggest drug lords in LA's history."

"Sir—" I started to argue.

"Look, I know she can be difficult, but just do it, Kendrick. Share information."

I sighed. "Fine. Who's point?"

"You stay point. This is still a homicide first. And I want to know who leaked those photos and talked to the press."

"Already have Garcia and Braun questioning the reporter, sir."

"Excellent. Keep me updated."

"Yes, sir." I hung up.

"Told you it's my case," Valerie muttered as she pushed past Kim and Desmond.

I mouthed, "Sorry," to them as I followed her. "The case is mine. I'm the lead detective; you follow my directives, got it?"

She folded her arms and huffed again. "Fine."

With a nod, I finally made it to the hotel room and opened the door. It seemed a bit crowded with a few patrol officers, a couple of crime scene techs, Lindsey Stone, head of CSI, and Damien Black, the coroner, as well as Angel. Though, Damien, Lindsey, and one of the techs were in the bathroom part of the room with the door open.

"Where the hell have you been?" Angel asked gruffly; his eyes flashed from me to Valerie. "Who are you, and why are you here?"

I put a hand up to stop Valerie from once again saying the scene was hers. "Angel Reyes, meet Valerie Burnett, Vice.

She noticed a connection to one of her cases in the pictures Channel 5 was showing in their report."

Angel pursed his lips and gave me a sour look. "So we're handing it over to her?"

"No, the case is ours, but we're sharing information with Vice. Captain called it a joint operation."

He folded his arms across his chest and stared at Valerie. "So what exactly did you see?"

Instead of answering immediately, Valerie pushed between us and headed for the bed. She pointed at the card lying on the dress. "That. It's El Gato's calling card. He has his assassins leave them at the site of anyone he's ordered taken out as a warning to others to not step out of line."

"What does a Hollywood starlet have to do with this drug lord? Was she a dealer?" I asked Valerie.

"Not that I'm aware of." She shrugged.

That was helpful. Not. I rolled my eyes. "Okay then. Angel, what can you tell me? Catch me up to speed."

"Body's in the tub. As you most likely saw, Damien's with her now. Lindsey's in there too, collecting samples. She's going to have her techs go over the room more thoroughly once we're all out of the way."

"Okay, so do we know anything yet?"

"I know there's an overwhelming smell of bleach in that bathroom," Angel muttered.

"Is that what has you so grumpy?" I narrowed my eyes at him, tired of him being short with me for no reason.

"Yeah, maybe. Also haven't had any coffee," he replied.

I stared at him for a moment. "Okay, why don't you go down to the restaurant and get a coffee, then talk to the front desk. I want to know who this room was registered to and for how long. I want to know why the bed has been stripped and if the bleach came from the hotel."

Angel hesitated for a moment, but without a word, he turned and walked out the door.

I sighed. There had been a strain between us lately, and I couldn't figure out why. If we were in any other kind of work situation, I would say that Angel and I might have ended up as lovers, but because we were on the job, that would never happen. Being a cop was hard enough; being involved with a cop on the job at another precinct was also troublesome at times; but to date where you worked, let alone someone you worked closely with, that was just borrowing trouble. Angel and I were best friends, but there was an added layer of attraction there that normally we both ignored. However, from how his mood had shifted after I told him I was with Frank this morning, I'd lay a guess that me telling him that had irked him for some bizarre reason.

It wasn't as though Angel was single. He and Callie had started dating months ago, just as the Broken Badge Killer case had gotten started. It wasn't the most ideal time to start a relationship, but I couldn't blame them. I'd met Frank around the same time. Angel's recent behavior made me wonder if there was trouble in paradise between him and Callie.

"Marce. Earth to Marcy."

A hand waved in front of my face, and I blinked and then smiled at Lindsey. "Hey, sorry, caught up in my thoughts. What have you got for me?"

"Hey, yourself. So, the water is a mix of the hotel's bubble bath, lavender scented, and judging from the smell, an entire bottle of bleach. I've got samples."

"Why bleach?" I asked. "Is it some sort of MO for this supposed assassin?" I looked over at Valerie.

"Are you talking to me?" she asked. "I don't know. El Gato uses different assassins for different things."

I gritted my teeth. For someone who specialized in this particular field, I would have thought she'd know every last known associate of El Gato and their MOs. Maybe that was why she hadn't been able to catch the bastard. I looked over at Lindsey. "Was she alive when she went into the tub?"

"That's a question for Damien. He hasn't said much, just made notes in his phone."

I moved to the bathroom door and poked my head into the spacious room. "Hey, Damien, got cause of death?"

He shook his head. "Not yet, but I can tell you she was already dead, or at least unconscious and near death, when she went into the tub."

"She didn't struggle at all?"

"Nope."

"When will you know more?"

"You already know the answer to that," he said wryly.

"After you get her on your table, got it." I nodded. "Anything else unusual about the scene or the body?"

"Not so far," Damien replied. "If it weren't for the bleach, I might have ruled this an accidental overdose."

"And the playing card," Valerie mumbled.

"Playing card?" Damien asked.

"Queen of hearts left on her dress in the bedroom. Apparently, it's some drug lord's calling card." I shrugged. "If that's all you got for me, then I'll release the scene to you."

"We're going to be here for a while," Lindsey said. "I want every inch of this room dusted for prints. Maybe we'll get lucky."

"Sounds like a plan," I agreed. "How long do you think before you've got everything from here and reports ready?"

Lindsey rolled her eyes and deadpanned, "Seriously? You want an exact hour?"

I laughed. "Just a ballpark. I'd like Detective Burnett to be there as well, so I thought we could work out the details now."

"I should have the majority of it ready tomorrow morning. That's the best I can do."

"Okay, we'll see you then." I turned to Valerie, who seemed to have spaced out during our conversation. "You have anything to add, Detective Burnett?" I waited patiently, slightly annoyed that she was still here.

"Huh?" She looked up from her phone and then shook her head. "Oh, no, not right now."

Of course not, I thought. "Then we'll leave you to it, Lindsey, Damien." I gave them each a nod and directed Valerie out of the room. "Look, I'm sure you've got things to do, so why don't we plan to meet up at the lab when Lindsey and Damien have their reports ready in the morning."

"All right, I can do that." Without another word, Valerie turned and brushed past Kim and Desmond, then headed for the elevators.

I didn't want to ride down with her, so I stopped next to Kim and Desmond. "I don't want her back in the scene, so if she shows up, call me."

Kim nodded. "Sure thing, Detective. Any reason to believe that she will show up?"

I pursed my lips and thought about it. "No, but just want to err on the side of caution."

"Okay, we'll call should she find her way back up here."

"Thanks." I gave them a wave and pushed the button for

the elevator. When the doors opened, Angel was inside, holding two to-go cups. "Hey," I said, stepping on with him.

"We all finished up here?" He handed me a cup and pushed the ground-floor button.

"Yeah, for now. What did you find out?"

He sipped his coffee and then said, "The room was registered to a Bill Smith. I've got a copy of his credit card and ID, so we'll need to track him down."

"That's a good start; did they say anything about the missing bedding?" We stepped off the elevator and headed for the exit.

"No, they don't know what happened to it."

"Great. Well, maybe CSI will find it."

"Where's Burnett?" He looked around, beyond the yellow tape toward the news vans.

"Sent her on her way. She's going to meet us tomorrow at the lab to get the reports."

"Okay, so where to now?"

"I figured we'll go brief the captain and then get started on backgrounds?"

He nodded. "I'll meet you there."

"Okay, and Angel?"

"Yeah, what's up?"

"We good?" I asked, trying to get a feel for where his mind was.

"Peachy." He smiled. "See you back at the precinct."

I waved and headed to my car, but paused and turned to look for Garcia and Braun. I wondered if they'd found our leak. I saw them over near the reporters, in the opposite direction from where I was going. Sighing, I turned back and called them over.

"Ma'am," Officer Garcia said, joining me.

"Morning, Detective," Braun greeted me. "We asked about the photos the reporters had. Turns out they were sent anonymously via a now deleted email account. I called it in, and tech is trying to run it down, but I haven't heard anything back yet."

"Okay, I'll check in with them and see what they've found. Thanks for running that down for me. Appreciate you doing that," I said. "Stay safe out there."

"You too, ma'am."

I gave them a wave and headed for my car again. As I climbed in, I heard my phone chime, and I thought it might be Angel, but saw I had a new message from my brother.

Lunch?

I texted Stephen back, telling him I'd meet him at Alebrijes Mexican Grill, our favorite place to eat, at eleven thirty. It was going on nine now, so I figured I'd be starved and ready for some good food by then.

He sent back:

See you then

I debated inviting Angel, but then decided to play it by ear. He might already have plans for lunch, or despite him saying we were peachy, he was still pissed at me for some reason. I didn't really want to look too close at that because I really feared that it wasn't me that he was pissed at, but himself and his jealousy over me being with Frank.

I shoved those thoughts aside and headed for the precinct.

4

CATCHING UP OVER NACHOS
MARCY

The precinct was busy when I arrived, it always was, but as I pulled into the lot, a call came in to all available patrol to head to the 101, as there was a ten-car pileup. My heart sank hearing it. Officers flew out of the lot like a jar of fireflies being opened, with their lights blazing. I really hoped there weren't too many injured and that they stayed safe out there.

I headed in and met up with Angel near our desks in the detective pool. "Hey, let's go talk to the captain." I smiled at him tentatively. I hated feeling like I was walking on eggshells around him, it made things awkward, and I didn't want things to be awkward between us.

"One sec," he said as he typed something on his phone. "Texting Callie."

"How is she doing?" I asked as I put my purse away in my desk.

He glanced up and grinned. "She's good. I'm meeting her for lunch." He paused and then offered, "You want to join us?"

"No, thanks, I'm meeting Stephen; he's back from that trip to Mexico with Yazmine."

"Oh, cool, it'll be good for you to catch up with him." He stood up and put his phone in his pocket. "Ready?"

I nodded, and we headed for Jason's desk. He just waved us toward the door.

"He's expecting you," he said as he picked up the phone.

I knocked twice on the wooden door and heard Robinson call us in. "Good morning, sir."

"Kendrick, Reyes, come in. Burnett with you?"

"No, sir. She's going to meet us at the lab tomorrow morning to go over the CSI and autopsy reports and hopefully give us what she's got on El Gato."

"Have a seat." He gestured toward the chairs in front of his desk.

I sat down and looked at Robinson. He was still a bit underweight, but he seemed to be in a good mood, which was nice. His divorce had taken its toll on him, and he'd been a little lost for a while. Now he was living in a fifty-five-plus condo community, and he looked like he was getting some sun. His face looked less stressed, and he seemed happier.

"What's the case look like?" he asked.

"So we've got a deceased actress, no known cause of death yet, but she was in a bathtub full of bleach and water, so she didn't get in there herself, though there are no marks of a struggle."

"Okay, and what's this connection Burnett found to El Gato?"

"A playing card left at the scene. The queen of hearts from a Black Cat playing deck," I shared.

"Sir," Angel interjected, "I don't understand why she's

horning in on this case. It's clearly a homicide and possibly connected to El Gato, I get that, but it's not like the victim was a drug dealer or anything."

"No, you're right about that, Reyes, but the playing card is concerning. She must have a bigger connection to El Gato than just a client for him to have sent an assassin after her. I've heard rumors that an assassin named El Vibora is in town." Robinson's voice was laced with concern.

El Vibora wasn't a name I was familiar with. All these Spanish nicknames were very gang-like in my opinion, and that just made me want to toss the whole case back at Vice and be done with it, but something made me hesitate suggesting that. It was the thought that maybe this assassin wasn't done, and there were going to be more deaths. In my opinion, assassin was just another name for serial killer. Assassins, though, were generally motivated by money rather than the actual killing, like most of the serial killers I was used to. In a way that made them more dangerous. Assassins had a unique understanding of law enforcement and were generally former military or government men— not necessarily from the US—who were either burned and went rogue, or cut loose for some reason that usually wasn't in our best interest. They generally sold themselves to the highest bidders and became mercenaries.

"Sir, what do you know of El Gato?" I asked. "And what is his connection with the assassin you mentioned?"

"As far as I know, we don't have El Gato's actual identity, though Burnett has been working on it for the past decade. Every time she gets close, her informant ends up dead. She hasn't been able to get close to the main man or any of his inner circle. His identity is very well protected. Drugs connected to him have been found with a black cat on the packaging. We're actually not even sure he is living here in LA, he could be down in Mexico, and his men here. Most likely whoever killed Ruby did it for El Gato."

"Valerie's been on this case for ten years and hasn't even identified exactly who this guy is?" I asked. "Could it be that El Gato is more than one person? Maybe it's a corporation?"

"That's a thought, but from everything I've heard, he's a man, people have met him, but they don't get his real name," Robinson replied.

"People are afraid of him," Angel added. "Him and El Vibora."

"I get that El Gato is cat, so the black cat makes sense, but El Vee Borda? What is that?"

"It's Spanish. It's not a *D* sound, but a rolled *R*," Angel replied. "Vibora. It means viper." He looked at the captain. "Sir, if El Vibora killed this actress, then she was most likely poisoned, probably via drugs."

Robinson nodded. "I agree. I know the DEA has also been after El Gato, so we may have to loop them in as well on this case if it proves to be bigger than this one death, but we'll hold back on this for now. Work the case as if it's a singular death until we know more. If El Gato is cleaning house, and using El Vibora to do it, we could have a lot more deaths coming."

"Great," I muttered.

"Or could just be a one-off," Angel said. "Maybe this actress got too close to him? Knew his real name or something? We should do that deep dive into her life, see who she associated with."

"That's a good idea. Maybe we can figure out what Burnett hasn't been able to do for ten years." The woman was a pain in the ass, and the idea of achieving something she couldn't made me smile. Was that petty? Yes, but I still wanted to do it.

"Speaking of Burnett," Robinson started, a look of annoyance crossing his face, "tread lightly with her. She's temperamental and very territorial when it comes to anything related to El Gato. She's outlived numerous partners over the years in the chase. She's become paranoid and hard to work with because she doesn't trust others."

"We'll stay respectful," I replied, not willing to do more than that. I didn't like Valerie, and I wouldn't pretend otherwise.

"Thank you. Keep me updated on what you find."

I took that as our dismissal and stood. "We will, sir." I tilted my head toward the door as I looked at Angel. "Let's get started."

Back at our desks, Angel said, "I'll get started on her financials; you want to take her social media?"

"Sure, that works. What kind of actress is she, anyway?" I asked. "You ever heard of her before today?"

Angel snickered. "Oh yeah. She wasn't a mainstream actress; she was best known for doing porn."

"She was a porn star?" I rolled my eyes. "Because of course she was."

Angel's snicker turned into a full-blown laugh. "She was known for doing a lot of the kinky stuff."

"Great. Incognito on my browser it is. Lord knows I don't need to be inundated with ads for whatever crazy stuff she was into." I sighed.

I set up my browser to keep the search engine from sending my research to third and fourth parties. I typed the name Ruby Gold into the browser and started looking into who she was and what her life was like online. Wikipedia said she was born Brenda Sheller; she was twenty-six years old, had blonde hair, brown eyes, stood five feet seven, from Lansing, Michigan. Her parents were both deceased. She'd come to LA about six years ago, changed her name and her looks to match a Kardashian, and shot to international fame by doing porn. I scrolled through some of the titles of the shows she'd done.

"*All the King's Men*?" I murmured. My eyes widened as I realized what kind of porno that was, but then I saw another titled *All the Queen's Maidens* and noticed that Ruby Gold would have sex with anyone who had a pulse, it seemed. I looked over at Angel. "She didn't do anything with animals, right?" I asked before looking further. I didn't want to see that.

He guffawed. "No, she didn't do bestiality. Just about everything else though."

I shuddered. "She's got, like, three hundred shows to her name," I said, shaking my head.

"You wouldn't know it by looking at her bank account. I mean, yeah, she had a lot of incoming money, but it went out almost as fast as she made it."

"I'm moving on to her socials; keep digging, see what the pattern is."

"I will, looks like her house payment was the biggest logged debt, but there are cash withdrawals for high sums of money. I'll keep digging."

I moved on to her Instagram page and found she liked to post shots of her shopping trips to Rodeo Drive. She bragged about spending $40,000 on a dress. That was more than some people made in a year. To spend that amount on a dress was insane. It wasn't even that nice, and it looked really uncomfortable.

I scrolled through her page, making notes of the people she mentioned. Samson Martinez was mentioned often, and I realized he was her manager, so that made some sense. There were other actors she was associated with and a few very wealthy businessmen. I wrote down all the names, no matter who they were.

At eleven fifteen, I shut down my computer. "I'm going to head out and meet Stephen; what time are you meeting Callie?" I asked Angel, and grabbed my purse from the drawer.

"At noon."

"Hey, when you were talking to the front desk, did you happen to ask about surveillance cameras?"

"No, I was"—he paused and looked back at his computer —"I wasn't thinking. We should go back over there after lunch."

"I was just thinking the same. Maybe Lindsey will have found something for us to run on as well, if they're still there."

"I'll keep digging until I have to meet Callie. Have a good lunch. Tell Stephen hey from me."

"I will." I waved and headed out.

It didn't take me long to reach the restaurant. Stephen was already there at a table with a plate of nachos waiting for me.

He stood up when he saw me and gave me a hug. "Hey, sis. How's work?"

I sank down and grabbed a chip, eating it as I realized I was as starving as I'd thought I'd be. "Busy, as usual." I gave him a quick rundown on what I'd been up to, but really no more information than what he'd see on the news. "Angel says hi."

"Hi back to him. How's he doing? Is he still dating that hairstylist? What was her name?"

"Callie. Yeah, he's meeting her for lunch, but..." I stopped myself from voicing the troubling thoughts that came to mind.

"But?"

"I don't know. He's just been a bit..." I shook my head. "He's been acting a bit annoyed or jealous or something whenever I mention Frank, which makes me think that maybe he and Callie aren't doing as well as he makes it seem."

"You think he's jealous of your relationship with Frank because he doesn't have that with Callie?"

"Maybe?" I wasn't sure if that was it or not. It felt more personal, but I really didn't want to put that in words.

"He'll get over it, whatever it is," Stephen suggested. "How's Frank?"

A grin swept over my lips. "Frank is great. We were supposed to go to the beach today, but I got called back in to work."

"That sucks."

"It is what it is. Goes with the territory," I said as our waitress approached. We both gave her our orders, and then I said, "So how's Yazmine? How was Mexico?"

"She's great. Mexico was amazing. We went deep-sea fishing. I caught a huge mahi-mahi; you should have seen it, Marce. It was incredible." He went on to describe the experience and all the things they did, and showed me pictures on his phone from his trip as we ate.

"I'm glad you two had a great time." I smiled at him. "Hey, I was thinking of having a barbeque soon at my new place. You and Yazmine up for that?" I had met her about a month ago, and she was still a bit shy and standoffish around me, being afraid of the fact I was a cop, but she was making an effort and so was I.

"Yeah, that sounds nice. Do you like having a house now?" he asked, eating the last of his food.

"It's different, certainly. No neighbors directly on top of me, nor below me, nor on the other side of the walls. So weird. And the space, I still have empty rooms." I grinned. "I'm thinking of turning the third bedroom into a workout room."

He grinned. "You mean I could come work out at your place instead of going to the gym? That would be great; they raised their prices again."

I shook my head and laughed. "I was thinking a yoga mat and maybe a treadmill and some light weights, not lifting benches and stuff, but sure." I thought about the large room, it would hold those as well, and I could probably pick up some used ones fairly cheaply.

"One of those stationary bikes with the electronic course programs might be good too."

"We'll have to measure the room and see if it will all fit. You want to help me?"

"Sure."

My phone buzzed for the twentieth time in my pocket. I'd been attempting to ignore it, but I knew he wasn't going to stop, so I pulled it out. Jordan. "Damn it. I'm going to have to block him," I muttered.

"What's going on?"

"It's Jordan. He keeps blowing up my phone, blaming me for everything wrong in his life. He's gotten more and more unstable since he was fired." I was annoyed by the distraction he was causing in my life.

"You haven't been answering him, have you?"

"No, mostly been deleting them without reading them."

"You should get a restraining order. I don't like that he's harassing you. Forward that shit to me, and I'll keep a record of everything for you so you don't have to deal with it."

"Okay, thanks," I said and sent the messages that had accumulated over the last couple of hours to him. It was nice having a brother who was an IT specialist.

We finished up our meal and paid our tab, then headed out. "I'll let you know about the barbeque, okay?" I said as I hugged him goodbye.

"Sure, and I'll stop by sometime and measure the room."

"Be safe; there was a big accident on the 101 this morning," I said, opening my car door.

"I heard about that. No deaths, thankfully. You be safe too, sis."

I watched him in my rearview mirror as I pulled out of the parking lot. It had been nice to catch up with him, but now my mind was back on the case. I really hoped there was something in those surveillance videos that would help us catch this viper assassin. I didn't like the thought of him running loose in my city.

I needed to catch him fast.

5

BACK AT THE SCENE OF THE CRIME
ANGEL

Lunch with Callie had been nice and helped me to let go of the jealousy I'd been dealing with all morning over the fact that Marcy had spent the night with Frank. I was glad she was happy and in a good relationship. Honestly, I was. But a small part of me wished it were me she was with, and occasionally that green-eyed monster got the best of me, and I couldn't get thoughts of her out of my head. This morning was one of those days.

We were best friends, partners. I loved her, and I'd do anything for her. She held a good chunk of my heart in her hands, but I didn't think she was aware of that. No matter how much I wished things could be different for us, that we could be together, it just wasn't going to happen. Not only had the brass implemented a new departmental policy about significant others not working together—all thanks to Jordan and his bizarre behavior over the last year—we both knew it was a very bad idea because we worked so close together. It was for the best that we stayed just friends.

However that didn't stop my brain from reacting when

she mentioned being with Frank. Most days I could control it, could be happy for her, but this morning I hadn't been expecting her to tell me she'd spent the night in Santa Monica with him. Of course, I knew that they were together, that she'd stayed at his place before, and he at hers, but normally I could compartmentalize those thoughts. It was just that I had been blindsided by it today.

As I walked into the precinct and into the detective pool, I saw her seated at her desk, her hair, which was in a bun at the base of her neck, doing its best to escape the confines she'd put it in. She looked different in her casual attire than she did on the daily in her suit. She seemed more relaxed and approachable. Softer even. I liked seeing her like this.

Marcy looked up and smiled, but it seemed almost hesitant, like she was afraid I was going to jump down her throat. I regretted once again how I'd treated her this morning. She didn't deserve that. She'd done nothing wrong.

"Hey, ready to go?" she said as I got closer.

I smiled at her, a genuine smile. "Sure, you wanna drive?" I knew she preferred to drive, and I didn't care either way.

"I can," she replied, picking her purse up.

We were quiet in the car for the first few minutes, and I wondered if she was still feeling like she had to tiptoe around me. I hated that I'd made her feel that way. I did my best to get us back on proper footing. I wanted her to be easy around me. I didn't like this awkwardness between us. It made things tense, and I just wanted our friendship back on course. Maybe I needed to take another trip with Callie, get my head and heart refocused on her.

To break the silence, I asked, "How was Stephen? Did he have a good trip?"

"Sure did; he caught a mahi-mahi." She smiled over at me, and her entire face lit up.

"Nice. I've been thinking about taking a vacation down there, visiting some relatives, take Callie and introduce her to them. Maybe I'll do some fishing too."

Her smile widened to a grin. "I bet she'd love Mexico. Meeting your abuela, that's a big step."

She was talking about my grandmother, and she wasn't wrong. My abuela hadn't liked any of the women I'd brought to meet her other than Marcy, but then I'd introduced Marcy as my work partner, not my girlfriend. "Yeah, maybe we'll skip the meeting-relatives part," I said with a chuckle.

"Oh come on, Callie is super sweet, owns her own business, can style hair like nobody's business, and knows her way around the kitchen. Your abuela will love her."

"You think so?" I looked at her curiously.

"I do; she just wants a strong woman who has her own mind, who's loving toward you and willing to learn how to cook like her. If anyone can sway your abuela, it's Callie."

She wasn't wrong.

"Besides, your abuela is looking forward to the day you start bringing your offspring around, and you're not getting any younger," Marcy teased.

"And there it is. You just want to marry me off and settle me down with a pack full of kids." I grinned.

"Better you than me," she replied, laughing as she turned her gaze to me for a moment.

"Uh-huh." I nodded. "So what about you and Frank? You talked about families yet?" I questioned, because I wasn't going to let jealousy spoil our friendship. Frank was in her life, and I could see they had something special between them. I wanted that for her.

"We've talked about what we want and don't want. He knows I'm not about to quit my job and play happy housewife, but that I'm not against kids should it happen at some point down the line. We're not exactly there yet though. We're just enjoying where we are right now, you know?"

"I get that. Have you met his parents? I mean officially?"

"Yes, they're good people. Still messed up over what happened though." Her tone got quiet, and I understood.

"You like them?" I said, keeping my tone light.

"I do." She nodded as she pulled into the hotel's lot and parked. "Frank said they like me and are impressed." She smiled as if she was remembering his words.

"That's good." I put my hand on the door handle. "Looks like Lindsey and the CSI team are still here. Shall we?"

We headed in to the front desk. Marcy requested to speak to the hotel manager and then explained we needed all the surveillance tapes from the time Bill Smith checked in until this morning.

"I already anticipated that, so I've had copies made for you," the manager replied. "My staff and I are appalled that something like this took place here. We'd like this individual caught and brought to justice."

"We would as well," Marcy replied.

"Let me get the discs for you," the manager said, turning back toward the counter. He picked up a thick, plastic CD case and then handed it to us. "This is everything from the lobby, the elevators, and the fourteenth-floor hallway."

"Thank you so much."

"My pleasure," he replied. "If you need anything else, feel free to ask."

"We will, thanks." I gave him a nod; then Marcy and I headed for the elevators.

"I do like when they cooperate so easily," Marcy said, grinning.

"It does make our job run more smoothly." I pushed the button for the fourteenth floor.

When the elevator doors opened, we noticed CSI was packing up and heading toward us.

"Lindsey, hey," Marcy called.

Lindsey turned around and smiled. "Hey, you two. Couldn't wait for tomorrow?" she teased; her eyes were bright and matched her cheerful tone.

I grinned. "Doesn't seem so," I answered.

"We came for the surveillance video from the hotel, forgot to ask before. Thought we'd see if you found anything?" Marcy said.

"Well, we checked with staff on the bedding. They did a thorough count of all the sheets, blankets, and bedspreads, but nothing is missing. And none of the staff removed it from the room."

"So our perp somehow managed to get it to the laundry area?"

"Looks that way. We might want to check with the manager about getting footage of that area just in case," I suggested.

"We can do that on our way out," Marcy replied. She turned back to Lindsey. "Anything else unusual?"

Lindsey turned and picked up an evidence bag. "Found this on the floor next to a leg of the dresser. It was underneath and seems our perp missed it when he was cleaning up." She held the clear bag up for us to see.

I noticed a small, clear baggie, about the size of my index finger in length, inside the evidence bag. On the baggie was a small black cat. "Is that a dime bag?" I asked.

"It is, but it didn't hold weed. It was something white, not sure exactly what though until we test it."

"Okay, let us know. What about prints? Did you find any?"

"Not a one that wasn't accounted for. The room was mostly wiped down, but we dusted everything and ran them on my laptop. Found prints on the TV, window, lamp and in various spots on the door, but they matched staff. Thankfully, the hotel has a digital file with employee prints that they shared with us; otherwise I'd still be running checks."

"The hotel prints their employees?" I was a bit shocked.

Lindsey shrugged. "These days, can you blame them? They deal with people's valuables on the daily; if anything goes missing, they want to identify the culprit quickly and recover whatever was taken and hand them over to us."

"Makes our jobs easier, I guess," Marcy replied.

"Feels like an invasion of privacy to me," I muttered.

"Maybe so, but it's their business, and the employees are paid well. If they aren't doing something wrong, then they've got nothing to worry about," Lindsey replied.

I didn't say anything more. I doubted we'd agree on this. I just remembered a time when people were more trusting of one another, but then they were also nicer too, and we didn't have all this gang activity and drugs invading every bit of our lives, so maybe they had the right of it. I didn't have to like it though.

"Okay, we'll go back and see if the manager can add the video of the laundry area and head out unless you have something more?" Marcy asked Lindsey.

"Nope, not right now."

"See you later, then."

We returned to the lobby and spoke to the manager once

more, and he was happy to get those videos as well. As we headed out the doors to the walkway in front of the hotel, we were accosted by several reporters shouting questions.

"Detectives! Over here! Do you know how she died?"

"Was it suicide?"

"Is El Gato involved?"

That last one nearly had me spinning around to see who asked, but I kept facing forward and waited to hear the voice again. It took me a second to recognize it was Mario Juarez from Channel 4. Of course he would have recognized the significance of the playing card. He'd covered Vice news for the last five years.

"Bunch of vultures," Marcy murmured.

I glanced at her as we strode quickly to her car. "Don't let them get to you. Just ignore them."

"They feed on this stuff. It's disgusting," she said, her voice full of venom.

I agreed with her. Most of these reporters always reported on the deaths, the destruction, the gangs, the violence, the drugs—it was a cycle of the degenerate side of life, and they kept people focused on it. Hyping things up, making people fear for their lives. Rarely did they run heart-warming stories that showed the good in life. Probably why I tended not to watch TV anymore unless it was a ball game or the occasional movie.

"Let's just get out of here, yeah?"

She clicked the button to unlock her car, and we got in. "Yeah, we've got hours of surveillance to go through."

"Oh yay, my favorite," I said sarcastically. "I'll pop the popcorn."

It was going to be a very long afternoon.

6

NO-SHOW
MARCY

I woke to my phone playing "Adore You" by Harry Styles. Yawning, I glanced at the clock to see it was barely six a.m. I had a while before I had to be at work. Grabbing the phone, I answered, "Hey, you're up early." I stretched and leaned back against my pillows.

"Did I wake you?" Frank asked.

"You did, but I needed to get up anyway," I replied, but I couldn't help the smile that touched my lips at the sound of his voice.

"I'm sorry, babe. I was just missing waking up with you in my arms and wanted to hear your voice."

His words were so sweet and one of the reasons I really adored being with him. "Miss you too." I snuggled deeper into my bed. "I'm sorry I didn't come out to Santa Monica last night, but figured I shouldn't with this case."

"I get it, TT, you're on an active case."

TT stood for tiny tornado, and it made me smile whenever he called me that.

"That's one of the things I wanted to ask you about, actually. I was looking at that news report again and noticed something. You might already know by now, but just in case."

I had a feeling where this was going. Frank was a good cop and was pretty aware of various things going on in the state. "Okay, what's up?"

"That picture of the dress with the playing card."

"Yeah, it's probably exactly what you think. El Gato."

He sucked in a breath. "Babe, you need to be really careful. He's not someone to mess about. If he put a hit out on that woman, he had a reason. As much as I don't like it, he's nearly untouchable."

"You know me. I'm not going to walk away from this investigation just because some drug lord put a hit out on her."

"I know. I just want you to be careful. Keep your eyes and ears open because cops go missing or end up dead around him."

I thought about Valerie and wondered about that. If that was true, then why was she still alive? Was she just incompetent? Or maybe just lucky? I had to wonder.

"Absolutely, I will." I was glad he cared about me. "I've been thinking about having a barbeque soon. Kind of a housewarming party?"

"Sounds good; when are you thinking?"

"Not sure yet, but you up for it?"

"Anything you want to do, babe, you know I'm up for it." I could hear the double entendre in his voice as he chuckled. "Listen, I got to jump in the shower. I'll text you later. Be safe, okay?"

"You too," I murmured. "See you."

"Bye, babe."

I continued to lie in bed for another five minutes before setting my phone down and heading for the shower. When I got out, my phone was ringing again, but this time it was "We Are Family" by Sister Sledge. "Hey, Stephen," I answered. "What's up?"

"I was just checking out your social media—wanted to check and make sure Jordan wasn't leaving shit on your page, and discovered your pages have been hacked. Wanted to give you a heads-up."

"What?" I frowned. I didn't often go on my Facebook or Instagram pages, mostly they just allowed me to share things with friends, and I tried to keep things private on there. "How?"

"I think Jordan guessed your passwords; have you changed them since you opened them?"

The last time I'd changed my passwords had been while the face flayer copycat had been active. "It's been a while; guess I need to change them."

"I'll take care of it; don't try to log in. I'll give you a secure password once I get everything cleaned up."

"Wait, what did he do?" I started, but then realized maybe it would be better if I didn't know. "Never mind. Thanks for taking care of it for me."

"No problem. I'm going to take screenshots of everything he did, and add it to the messages he's been sending. You really need to consider getting that restraining order. I know it's just a piece of paper, but it will help establish his harassment and threats, Marce."

"I'll talk to the captain. Thanks, Stephen."

"No problem. Talk to you later, sis." He hung up.

I was really worried about how far gone Jordan's mind was now. He seemed to be spiraling. I'd seen it before; hell, Frank had just seen it happen with his brother, Daniel, a few months ago. Granted, he'd gone way, way off the deep end, and I didn't think Jordan was quite that far gone, but he seemed to be getting closer each day. A tiny portion of my brain was concerned for Katie, Jordan's wife, considering I was his target for his anger.

Sighing, I got dressed, made an egg sandwich, and ate on my way to the coffee shop and then headed into the precinct. Angel and I were going to finish watching the videos and then head to the labs to see what Lindsey had for us and meet up with Valerie.

I set Angel's coffee on his desk and sat down at mine. He walked in as I was putting my purse away. "Hey," I started as I looked up at him. He looked to be in a better mood than he had been yesterday morning. "Did you have a good night?"

"I did," he replied, lifting his cup and taking a sip, then sighed happily. "Went out to dinner with Callie and then back to her place. Talked to her about taking a trip down to Sayulita; she's up for it."

That made me smile. "When are you thinking?"

"Maybe this fall."

"That's probably a good time to go." I turned on my computer and unlocked the drawer where I had put the surveillance videos the night before. "Let's pick up where we left off on these videos. It's weird how this guy just looks and acts normal. Coming and going as though he hasn't a care in the world, right?"

Angel stared at the screen but didn't comment for a

moment. Something about his gaze seemed strained, and I wondered what was on his mind.

"Angel?"

"Hmmm?"

"Everything okay?"

He glanced at me. "Yeah. Fine. Sorry, just spaced for a second. Let's see if we can find out what he did with that bedding."

We spent the next three hours combing for every sight of the man we knew was Bill Smith on the tapes. He had been in and out of that hotel numerous times over the three days he was staying there. If I had passed him on the street, I never would have noticed him. He was just an average-looking guy. Wavy dark hair, glasses, not super handsome, but not ugly. He was just normal. It was almost unnerving. He had a wide smile with large, straight teeth, and though there was no sound on the videos, I could see him laughing heartily with one of the bellhops at the hotel. I made a note of wanting to speak to them.

My phone rang at ten, and I picked it up. "Kendrick."

"Hey, want to come down to the lab?" Lindsey asked. "I've got some things to show you."

"We'll be there soon. Did you call Burnett, or need me to?"

"I'll give her a call."

"Okay see you in a few."

"Lindsey ready for us?" Angel asked.

"Yeah, let's shut this down and head over there."

Fifteen minutes later we stood in the doorway to the lab. I waved to Lindsey, who came over to join us. I looked around to see if Valerie was there yet, but she didn't seem to be. "Did you get a hold of Burnett?"

"Um, yeah. She said to just send her the report."

Annoyance filled me for a moment. Valerie had demanded to be a part of our investigation but was now ghosting us. She had information that I needed, but I didn't want to go chasing her down. If she was going to be uncooperative, then I could be too. "Whatever. No, you know what, don't send her anything. It's not her case, and I let her in as a courtesy, so if she can't be bothered to come down here, then she doesn't need it."

Lindsey arched a brow. "You sure?"

"Absolutely. I'm the lead on this. If she wants the information, she can come get it from me."

Grinning, Lindsey nodded. "Okay, let me show you what we've got." She walked us over. "This is a single strand of hair we found on the floor in the bathroom. It's synthetic, from a wig. From the length of it, I'd say either a woman's short-haired wig or a man's toupee or wig."

"A wig?"

Angel sucked in a breath, and I glanced over at him, wondering what had him pale looking.

"And that baggie? It contained fentanyl."

"Fentanyl, that's highly toxic, right?"

"Deadly in small doses. There were only a couple of crystals left, and even those could do some serious harm to a person."

"So Ruby was poisoned with fentanyl?"

"I can't tell you that for sure; that's a Damien question."

"Right. Anything else?"

"Just that every print we found in that room was accounted for, as I told you yesterday. There weren't even any of Ruby's prints in the room or on her shoes. It was like she just appeared in that bathtub."

"Awesome." It really wasn't. I was being sarcastic out of frustration, and I was sure Lindsey knew it.

I glanced at Angel again and noticed that he was even paler than he'd been a moment ago. It was like he'd just seen a ghost and couldn't move. "Angel?" I said, gently reaching for him, suddenly afraid to know what was on his mind.

7

TRACK MARKS BETWEEN HER TOES
MARCY

"Angel? Are you okay?" I gently shook his arm. Was he having some kind of stroke? I wondered, very worried about him.

It took him a full ten seconds to snap out of it and nod. "Huh? Oh, sorry. Just sort of lost in my thoughts. You were saying?"

A knock sounded on the door behind us, and we all turned to see Damien with his head popped through the opening. "Hey, I'm ready for you when you've finished up here."

I turned back to Lindsey. "You have anything else?"

"Not right now."

"Okay, thanks," I said and looked back to Damien. "We'll come with you now."

Following Damien down the hall, we entered the morgue. He had Ruby on the metal table under the sheet. I could see the beginnings of the Y cut he'd performed to check out her internal organs peeking out from under the white sheet.

"What can you tell us?" I asked. "Lindsey said she found a packet with some fentanyl; was that what she was given?"

"Patience, young padawan." Damien smirked. "Take a look at this." He moved to the end of the table and spread her toes.

"Track marks? She was an addict?" I asked in surprise.

"Looks like it. Her organs show signs of serious heroin abuse."

"So not fentanyl?" Angel asked.

He grinned. "I didn't say that."

Sighing, I gave him a look, telling him to get on with it.

"Okay, so yes, she died of a heroin and fentanyl overdose. Also there are signs that she had sex shortly before she died. No signs that she was raped, no sign of struggling at all."

I turned to Damien. "Anything else?"

"I can tell you she was allergic to latex. She was slightly irritated from the condom that was used. There was no DNA found on her that wasn't hers. No skin particles, no saliva, no semen. I hate to say it, but this guy is good. Very meticulous in cleaning her up. My guess is he's a professional. Knows exactly how to scrub a scene and a body. Actually, I would speculate that he wanted her found, which isn't surprising given the playing card he left behind. If he hadn't, she would have been just another missing person. He'd have made her disappear. El Gato wanted to make an example of her. She's a warning to others."

"El Vibora," Angel murmured under his breath.

"That's not a name I know." Damien gave Angel a curious look.

"He's a ghost. An assassin and it seems he's currently working for El Gato, according to Vice."

"Speaking of Vice, wasn't Detective Burnett supposed to join us?"

I rolled my eyes. "Yes, but apparently she couldn't be bothered to show up."

"Typical," Damien said. "She usually avoids the lab and morgue like the plague. All she wants is the report most of the time."

"How often do you have to deal with her?" I asked curiously.

"Surprisingly, not very often. She doesn't have many cases that deal with a death unless it's an informant. Even then she doesn't look in on the autopsy."

"Maybe she has an aversion to seeing the dead?" Angel suggested, giving her the benefit of the doubt.

I supposed that was possible, but something about Valerie rubbed me wrong. I guessed it was because I found her unprofessional and irritating.

"I think Ruby was there for a good time," Damien concluded, returning to the subject at hand. "The man laced the heroin with fentanyl to kill her. She probably didn't suffer, at least not until the very end when she gasped for breath a few times before her lungs shut down and she passed. She might have even thought it was from the act of having sex and still not realized anything was wrong until she breathed her last breath. At least I hope so."

"You've given this a lot of thought," I said, giving him a curious look. Damien didn't usually get so emotionally involved, but this time, as he spoke, he sounded almost like Ruby Gold was a personal friend.

Damien shrugged. "Normally I make jokes, but it's just a way to keep my sanity. This one hit different. She was young; she didn't deserve this. I hate to see that she was messed up on drugs prior to her death, but it's not surprising given her profession. Do you know how many young wannabe actors and actresses end up on my table because of accidental overdoses? She'd have been written off as the same if it weren't for the bleach and the playing card. Somebody took her life, and just like that"—he snapped his fingers—"her light was snuffed out."

He wasn't wrong. Too many young lives were destroyed by drugs and violence, especially in Hollywood. I wanted this assassin and the drug lord he worked for off the street. Maybe then we'd save a few lives from Ruby's fate.

"We need to catch these assholes," Angel muttered, staring at Ruby's face.

I glanced at Angel, and I could see the same determination in his gaze as I felt. It was one of the things I enjoyed about working with him. We were almost always on the same page as far as work was concerned. He might err on the side of caution more than me, but he always had my back, same as I had for him.

I nodded. "We will."

8

DEA DEALS IN

MARCY

When Angel and I returned to the detective pool, Jason was waiting for us next to our desks, scrolling on his phone. I gave him a curious look, wondering what was up. I looked over at Angel, wondering if he knew what it might be about, but he shook his head.

"Did you need us for something, Jason?" I asked.

He looked up from his phone and nodded as he pocketed the device. "Oh, yeah, sorry, got distracted. The captain wanted me to tell you he's been contacted by some DEA agent about your case. He wants to see you."

"Okay?" I said, waiting for further information. "Now?"

"He's in a meeting with Warren at the moment, but he wanted you to have a heads-up. He'll be back in about an hour, so don't go anywhere."

"There goes lunch in Tijuana," Angel joked.

Jason blinked, and then his brow furrowed. "You were going to lunch in Tijuana?"

"No, he's kidding, Jason; we'll stick around."

"Okay, good." With that, he pulled his phone back out and strolled to his desk.

"A DEA agent?" Angel questioned. "That can't be good."

"Nope. Though if they want to take over, I'm tempted to let them."

"You are?" He looked at me as if I'd suddenly lost my mind.

"Not really, but kind of. I mean, this isn't our normal kind of case. Feeling a bit out of my element, I think."

"Hey, he's just another serial killer. You're good at nailing them; we'll get this guy."

I smiled. "You're right. He's just another serial killer; we've got this." I sank down in my chair. "So I want to know Ruby's movements. How did she meet up with our killer? Where was she prior to the Bradford?"

"I'll see if I can track her timeline down. I'll go through her credit card and debit card history; maybe that will tell us something."

"That's a good idea. I'm going to keep digging into her social life. Maybe there's something there I'm missing."

I started with her Instagram page. Anyone who wasn't named in the caption of her pictures or that I didn't recognize, I ran facial recognition on to get a name. Turned out she was connected to a lot of powerful people. Most were Hollywood executives, actors, and actresses, but a couple were businessmen in the tech industry. There were a few men who were just rich playboys. I couldn't pin down where their wealth came from, though it seemed a couple had inherited it. I was curious how they maintained that kind of wealth.

I tapped my pen on the desk, looking at my list of names. I wondered if it was worth diving into their lives. How likely was it that one of them was connected to Ruby Gold's death? Probably not very likely unless one of them was secretly El Gato. However it would be hard to uncover that information with any kind of deep dive. No, I'd need to flip someone close to him to garner that information. If I could catch this assassin, El Vibora, maybe that would allow me to nail the drug lord too.

"Kendrick! Reyes!" The captain's voice carried across the room.

I hit the keys on my computer to shut down my search, then rose. Angel and I headed to Robinson's office. "Sir, you wanted to see us?"

"Come in," he said. "Have a seat," he added as he closed the door behind him and then took his seat behind his desk. "While you were down in the lab, I received a call from an agent with the DEA. He's got some information to share on both El Gato and El Vibora, and I arranged for us to have a Zoom call with him."

"That's great, sir. Are they wanting to take over the case?"

"That wasn't what I got from this agent. More that they're trying to be helpful." He typed something into his keyboard and then turned his computer screen so that the three of us could be seen on the call.

A moment later, the agent joined us. "Good morning, Captain Robinson, Detectives," he said with a nod.

"Agent Darwood. Thank you for doing this."

"Sure, no problem. When I saw you could be dealing with El Vibora, I thought you could use all the help you can get. We've been chasing him for years now, but he's like a ghost."

"Has he always worked with El Gato?" I asked.

"No, not that we believe. He came across our radar about

ten years ago down in El Salvador. He was working for a merc group at the time, took out a few major players there. We next encountered him in Mogadishu, where he is suspected of poisoning a couple of US federal agents."

"So this guy gets around, then?" I asked.

The agent hesitated and then nodded. "He has in the past. We think he's been working with El Gato now, mostly killing rivals in Central America and Mexico. This is the first we've seen evidence of him in the continental US. We've caught him a couple of times, but either he escapes custody, or the man we thought was El Vibora died in custody. So we can't even say we were correct on the times he escaped. He's slippery as an eel and can change his appearance easily."

I recalled what Lindsey said about the hair they found and shut my eyes, swallowing the slew of swear words that wanted to spill from my lips. "We've got video surveillance of him and a couple of still shots. Sir, do you have the copies I put on your desk yesterday?"

Robinson found the file and opened it, then held the still shot of the man we suspected to be El Vibora up for Agent Darwood to see. "This is who we suspect; he checked in under the name Bill Smith."

"Alias, probably voided now. He won't use it again, and I'll guarantee he no longer looks like that."

"Great. So he's a literal ghost." It crossed my mind that it would probably do me no good to ask the bellhop about our suspect now. Anything he'd noticed would be a dead end.

"Pretty much. If you can catch him in the act, then you might have a chance of nailing him, but it's hard to say if he plans to kill again here in the States. He could be on a plane back to Mexico or Guatemala for all we know."

"Okay, so what do you know about El Gato?" Angel asked.

"Cartel drug lord. His name popped up in El Salvador about fifteen years ago. His power grew, and he moved up the coast into Mexico. For the past ten years he's been rumored to have ties in Los Angeles, and of course, as you are now aware, drugs with the black cat logo have been showing up there for about that long as well. We've intercepted shipments of heroin and cocaine that belonged to him, but we don't have a name on who El Gato actually is. Anyone who gets close to his inner circle ends up dead. He keeps things tight around him."

"You've gone after him?"

"I haven't personally, no. We lost a couple of undercover agents who got close to what we thought was his inner circle, but then lost them in a plane crash in Mexico before we could find out if we were right."

"How is this guy so untouchable?" I murmured. "He's got to have help," I theorized out loud.

"We suspect that as well, Detective. Which is why we're really hoping you can nail him. You're not the typical kind of cops he deals with, and maybe this time he's made a mistake. I'm just going to warn you both to watch your back."

"We will, Agent Darwood."

"Thanks for the information," Captain Robinson added.

"Good luck," Darwood said before closing his side of the Zoom call.

Robinson shut down the call on his end and looked at us. "Did you meet with Burnett and get whatever she's got on El Gato?"

"She didn't show up," Angel replied.

He sighed. "Not surprising. I did warn you she was difficult."

"What do you want us to do about her, sir?"

"Has she said anything? Did she give a reason for not meeting you?"

I pursed my lips and shook my head. "Not exactly. She asked Lindsey to send her a copy of the report, but I told her not to."

"Kendrick, I asked you to play nice with her."

"I know, sir, but—"

"No buts. I know she's difficult, but you have to admit, you're a bit intimidating yourself. Send her a copy of the report. She might see something that you don't."

"Yes, sir." I gave in. I didn't want to, but it was easier than trying to argue my point when it was a losing battle from the start.

"I'll let you get back on it; see what you can find out about Ruby Gold."

I nodded; then Angel and I returned to our desks. "Did you get anywhere on her cards?" I asked as we sat back down.

"Actually, yeah. So the day before she was found, she made some purchases on Rodeo Drive. But the best thing I found was a cover charge to a club downtown, just down the street from the Bradford. Wanna bet that's where she met our killer?"

I turned to look at him. "Seriously?"

"Total cereal." He grinned.

"You're a goof." I laughed and pulled open my desk drawer to get my purse out. "Let's go check it out."

"I'll drive," he commented.

I didn't even care. I was just happy to have an actual lead to something pertaining to the case. "Lunch on the way?"

"Sure, where do you wanna go?" he asked as we headed out of the building.

"Driver's choice."

"There's a Jack in the Box over there; sound good?"

"Perfect," I replied as my phone buzzed. Picking it up, I noticed a text from my brother with my new passwords. I sent him back a thank you and pocketed my phone before getting out of the car.

After eating in the parking lot, we headed to Exchange, one of downtown LA's hottest night clubs, or so I'd heard. I didn't really partake in the club scene. We knocked on the glass door and flashed our badges so they'd open up for us.

"We aren't open, officers," the woman said as she cracked the door to speak to us.

"We're aware. We need to speak to the club manager, please."

"Cassandra's in the back. Let me get her for you." The woman closed and relocked the door, leaving us standing out front.

"Looks like they take their safety pretty seriously," I smirked.

A few minutes later, another woman, probably in her mid-thirties, approached the door and unlocked it, then pushed it open. "I'm sorry, officers; please come in. I'm Cassandra Sanderson, the club manager."

"We're actually detectives. I'm Detective Kendrick; this is Detective Reyes. You may have seen on the news that Ruby Gold died the night before last?"

"I did, such a shock. She was kind of a regular around here. Is that why you're here?"

"Yes, actually. She was here shortly before her death, and we wanted to see if you had any video surveillance of that night?"

"You mean she was murdered?" the woman gasped.

"It looks that way, yes."

"That's awful. We do have video cameras set up around the place. I'll happily get you copies of everything from that night. It might take a few minutes though. Can my bartender get you anything? Robbie, get the detectives anything they want."

"Sure thing," he called back.

"We're good. We just need the video surveillance, but was Robbie working that night?"

"I'd have to check the calendar, or you can ask him, he'll tell you." Cassandra smiled. "I'll be right back."

Angel and I headed for the bar. "Hey, Robbie, was it?"

"That's me; what can I get you?"

"Nothing for me," I started.

"Actually, can I get a water?" Angel asked.

"Sure, man, no problem. You want a glass with ice or a bottle?"

"Bottle is fine," Angel replied.

"So, Robbie, were you working the night before last?"

"Sure was."

"Was it busy in here?" Angel asked as he took the offered bottle of water.

"Slammin', man. We were packed."

"Did you notice anything unusual?"

"Not really, everything seemed normal, you know? Just busy."

"Okay, well, thanks," I murmured.

"So did you know Ruby Gold?" Angel asked, like he was making conversation rather than interrogating.

"Oh yeah, Ruby was in all the time. She was, like, a huge draw when she showed up. Hey, she was here the night before last."

"What was she doing? Did you notice?"

"Same as she always does, dancing, drinking, doing a little bl—" He stopped, and his eyes widened. "Um..."

"It's okay, we're not Narco, we're homicide, and I'm going to assume drugs just show up in a place like this, not your fault."

"Yeah, but Cassandra doesn't put up with drugs in the club. She removes anyone dealing in here, but I don't think she knew Ruby was buying shit in the club from people."

"You know for a fact she was buying here in the club?"

Robbie shrugged. "Not for sure. I didn't see it going down or nothin', but you could see it in her eyes. She'd be normal when she came in, and within a few hours she was higher than an airplane. She had to get it somewhere, right?"

"Makes sense. Unless she brought it with her," I suggested.

His face brightened. "You think she was doing that? Bringing her own?"

"I have no idea, but it's a possibility, especially if you say that your boss kicks out anyone she finds dealing."

"That's true, that's true. Still, sad that she OD'd, man. I, like, really liked her. She was a fun girl."

"I've heard that," Angel replied, sipping his water.

"Here you are, Detectives," Cassandra said as she joined us. "I trust Robbie has been accommodating?"

"More than," Angel agreed, lifting his bottled water.

"Thank you, Ms. Sanderson, if we have any questions, we'll be in touch," I said, taking the discs from her.

"My pleasure, Detectives. Come by sometime when the club is open and you're off duty. Your first drink is on me." She smiled as she walked us back to the door.

"Thanks for the offer." I gave her a nod, and Angel and I left.

We spent the remainder of the afternoon watching the surveillance videos, noting every movement Ruby made. Around midnight, a man approached her to dance. He looked a lot like the video surveillance of Bill Smith from the Bradford. Sure enough, about forty minutes later, he left with her.

"So now we know how she connected with him," Angel said, rewatching that section of the video.

"Seems that way. Not sure it helps us though."

"Let's go back through the video, only this time look for him; maybe there's something there," he suggested.

"Couldn't hurt," I agreed as my phone buzzed in my pocket.

Pulling it out, I saw it was Frank texting.

Hey, I know you're working the case, but wanted to touch base. See if you were open to going out this weekend? Maybe Saturday night?

I smiled.

I'd love to if I'm not caught up in the case. You have something planned or want to play it by ear?

Let's play it by ear. I have a few ideas, but
depending on what you've got going on, we
can change things. Better get back to work,
my tiny tornado, I'll call you later.

Okay, talk to you tonight. :)

I put my phone away and glanced at the screen Angel
was flying through. "Pause it there, go back a little bit... yeah,
right there. Isn't that him at the bar, talking to Robbie?"

"Yep, I think it is." He played the video from there, and
we watched the man we knew was El Vibora, aka Bill Smith,
leaning against the bar as he sipped his drink, his eyes
trained on the dance floor. "I think he stood there and
watched her for a while before approaching her."

"Looks that way."

"So what was that about?" He nodded toward my phone.

"Just making tentative weekend plans with Frank."

"Doing something fun?" he asked, keeping his eyes on
the screen.

"We're going to play it by ear, so if our case has us
working overtime, we don't have anything set in stone."

"Good idea," he murmured and then glanced at the clock
on the computer. "We should call it a day. Not much more
we're going to learn from these right now."

"Okay. We'll pick back up tomorrow."

"Don't forget to send Burnett the lab report," he
reminded me.

Sighing, I had forgotten. So I said, "I'll do it now." I took
the physical report to the copier on the other side of the
room and made copies for Burnett. I shoved it all in an
interoffice envelope, put her name on it, and dropped it in
the delivery slot. I wasn't about to deliver it in person.

Later that evening as I sat on my couch, Frank called. I'd poured a glass of wine and was watching an old episode of *Friends* while I waited for him. I answered as soon as the first notes of "Adore You" started.

"Hey, TT. Did you have a good day?"

"Not bad, how about you?" I asked, snuggling back into the pillows on my couch and tucking my legs under me.

"Had to chase a guy down the beach today, got sand everywhere. I think I'm going to be scrubbing it out of my hair for the next year."

I laughed at his exaggeration. "Wish you were here."

"Me too. Or you here at any rate. I miss having you in my arms."

That made me smile. "I miss being in them."

"So how's the case going?"

"Kind of at a loss right now. Turns out our killer is a man of many disguises. At least according to the DEA. An assassin named El Vibora."

"Marce, listen to me. That guy is extremely dangerous. He's like a ghost, and he doesn't leave behind witnesses."

"I know, Frank. I'm fully aware."

"I'm not saying you aren't capable of capturing him and El Gato, if anyone can, I know you can, but I want you to be very careful. Damn, I wish I could be there to back you up on this."

It warmed my heart that he felt that way. "As much as I love hearing that, this is my job."

"I know. I just worry when it's a guy like El Gato. Nobody even knows what his real identity is. You could be standing right next to him and not even know it." He sighed, and I could imagine him running his hand through his hair in frustration.

"I'll be careful. Promise." I went on to tell him about Valerie and how she hadn't shown up today. "The captain told me I had to send the report to her anyway."

"I asked around about her, just, you know, to get a feel for who you were working with; I got the feeling that she's on the outs with the brass. I think she's about to lose rank or have the El Gato case taken from her because she hasn't nailed him yet, and she's been after him for a long time now."

"Really? Robinson didn't say a word about that. Only said she was difficult to work with."

"Maybe he couldn't say anything?"

"Maybe, you could be right. Anyway I've found her rude and unprofessional, and it just rubs me the wrong way. I really don't like her."

"I bet she's pushing back and being rude because you're good at your job, babe. You've closed more serial killer cases than most, and you've got a great track record. She's got nothing in comparison."

"So you're saying she's jealous of me?"

He chuckled. "Hell, babe, I'm jealous of you. What cop wouldn't be? You make it look easy, when I know damn well it's not. It takes a lot of hard work to do what you do."

"You do realize it's not just me, right? It's all of us, Angel, me, Lindsey, Damien, several patrol officers, heck, even Hummel and Vance contribute... I'm not this supercop who does it all on my own."

"I know, but it's your name in the papers. You're the one getting the accolades. It can be intimidating to someone like Burnett."

"Funny, you're the second one today to say I'm intimidating." I grinned.

"Who else told you that?"

"Captain Robinson."

"Well, it's true."

"I didn't intimidate you, though."

"No, you didn't. You intrigued me, and the more I've gotten to know you, the more impressed and enamored of you I become."

"Enamored, hmmm?" I couldn't help the smile that spread across my face.

"Very enamored," he agreed.

"I'd say the same goes for me about you." It was true. I'd never met a man quite like Frank before, and every day I fell just a little bit more for him.

"I'm glad to hear it." He chuckled. "So, this weekend... you mentioned you wanted to have a barbeque; how about we set it up for Sunday? We'll go out Saturday night, and if you're okay with it, I'll stay with you, and we can get everything ready Sunday morning?"

"I like that idea. You've not stayed with me since the night you helped me move in."

"I know. Sorry about that—"

"No, it's okay. I've been to your place more because I like getting out of LA, and you've got the beach right there. But I have to admit, I'd like to have you come stay here more too," I tossed out there, hoping he took the hint that I'd like to see him more than once a week.

"Babe, if I can arrange it and you're up for it, I'd be happy to come over a few times a week. Just depends on our schedules. You know I don't want to interfere in your cases."

"Your being here with me at night isn't interfering."

"I'm glad you think that way. Let me see what my

schedule looks like after this weekend. Maybe we can find a few days it'll work."

"I'd like that, Frank."

"So would I, tornado, so would I."

I yawned and picked up the remote to turn the TV off. "I should probably head to bed."

"Me too. You have sweet dreams, okay?"

I smiled. "You too."

"I'll be dreaming of you, so of course they'll be sweet, and maybe a little naughty," he said with a laugh.

"Good night, Frank," I said, laughing. This man was good for my soul. I hoped that we could work things out so we could see each other more often. I really needed him in my life.

9

LIKE A TERRITORIAL CAT

MARCY

I pulled into the station just before seven. I didn't even stop for coffee, which in hindsight was probably a mistake. The coffee in the precinct wasn't anywhere near drinkable unless you liked drinking tar water, which I didn't. Thankfully, I saw the beignet truck parked close by, and I headed for it.

After grabbing a box of powdered beignets and two coffees, I went inside. I'd seen Angel's car in the lot, so I had gotten him one as well. "I come bearing gifts," I said as I reached my desk.

Angel looked up, and his eyes brightened. "You're brilliant, thanks," he said, taking the coffee I offered. "So, what's the plan for today?" he asked, sipping his drink.

I'd been thinking about that since I woke up this morning. As much as I hated the idea of working with Valerie, I knew we needed to get her take on El Gato. I wanted to know what she knew about him. She'd been chasing him for a decade; she had to have a file on the guy as fat as Elon

Musk's bank account. The question was, could we get her to share that information with us?

"We need to talk to Detective Burnett."

Angel frowned. "What do we need to talk to her for? She's the one who chose not to show up."

"I know, but she's also the one who's been after El Gato for ten years. She's got to have more information on this guy, right?"

"Okay, yeah, probably. Is that why you got me coffee and beignets?" He looked at me suspiciously. "You trying to butter me up?"

I grinned. "It didn't hurt, did it?"

He popped a beignet in his mouth, and powdered sugar dusted his lips. "Nope." He chuckled. "Okay, let's go."

I gulped down some of my coffee and one of the beignets, then dusted off my hands. "Okay."

We headed for the elevator and pushed the button. Five minutes later we entered Vice and found Valerie seated at her desk. "Glad we caught you," I said, approaching her.

She looked startled to see us, and her gaze shifted around the room and back to us. "What are you doing here?"

"Well, you didn't show up yesterday, and you have information we need on El Gato."

"I don't know why you'd need anything on him. It's my case." She sounded like a territorial cat, ready to defend the area she perceived as hers.

I could feel my cheek twitch at that. "We're not going over this again. I am the lead on this case, not you. You have information on our suspect, and I'd like it, please."

Valerie leaned back in her chair and folded her arms across her chest and stared at me mulishly. "She's just some dead junkie actress; it's not like she was all that important," she said, but her words sounded slightly slurred.

I looked over at Angel as he grabbed my arm, probably holding me back from throttling this woman. I gave him a single nod. I wouldn't touch her, but she was about to get the sharp side of my tongue. He let me go.

I slammed my hands down on her desk and leaned forward, almost getting right up into her face. "Listen, we don't talk about victims like that. Ruby was someone's daughter, someone's loved one, someone's friend. She was a person, and she was important. You do not get to pass judgment on her. Got it? And you also don't get to gatekeep information about this case. I want everything you've got on El Gato by noon today. And if you don't cooperate, I'll go to the captain about it."

Her eyes widened, but they were glassy and seemed off. When she said, "Fine, whatever," I could smell alcohol on her breath.

I drew back and narrowed my eyes at her. "Noon." I stood back up and looked at Angel. "Let's go."

Turning, we left Vice and returned to the Homicide Special Section Unit. I was seething and unable to speak my thoughts while we were on the elevator, but back at our desks, I said, "I can't believe her. She's drinking on the job."

"I wondered. Her words sounded pretty slurred." He shook his head. "Do you think the captain knows?"

I shook my head. "Doubt it. Maybe it's a one-off, but I don't like it."

"Maybe she's a struggling alcoholic?" he suggested.

"Doesn't excuse her drinking before nine a.m."

"So what do we do in the meantime?"

"Let's keep looking at Ruby's life. I want to know everything about her. I want to know where she was all day before going to the club. I want to know who she spoke to. I want to know what she ate and where she ate it."

He nodded. "Maybe we should take a trip over to her house? Start there?"

It was an idea I hadn't thought of, but he was right. Maybe we'd find answers there. "Yeah, let's do that." I yanked open my desk drawer and grabbed my purse, then slammed it shut. I was still angry about Valerie. I stood still for a moment and took a few calming breaths. Glancing at Angel, I added, "Do we have the keys to her place?"

"Yeah, they're with her effects, which were delivered to us sometime yesterday. Let me grab them." He turned and pawed through the things on his desk and opened an envelope, then pulled out a set of keys.

"You'd better drive. I'm already pissed off enough. I don't need to get behind the wheel of the car."

"Sure thing," he said, pulling his keys from his pocket.

"Know where we're going?" I asked, just to make conversation as we got in the car.

"Yep." He plugged the address into the GPS, and we took off toward West Hollywood.

"Did she have an apartment?" I asked. I hadn't actually looked into where Ruby lived, or what her finances were; Angel had taken that task on.

"No, she was probably living way beyond her means. Her outgoing house payment was nearly thirty-five thousand a month. She missed the last two payments."

"Whoa, that's crazy money. Where the heck did she live?"

"On La Jolla Avenue."

"In one of those multimillion-dollar homes? Did she really do that well in her career?"

"She did at first. She was pulling in a couple of million per video, but her spending habits were high. She pulled cash a lot. My guess would be for drugs unless she has a whole lot of assets at this house that she bought with cash."

"Considering the track marks that Damien showed us, I'm going to go with you on that."

Twenty minutes later we pulled up to a Spanish-style home. It had a Mediterranean feel to it that I actually liked. Angel pulled the keys out, and we entered through the front door.

"Wow, this place is pretty snazzy," I murmured as the lights came on automatically.

Angel was standing by the door, staring at a panel. "Looks pretty high tech too. Everything is automated, it seems."

"Let's check it out." I didn't really have an occasion to be in a home like this often, especially without owner supervision, it was kind of cool to just wander a bit, but we were here to discover if there were any clues to what Ruby was into that might have led to her death. I doubted I would find it by sitting on her plush sofa and watching a movie, like I wanted to do.

We walked through the living area, toward the kitchen. "How big is this place?" I wondered out loud.

"I looked it up." He held up his phone. "It's got four bedrooms, five bathrooms, and a pool with a cabana out back."

"Wow. I'm almost envious of her. Almost. Wouldn't ever do porn to get it, and certainly wouldn't do drugs and lose it if I had it." I shook my head.

Angel grinned. "I can just see you living here now, Marce.

Throwing Hollywood parties, mingling with the upper echelon, Brad Pitt on your arm..."

"Not Brad Pitt, Ryan Reynolds." I grinned back.

"His wife, Blake would never allow it." He shook his head and laughed.

"Hey, it's my fake life. I can fake marry Ryan Reynolds if I want," I returned with a wink.

We continued into the kitchen, and I stopped just inside the doorway. The cabinets were a light wood, as were the countertops. Even the double-door fridge looked like it had wooden doors over stainless steel. We started opening drawers, looking for anything that stood out.

"Anything?" I asked, closing the drawer I'd sifted through, coming up empty.

"Nothing over here. You?"

"Nope. Let's look for an office and then maybe check the master bedroom?"

"Sounds like a plan." He nodded and started across the room, but stopped short as he looked through the rounded glass doors to the patio. "Come look at this."

"What is it?" I moved next to him and stared out to the backyard. It was an oasis of luxury. A pool with a natural waterfall, a cabana that had ivy covering the sides and trees on either side of it, and lounge chairs that were probably more comfortable than my sofa. "She really had it all here, didn't she?"

"Must have been nice. Too bad she ruined it all by taking drugs."

"Sad, really," I acknowledged. "Come on, let's finish up."

We found a room near the bedrooms set up like an office, well, sort of. Mostly it held a desk and a chair and then bookcases with awards and a collection of her movies and some posters. Angel went through the desk, and I headed for the master suite.

I started with her dresser and found a glassine packet of white powder, another with weed, and several pictures with various people scantily dressed or flat-out naked. I confiscated all of it. I'd need to identify the people in the photos, and the drugs needed to be logged into evidence. I went through the rest of the drawers, then hit her nightstand and found another packet of weed. From there I headed for her bathroom. I found some drug paraphernalia and added that to my confiscation pile.

"You find anything?" Angel asked, coming into the room.

I pointed to the bed, where I'd put everything. "Some."

Angel headed over and picked up the photos. "Hey, isn't this Carmen Veraga?" He held up a photo of two women making out.

"Looks like it. I didn't know she swung that way." I shrugged. The woman was a pretty big-name actress who'd starred with some of the biggest names in Hollywood. Last I'd heard she was dating Devon Michaels, a massive action star at the moment.

"Think Ruby was blackmailing these people?"

I tilted my head as I thought about it. "Maybe. Did you see anything like that in her accounts?"

"There were a few cash deposits every few months, not a lot, at least not for her, so I guess it's possible."

"That could be an avenue to pursue. We'll need to check out all of these people in the photos."

"They'll be thrilled."

I blew out a breath. "Yeah. Probably every one of them will lawyer up."

"Maybe. Did you find anything else?"

"Just those and the drugs. Figured we should take them with us."

"I'll grab an evidence bag from the car." He set the photos down with the rest and jogged out of the room.

I heard the front door open and close. I looked around the room a bit more, but didn't find anything else that was worth our attention.

Angel returned, and we bagged everything separately. The drugs in their own bags and then the photos in another.

We locked the house back up as we left and then headed back to the station. It was nearly noon, and I was anxious to see if Valerie had complied with my demand. If she hadn't, I was ready to go straight to the captain.

I wanted that information, and I was going to get it come hell or high water.

10

DOING A 180

MARCY

As Angel drove, my phone rang, but as soon as I saw the number, I hit decline. I wasn't going to put myself through another of *his* harassing calls. A moment later my phone dinged, saying I had a voicemail.

"Everything okay?" Angel asked, glancing over at me.

"It's Jordan. He's been harassing me since he was fired."

Angel gave me a concerned look. "Why didn't you tell me?"

I shrugged. "It hasn't been a big deal until just recently. I've got Stephen handling it. I just forward everything to him, and he's been consolidating all the evidence for me. He wants me to file a restraining order, but you know how that goes."

"Yeah, I do, but you should still do it. You want me to talk to him?"

"You don't have to, Angel. I know you're friends with him—"

"No. I'm not anymore, Marce. Haven't been for some time now. That being said, I can still talk to him as a former friend concerned for his behavior. You know I don't like the way he treated you, not then and not now."

"Yeah, then. If you can talk some sense into him, I'd be glad for it."

"And you really do need to file that restraining order."

"I will," I murmured as we pulled into the precinct. My stomach rumbled loudly, and I gave a self-deprecating laugh. "Maybe we should hit the food truck before we go in?"

"How about you grab us food, and I'll go make a call to Jordan? Get him to back off and leave you alone."

"If you can manage that, I'll buy you lunch for a week," I said with a grin. "Which do you want?" I asked, looking at the couple of trucks parked on the street nearby.

Angel followed my gaze to the Lobsta Truck and Tropic Truck. "Let's go with Lobsta. Get me a Lobsta roll, the clam chowder and some Cape Cod potato chips."

"And lemonade?" I asked, knowing they made it fresh squeezed.

"Sure."

He headed into the precinct with our evidence bags while I made my way over to the truck. I waited my turn and then placed his order and added mine. I went for the crab roll, the lobster bisque, and chips, as well as a lemonade for myself. After grabbing napkins and utensils, as well as a carrier for the drinks, I headed into the building with the food.

Angel met me at the door to the detective pool before I could even enter the room. He had a strange look on his face. He took the drink carrier and directed me to the hallway outside the offices. "Come over here for a minute."

"What's going on?" Concern swept over me, and a chill

went down my spine. "Is Jordan here? Is he planning to harass me in person since I won't take his calls?"

"What? No. It's Detective Burnett."

I relaxed and then rolled my eyes. "What about her?"

"She's in there waiting for us. She wants to cooperate and is ready to share everything."

I frowned. "Seriously?"

He nodded.

"Okay, so why is that a problem?"

"She wants us to come to her office, and she's being pretty adamant about it. She doesn't want to talk out in the open of the detective pool."

"We've got the incident room we can use, and you couldn't let her tell me this?" I felt like I was missing something.

"I just want us to be on the same page before we talk to her. She didn't bring the file or anything. She almost seems feverish about being helpful now. It's weird."

"Okay. Well, let's do this. We'll eat our food, go over what we found at Ruby's, and then tell her we'll join her in her office in an hour. Think that will appease her?"

"Maybe. I locked up the stuff we found. I didn't want her going through it before we had a chance to."

"Smart. Did you call Jordan?"

"No, sorry. She was waiting on me when I walked in, so no chance yet."

"It's fine. It can wait. This takes precedence."

Together we headed into the office, and I noticed right away what Angel meant by her acting squirrelly. She couldn't stop fidgeting. Her fingers tapped her arm, her feet kept shifting, and her eyes bounced around the room.

"Detective Burnett, Angel tells me you're ready to cooperate with us. I appreciate that. How about we meet you down at your office in an hour? As you can see, we're about to eat lunch, and we have a few things to wrap up before we talk."

"Oh? What things? I can help."

"No, thanks though. It's just running down a few alibis on another case. Nothing major."

"You're working on another case?" She seemed taken aback.

"It's an old case, but yes. We sometimes work on two or three cases at a time up here. Crime doesn't take a break, you know?"

That wasn't technically true. It was only occasionally that Angel and I found ourselves working multiple cases that weren't linked. And since Jordan had been fired, it was rare for us to have more than one case at a time. The captain liked to keep us focused on the major cases and sent Detectives Hummel and Vance off on the domestics and randoms that cropped up because they were generally solved quickly. The only time we did those were when we didn't have a major case, but Valerie didn't need to know that.

"Oh. Well, okay. I guess that's all right then. An hour? My office?" she asked, sounding jittery, like an addict jonesing for their next hit.

Suddenly I was glad that Angel had locked up the evidence. The way she was acting, I was afraid she'd steal it and use it for herself. It wasn't a pretty thought, but it couldn't be helped. I held up the bag and said, "If you don't mind. Our lunch is getting cold."

"Oh, right. I'll see you in an hour." She stared at us for a couple more seconds and then fled the room.

"So that was weird," I murmured and started unloading the bag.

"Very," Angel agreed.

We ate, and he pulled out the photos. We started putting names to the people in them, making notes and prioritizing whom we needed to call. Some of the photos were of other celebrities engaged in questionable behavior with people they weren't married to, and then there were photos of various men in suits that didn't seem to quite fit with the others, but it all seemed to be one giant party.

"Where do you think this was?" I asked, studying the background of the photos. "They all seem to have been taken at the same party in the same place, but not Ruby's house."

Angel looked at them as well. "Definitely not her place, but it does look like a home. An apartment maybe?"

"What makes you say that?" I asked, lifting another photo to look at the background.

"Look here." Angel rolled his chair over next to mine and held out a photo, where he pointed to the window in the background. "If you look out the window, you can see another high-rise out there. Looks like maybe the tenth floor? Maybe higher?"

"Good catch. So who in Ruby's circle has an apartment in a high-rise?"

"Maybe we can use this photo to triangulate the exact building?"

I looked at him with surprise. "You know how to do that?"

He shook his head. "Not me, but the tech department probably can."

"Then let's get this over to Howard on the way to Valerie's office."

Angel rolled back to his desk and began eating his chowder as he continued to write down names. "This guy"— he held up another photo—"he's in a lot of these. I think this is her manager."

I took the photo and looked it over. The man had medium-dark skin, brown eyes, and wavy, dark brown hair that seemed to be thinning just a bit. He was dressed in jeans that were distressed, and a fitted white T-shirt with a couple of gold chains. Despite how he dressed, he looked older, like he was probably in his mid-forties. "Samson Martinez."

"Yeah, that's him."

"Where does he live?" I asked.

Angel arched a brow and then turned to his computer and typed in Martinez's name. "Looks like he lives in a condo in Cascade Rise over on Doheny Road."

I was trying to picture the building. "Wait, isn't that near Sierra Towers? Could that be the high-rise in the background of the picture?"

"Maybe so, we'll have tech confirm it. Maybe they can pinpoint exactly which room this was taken from, and we can match it to Martinez's place."

Finally it felt like we were getting somewhere, at least on this part of the investigation. I finished my chips and tossed my garbage in the bin. "Ready?" I asked, glancing at him.

He drank the last of his lemonade and then nodded. "Yep." He stood up, dropped his garbage in the trash, then picked up the pictures. "I'll have them use a couple of these; maybe it will help with pinpointing the location."

As we started out of the detective pool, my phone rang

with "We Are Family." "Hey, this is Stephen. I need to take it. Can you take those to the tech and tell them what we want?"

"Sure thing," Angel agreed and headed down the hall as I hit the answer button.

"Hey, sis," Stephen said.

"Hey, what's up?"

"I got that last voicemail you forwarded to me. You need to be careful. Jordan sounds completely deranged. Have you gotten that restraining order yet?"

"No, but I will. Just been busy."

"Do it today. As I said before, I know it's just a piece of paper, but it will help if he tries something."

"You think he will?"

"I don't know. Maybe, yeah." He sighed. "Look, Marce, you're all the family I've got, so be careful, okay?"

I smiled. "Always. Thanks for having my back." I glanced around me in the hallway, and my mind flashed to Detective Burnett and her strange behavior. I couldn't officially look into her, but maybe... "Hey, do you think you could do some digging on someone for me?"

"What, like consultant work? Like I did before?"

"Well, sort of, but really more as just a favor to me?" I hedged. "I'll buy you dinner."

He chuckled. "Who is it you want me to dig into? Not Frank, right?"

That made me grin. "No, not Frank." I looked around again and then lowered my voice. "Her name is Valerie Burnett. She's a detective here, but with Vice."

Stephen paused, not saying anything, and I was afraid we'd lost connection.

"Stephen?"

"Why are you wanting me to dig into some Vice cop's life?"

"She's on this case with me, and something just seems off."

"Okay, I'll see what I can find."

"Thanks, Stephen. I appreciate it. I'd better go. Angel is on his way back to me."

"Okay, bye," he said and then hung up.

I slid my phone in my pocket as Angel walked up.

"All good?" he asked.

"Yep. Shall we go beard the lioness in her den?"

"No time like the present."

11

ASSASSINATING THE JACK OF HEARTS

EL VIBORA

I t was a little after one in the afternoon, but my boss was getting impatient. He wanted this killing done and feared it wasn't going to happen before the bastard got away. It wouldn't matter if he ran though. I'd still kill him. There was nowhere on the planet he could hide that I couldn't find him.

Besides, from everything I'd seen, the guy was broker than a 1970s Ford Pinto. His bank account was in the red, and he was about to lose the lease on his penthouse apartment here at Cascade Rise. I stared up at the building from the parking lot. It stood about ten stories high, about half the size of Sierra Towers across the street.

I was wearing a maintenance uniform, which would get me into the building without much comment. I'd donned a shaggy blonde wig, matching mustache, and a fake nose. Nobody would recognize me. Even the car I was using was one I'd acquired for the day, with a fake license and debit card to an account I'd close before the end of business hours.

Climbing out of the car, I checked to be sure I had what I

needed. I wouldn't be bringing a variety of syringes today. I only needed the one. It was a slowish-acting poison, one that would make my target have trouble breathing for a bit before he finally succumbed to the liquid fire that I'd fill him with.

I headed for the building, the capped syringe and playing card in my pocket. I used a handkerchief to push the button for the elevator, not that my fingers would leave prints, but better safe than sorry, in my book. When the elevator arrived, I stepped on, pulled on a pair of gloves, and pushed the button for the penthouse floor. There were two apartments on that floor, but I'd only be entering one. I reached into my shirt pocket and pulled out my lock picks. When the door opened, I stepped out and turned for Samson's apartment.

Using the lock pick, I had the door open within seconds. I was fully prepared to disable the alarm if it went off, but it didn't. Turned out Samson hadn't set it. My lucky day.

Silently, I made my way through the apartment to the doorway of the master suite. I stood in the shadows of the hallway, watching him for a moment.

Samson was hastily tossing clothes into a couple of suitcases laid out on the bed. It looked as though he was in a hurry to leave. He'd be leaving all right, just not the way he expected. I paused, listening as he muttered to himself.

"It was a stupid drug debt; why'd he have her killed?" Samson seemed completely baffled. "I can't be next. Surely, he won't come after me, right?"

I'd have to set him straight, but then I supposed the lethal injection he was about to get would be answer enough for that.

"I know he's loco," Samson continued as he tossed

another stack of clothes in the open suitcase, "but we're family. I'll just go away for a bit, let things settle down..."

It was a good plan, but he should have executed it a week ago, not waited. He wasn't wrong though. El Gato was loco. I thought it was foolish to do what he was doing, but it wasn't my call. He paid me to execute those he deemed unworthy of life, and I complied. I hated doing this to women, but money was money, and I had bills to pay just like everyone else. Thankfully, this one would be easier than the last one.

My thoughts went to Ruby and the pictures I'd sent off to the TV news station, anonymously, of course. El Gato had wanted her seen as a warning to others who might be considering doing what she'd done. I assumed the pictures had accomplished what he'd intended. Probably why Samson was trying to flee now. He knew his end was coming.

On silent feet, I moved behind Samson as I pulled the syringe from my pocket and uncapped it. Grabbing him from behind, I stabbed the needle into his neck and pressed on the syringe, sending the liquid into him. Letting him go, I stepped back.

Samson gasped and spun around, his hand clutching the spot where I'd injected him. "What? No! No, you didn't..." His eyes widened, and he started to gasp for breath harder. He dropped to his knees, his eyes on me as he sank back against the bed.

"'Fraid so," I murmured.

"Why?" he asked, shaking his head slightly.

"It's your own fault. You should have made her keep her mouth shut. Now you know too much, and you let her irresponsibility lead you astray. El Gato doesn't like people who run their mouths and don't pay him what he's owed on top of that."

Samson's eyes fluttered, and I knew he wouldn't be with me for much longer. His breathing was already slowing down drastically.

"Should never have allowed her to try to blackmail him," I muttered as I tossed the Black Cat playing card with the jack of hearts into his lap.

His mouth fell open slightly, and his head lolled to the side; his eyes closed permanently. Samson was gone.

I didn't regret killing him. He was just one of many over the years. I felt nothing. There wasn't even a thrill in killing him; it was just another job.

I glanced in the mirror above the dresser and adjusted the wig I was wearing, making sure it covered my own hair, before backing out of the room and returning to the front door. I used the handkerchief to open it and let myself out. I didn't bother to relock the door, as I was going to leave it ajar anyway. El Gato wanted him found, and the apartment was too nice to let it be corrupted with a decaying corpse. The sooner he was found, the better.

As I headed out of the building through the side entrance, I thought about triggering the fire alarm, but decided against it. The building staff or the neighbor would discover him soon enough. By that time, I'd be long gone and have a new appearance.

All in all, it was a good day's work.

12

VEXING VALERIE
ANGEL

As Marcy and I headed down to Vice, I glanced at her. She was wearing her hair in a low ponytail today. I liked it, but didn't comment on it. She wouldn't appreciate me mentioning it, and I knew it.

Instead, I told her what the tech guys had said. "So, spoke to Howard; he's pretty sure he can figure out where that building is from the photo. Said he'd have something for us by next week."

"That sounds good; we need to get on that. I really think we might be onto something with the blackmail angle. That does make more sense than her being killed over a drug debt. Maybe this killer is just mimicking one of El Gato's hits. We should check into the Black Cat card deck angle too, see if any have been sold recently to one of those people in the photos."

"I'll add it to our list of things to do." I nodded, jotting a note in my planner. It was a solid lead, and Marcy was right. It did make more sense, but still we were heading down to Vice to get information from Valerie about El Gato himself.

We stepped off the elevator and ran into the woman we were after. It looked as though she was leaving.

"Hey, are we late?" I asked, noticing she seemed in a hurry.

"Sorry, I do want to do this, but I'm being sent out on a call, so this will have to wait. Can we meet at the Short Stop after work? I can give it to you both then."

Marcy looked like she was ready to argue, but I stepped in before she could. "Yeah, we could do that."

"Great, see you at five thirty or so," she said with a wave and jumped on the elevator, stabbing the button repeatedly.

"I swear. That woman is very vexing," Marcy huffed. "She says she wants to cooperate and then runs away from us. I bet she doesn't even have a crime scene to head out to."

I chuckled. "Let's give her the benefit of the doubt. We can go make those calls to our potential blackmail victims and look into the Black Cat playing cards."

Marcy sighed. "Okay. At least we'll stay productive."

We spent the rest of the afternoon calling various shops around the city as well as certain Hollywood elites and asking them about those pictures. It turned out that the cards were actually pretty popular, and they'd sold a lot of them over the past couple of years. It would be difficult to identify exactly who had bought the deck that was being used.

As to the celebrities, only three admitted that, yes, Ruby had asked for money and, yes, they'd paid her off, but they'd been told the photos were tossed in the fire afterward. They were pretty shocked to find they still existed and asked for them back. Several claimed they would get their lawyers involved if necessary, which it wasn't; however, they would have to wait until the case was closed before taking possession of them, as they were still evidence.

At five, Marcy and I called it a day and headed to the parking lot.

"I can drive if you want," I offered.

"I'm gonna take my car. I don't want to have to come back here tonight. I'll just head straight home from the bar."

"Okay, I'll follow you, then." Getting in my car, I debated calling Callie. We didn't have any actual plans, and I knew she was probably working late. Still, it might be nice to hear her voice. And it would help get my mind off my best friend. I hit the number for her salon as I pulled out of my parking place.

"The Mane Event Salon, this is Rebecca; how may I serve you today?"

"Hey, Rebecca, it's Angel. Is Callie available?"

"She just finished with a client; let me get her for you."

"Thanks." I pulled onto the highway as I waited for her to come on the line.

"Well, this is a nice surprise. I wasn't expecting to hear from you until later."

I could hear the smile in her voice, and it made me happy. "I was just thinking about you. I have to go do a work thing, we're meeting a detective from Vice, but I thought afterwards, maybe I could pick up dinner, and we could meet at your place?"

"I'll probably be here until at least nine thirty tonight, late client," she said with a sigh.

"That's okay. I'll get something that will keep. Pizza maybe?"

"I'd like that. You know where I keep the key."

I smiled. "I do." Like Marcy, Callie had moved into a new

home as well. She had wanted more space and even had a room where she could style special clients. The key to her place was hidden in a fake rock in a flowerpot on her back porch. It wasn't really the safest place, but it was a gated backyard and not in plain sight. "I'll see you when you get home."

"See you then. Have fun at your meeting," she said before hanging up.

I doubted I'd be having fun, but the Short Stop did have some good memories. It was where I'd gone with Callie on our first date. I pulled into the lot and parked next to Marcy's car. Climbing out, I locked my car and joined Marcy by the bumper of hers. Together we headed into the bar.

I noticed Valerie seated at a table for four, two empty beer glasses were on the table, and she was drinking from a third. I glanced at Marcy. She didn't look happy to see that Valerie had been there drinking for who knew how long.

"Hey!" Valerie called out, but she drew the word out so it lasted a full five seconds.

"Evening, Valerie. How long have you been here?" Marcy asked, eyeing the beer glasses.

"Just got here about three minutes ago; have a seat." She rattled the back of one of the wooden chairs, and it clattered against the wood plank floorboards.

Marcy yanked the chair from her grasp and sat down, setting her purse on the table in front of her.

I took the seat next to her and opposite Valerie. We were seated right in the middle of the room. I thought it was an odd choice for a meeting about a secretive drug lord, but this whole thing with Valerie seemed just a little surreal.

"You said you wanted to cooperate?" Marcy started.

"Sure, sure. Let's get you some drinks first," Valerie said, waving to the cocktail waitress.

"Yes, ma'am, what can I get for you?"

"Beers all around," Valerie replied. "You can put them on my tab."

"Of course, ma'am." The waitress' gaze drifted to mine. "What are you drinking?"

"I'll have a Heineken."

"Blue Moon," Marcy said before the waitress could ask.

"Coming right up," she said as she started to turn away.

"And I'll have another Coors," Valerie added, catching the young woman's arm to keep her from hurrying off.

The waitress nodded, pulled her arm free, and drifted off.

I watched Marcy's face sour, but she didn't say anything, which surprised me. "So, did your case go well?" I asked, trying to make small talk until Valerie was ready to talk about El Gato.

"Yeah. Just a drug dealer we busted. It was nothing. Small potatoes."

"So they weren't connected to El Gato?" I asked.

Valerie's eyes widened, and she looked around the room to see if anyone was paying any attention to us.

However, as I followed her gaze, I couldn't make out anyone who seemed to have a vested interest in us. Of course, I could have been wrong.

Her shoulders relaxed a little, and then she said, "No. Just some lowlife selling dime bags of weed to underage kids. Wouldn't have been a problem if he was selling to adults." She shrugged.

The fact she'd said that without slurring had me

impressed because I knew she had been drunk earlier, and she'd clearly consumed three full beers since getting here. I wondered if she was a high-functioning alcoholic. I recalled there were certain people whose reflexes and possibly their thoughts improved under the influence. It was called hyperactive dopamine response, but I wasn't about to ask if that was something she had, though.

The waitress returned and set our beers down before us. "Let me know if you need anything else," she said, but didn't wait to see if we did indeed need something else.

I couldn't blame her, the place was packed, and a glance at the TV told me it was the pending ballgame that had drawn people in. The Angels were playing the Mariners in Seattle in less than an hour. I'd forgotten it was a game night. With all of these people around, it probably wasn't the best idea to be talking about El Gato or our case. Too many ears might overhear us. A glance at Marcy told me she was thinking the same.

"So, I wanted to tell you I'm sorry for not being a team player before," Valerie said. "I've been dealing with a lot of crap lately, and my aunt just died, so I've not been in the best mindset, you know?"

"Sorry for your loss," I said, but I nearly had to shout it to be heard over the group of eight men who had just walked in wearing Angels' jerseys.

"I'm glad you're going to be a team player, but meeting here probably wasn't the best idea. Especially considering the game and all these people here. Why don't we meet tomorrow and go over the case file?" Marcy suggested.

"Yeah, that might—" She stopped as her phone, which was on the table, began to ring; then so did mine and Marcy's.

I pulled mine out and saw it was dispatch. "Reyes," I answered, looking at them as an overwhelming feeling of dread filled me.

13

DEATH AND TRAUMA
MARCY

I knew the minute all three of our phones went off that someone was dead. "Kendrick," I answered as soon as I pulled mine from my purse.

"Detective, there's a dead body at Cascade Rise on Doheny Road. I was told it may pertain to a case you're working on and to send you to the scene."

I sighed. "Okay, thanks. We're on our way." I hung up. Dispatch didn't name the victim, but considering the address, I was pretty sure we were going to find Samson Martinez dead at the scene. I glanced at Angel. "I knew we should have gone to talk to him sooner."

He nodded. The look on his face told me he was thinking the same thing.

I turned to Valerie, who was still on the phone. She seemed to be arguing with Dispatch.

"You can send a car," she complained. "I came in an Uber. I'm not taking that to a crime scene."

"You can ride with me," I offered, but I did it through gritted teeth. I didn't want to drive her drunk ass to the crime scene. I didn't want her anywhere near the crime scene, but I figured better to have her with me, where I could control what she touched, than to have her off on her own.

Valerie looked up and seemed surprised to find us sitting there with her. "Oh, okay, never mind on the car. I've got a ride—" She paused and then added, "I'm with Detectives Kendrick and Reyes; they offered." A moment later she hung up. "Oh, I should pay the tab, right?" She looked around for the waitress.

I pulled three twenties from my purse and laid them on the table. "That should cover it and her tip. You can pay me back." I would be sure to collect that later because I wasn't going to let her off the hook. She had invited us, and on top of that, she'd had at least four beers at eight bucks a pop. Toss in mine and Angel's, that was six beers. I probably should have left more for the tip, but it was all I had in cash.

We hurried out of the bar and to our cars. Valerie got in my passenger seat and put the siren on the dashboard. As soon as I flicked it on, I pulled out of the lot and onto the street. It probably wasn't necessary to hurry, the guy was already dead, but we did get there faster than we would have without it.

I parked and moved to the entrance of Cascade Rise, flashing my badge at the patrol officer guarding the building. Luckily, news crews hadn't been contacted yet, but it was only a matter of time before they showed up and started shouting questions, making their own connections. I hated it when they speculated about our cases, but I hated it even more when they were given information they shouldn't have and instilled fear into the public. It just made our jobs harder.

"Deceased is in the penthouse, ma'am. Neighbor called it in," Officer Curtis shared.

"Thanks, when the news crews show up, give them nothing, got it?"

"Yes, ma'am."

"CSI or the coroner here yet?"

"No, ma'am, not yet."

"Send them up as soon as they arrive."

"I will, ma'am."

I gestured for Valerie and Angel to enter, and the three of us took the elevator up. At the top floor, I strode out to see there were two doors on this floor, but only one was being guarded by a cop.

"Hey, Lopez," I said as I reached him. "What have we got?"

Angel and Valerie flanked me, listening in, but not saying anything. Angel nodded at Lopez, but Valerie just stood there.

"Neighbor was returning home, saw the door ajar, and went to investigate, ma'am. Found the resident, Samson Martinez, deceased in the bedroom."

"Deceased how?"

"Not sure, ma'am. No sign of a struggle or anything. He is just on the floor; no sign of a gunshot wound or anything. The neighbor did attempt CPR, but wasn't successful."

That irritated me because that meant they moved the body. "Did they tell you exactly how they found him?"

"No, ma'am, but they are right across the hall with Officers Kim and Desmond, if you want to speak to them."

That calmed me a bit. I wanted to talk to them, but not until after I assessed the scene and the CSI crew arrived. "Okay, thanks." I turned to Angel and Valerie. "Let's go in." I pulled a pair of latex gloves from the bag of them I had in my purse, then looked at Valerie. "You have gloves?"

"No."

Sighing, I pulled another pair from my purse and handed them to her as Angel finished putting on his own pair.

We entered the residence, and I glanced into each of the rooms we passed, but nothing seemed disturbed. In the bedroom, we found Samson laid out on the floor, his mouth open, and his eyes glassy. His lips were tinged a light blue, and I knew he'd been dead for a hot minute. A few hours at minimum.

A cursory glance about the room showed that he'd clearly been packing suitcases, probably hoping to outrun what had found him. On the floor next to and partially under the body was the jack of hearts. I didn't have to turn it over to know it was from a Black Cat deck of cards. It was obvious to me that he had been killed by the same person who killed Ruby. I just didn't see the injection mark. I'd leave that to Damien to find.

"I want the suitcases taken into evidence. Bag the card, and then once the CSI team shows up, we'll go over this place like we did Ruby's," I said to Angel.

"You went to Ruby's place?" Valerie questioned, her eyes wide.

"If you had been cooperating, you would have known that."

She didn't look happy about that, but I didn't care. I was going to be having words with the captain tomorrow about her. I was pissed off that I hadn't reached out to Samson before he was offed. It was my fault he was dead. I could have had him in protective custody if I'd known he was on El

Gato's hit list. I felt like I was three steps behind on this case and going about things blind. I didn't like it. Part of that blame lay at Valerie's feet.

Angel closed up the suitcases and set them by the door. They were too big for evidence bags, so he just put stickers on the hard shells of the cases. The card he picked up by the corner and dropped into a baggie with an evidence label.

"I just can't figure out why El Gato would go after two of his customers like this. I mean, I get that maybe they owed him money, but you can't get money from a dead client. So why kill them?" Angel asked.

"Good questions. I'd like to know the answer to that as well. Valerie? You got anything? You've been after this guy for a while; why would he do this?"

"I don't know. Do I look like I have El Gato's ear? The guy is unpredictable."

I wanted to say more, but I heard the door to the apartment open and decided against it.

"This place is huge," a voice said from the hallway.

I turned to see Jeff Calhoun, who worked as the CSI team lead on cases Lindsey couldn't get to personally. He had Kimberly March, a CSI photographer, with him, a camera slung around her neck and her dark hair in multiple braids twisted up into a bun. Beyond them were a group of young CSI techs all dressed in their white scrub jumpsuits.

"Hey, Jeff," I greeted him, then turned to her. "Kimberly, good to see you."

"I know you were expecting Lindsey, but she had a thing tonight, so here we are." Jeff shrugged.

"I don't know why you'd think I'd expect her over you." I shook my head, giving him a confused look.

"Well, she usually takes these higher-profile cases, which is what you do. Just figured you expected her."

I had to wonder if he was a little bitter about that, because it sounded that way to me. Still, I assured him, "I'm just happy to have you and your team here. I don't expect that you'll find much here, considering the last scene. This killer is meticulous. I want the entire apartment dusted for prints. I want every inch of this place gone through; look for anything with a black cat on it."

"Okay, anything else?"

"Get someone on the video surveillance for the building."

"Got it."

Damien walked in a moment later with his kit. "You got a body for me, Kendrick?"

"Over here." I directed him to Samson. "Pretty sure he was given an injection like Ruby, but I'll leave you to figure out where. Also, noticed his lips tinged a slight blue, figure he's been dead for a few hours at least, but I'm hoping you can give me an exact time of death."

"Well, let's see what we've got." Damien moved toward the body and squatted down. He poked at the face, then lifted the arm and tried to move it, but it seemed difficult. From there he moved to the legs, and again that seemed difficult. "Okay, so judging by the way the body is stiffening, but not fully stiff, I'd say he's been dead between six and seven hours. I'll take a liver temperature to verify that." He opened his bag and got out his thermometer, then turned back to the body.

I looked away as he poked it into Samson's liver. I didn't like that part. "Well?"

"Given I looked at the thermostat before coming in here,

and the apartment is a comfortable seventy-one degrees, I'd say he died around one this afternoon."

"That helps, thanks." I turned to Jeff, who was chatting with Angel. "Hey, Jeff, Angel, when we get the building surveillance, we'll probably want to look between noon and two; that will give us a good window to find our killer."

"Do you want me to go talk to the staff?" Angel asked. "Get the videos?"

I shook my head. "Let Jeff's team handle it." I slid my gaze to Valerie, who seemed to be watching everything with wide-eyed interest and something that looked like suspicion on her face. "Can you—" I didn't finish my sentence because Angel picked up on what I was asking.

"On it." He nodded and then moved over to join Valerie.

I relaxed a little more, knowing she wasn't going to mess with anything since Angel was right there. I wasn't sure what it was about her that made me not trust her, but I didn't. Call it a gut feeling or whatever, but I didn't want her anywhere near this or any other crime scene.

I looked back at Damien, who was examining the body. "Anything else you can tell me?"

"Pretty sure he was injected here in the neck. There's a slight bruising around this spot. I'll have to get him to the morgue and do a full autopsy to be sure, but this does look like a possible injection spot."

"Okay, I'll release the scene to you and Jeff. How long are you thinking?"

"Probably won't have anything for you until midmorning at the earliest."

I gave him a nod. "Angel, Valerie, gather up the evidence we've collected so far. Jeff, let me know if you find anything else; you've got my cell, right?"

Jeff walked over to me and pulled his phone out. "I think so; let me check." He scrolled through his contacts and then nodded. "I've got you."

"Great. If you don't call tonight, I'll look for your report tomorrow morning."

"Yes, ma'am. I'll have it to you before noon."

"Thanks."

Back outside, we headed for our cars, avoiding the news crews who had shown up to take in the scene. Angel put the suitcases in the trunk of his car. "I'll take them to the precinct and get them logged in, along with the card."

"Thanks, Angel," I said with a yawn. "We'll write up the reports in the morning and confer with the captain then too."

"Sounds like a plan." He waved and got in his car.

I unlocked my car and gestured for Valerie to get in. "Can I drop you at home?"

"I guess. Unless you want to go back to the Short Stop?"

"I don't think so, but I'm happy to drop you there if you want." It was on the way to my place, so I didn't mind.

"Would you? That'd be great."

It was her life; if she wanted to spend it drinking until her liver deteriorated, then that was her choice. I just didn't want her anywhere near me if that was what she was going to do. Still, she was a fellow officer; maybe I should try to talk her out of it. "You sure? It's kind of late, and we've got an early meeting tomorrow."

"I'll be fine."

I did as she asked, dropping her at the bar, and then headed home. I sent Frank a text telling him I was home, then got ready for bed. He replied as I was in the shower, telling me to get some rest and we'd talk tomorrow. I smiled at his "have sweet dreams" comment. I doubted I would, but it was nice of him to wish that for me.

The next morning, I swung through the coffee shop drive-thru and picked up coffee for me, Angel, and the captain. I thought about grabbing one for Valerie, but decided against it. I had no clue what she drank, and I didn't want to waste my money. I'd already forked over sixty dollars on our drinks the night before.

"Coffee, you're the best," Angel said, taking the cup and gulping it.

"Valerie here yet?"

Angel shook his head. "I bet she's a no-show again."

I wasn't about to take that bet. I didn't think she'd show either. We waited another few minutes, but when she didn't show, I said, "Let's go see Robinson. His coffee is getting cold anyway."

I knocked on his door, since we were there before even Jason showed up. "Sir? It's Kendrick and Reyes."

"Come in," he called. As we walked in, his gaze landed on the two cups in my hands. "One of those for me?"

I smiled and handed him his coffee. "Yes, sir. Wanted to catch you up on the case."

We spent the next fifteen minutes going over both where we were with Ruby's murder and what we knew about Samson's. I explained that once again we were waiting on Valerie and what she knew about El Gato.

"Sir, about Detective Burnett... I'm a little concerned. She seems to be drinking a lot and—"

"Kendrick, you know better than most how many cops

use alcohol as a coping tool. After the last year, can you blame her for turning to that to get through her nights?"

I frowned.

"Think about it. Her team was decimated by what Selene Webb brought to light. She's one of the few Vice detectives who wasn't under indictment. And that's because she's been on this El Gato thing pretty deeply for years and probably because she's a woman. Hard to break into the boys' club over there in Vice."

I felt like he was making excuses for her, and I didn't like it. "I know that, sir, but—"

"Just give her some time. Be patient with her. She's not used to the way you work. Not many are, if you recall."

I pursed my lips. I didn't know why I had to baby her. Other cops didn't need me to hold their hand when they worked with me. My thoughts turned to Frank, who had jumped in whenever I needed him to, and he had been right there in that last big case all the way to the end... of course, how that ended hadn't been great.

"Sir, I think what Marcy is trying to say is that she's concerned for Detective Burnett's welfare. I smelled alcohol on her breath yesterday; if she's drinking during working hours..."

"I take your point, Reyes. Perhaps it was a one-off; just try to give her the benefit of the doubt. Do your best to work with her, Kendrick."

I didn't agree with Robinson, but I wasn't going to argue with him. "Yes, sir."

"Keep me in the loop and get me your reports before the end of the day on the scene."

I stood and gave him a nod. "We will, sir."

As we headed out of Robinson's office, I stopped short when I noticed who was waiting for us next to our desks.

Valerie.

14

CHASING EL GATO

MARCY

"Valerie, you're late."

"Sorry 'bout that. Couldn't get an Uber that early."

I pressed the spot on the bridge of my nose. "Why are you taking an Uber to work?"

She shrugged. "My car's in the shop."

"So, did you bring the file?"

"What file?" She looked bewildered.

"Patience," Angel murmured next to me.

"The file you've compiled on El Gato?"

"Oh. That. Well, no. It won't help you anyway. It's just full of random things, nothing concrete."

"What do you mean?"

Valerie sank down in the chair next to my desk. "It's a long story. Maybe we could go eat, and I can tell you all about it?"

Before I could answer, one of the CSI techs showed up with a file folder. "Detective Kendrick? Officer Calhoun asked me to bring this to you immediately."

"Thanks, appreciate it. Is he down in the lab? I'd like to go over his findings in person."

"Yes, ma'am. He said he's ready for you whenever you're ready."

"We'll be right down." I glanced at Valerie and then Angel. "We'll put a pin in our conversation and circle back to it after we talk to CSI and Damien. Let's go."

Down in the lab, we found Jeff waiting for us. I noticed Lindsey in her office, and I waved, but didn't go over to chat. I'd talk to her later. "Hey, Jeff, can you walk us through your findings?" I asked with a smile.

"Yeah, of course. Have you looked at the file yet?"

"Only briefly on the way down."

"Okay, so you asked us to dust the entire place for prints. We managed to find a number of prints, but they all belonged to Samson and his friends. There were a couple of Ruby's prints in the living room as well, on a picture frame of the two of them. All prints were accounted for."

"So was anything wiped clean?" I asked, confused.

"No, ma'am. But I did discover a couple of things. One, the door to the apartment; the lock was picked. We could see the scrapings of the pick on the tumblers. Two, we've got the guy on the elevator camera, and while in there, he pulls on gloves."

That gave me pause. "But he didn't wear them as he got on the elevator?"

"No, ma'am. He used a handkerchief to push the button to the penthouse. He did the same to call the elevator."

I sighed. Of course he did. This guy was too smart. "Okay, do we have a description?"

"Yes, ma'am. He was wearing a Cascade Rise mainte-nance uniform; he had shaggy blond hair and a full mustache. I took some screenshots of him, and they're at the back of the file."

I flipped to the back of the file and scanned the photos. This guy looked nothing like the guy with Ruby. It had to be another disguise, or someone else murdered Samson. I glanced at Angel and Valerie. "This isn't the same guy as before, is it?"

"El Vibora is a master of disguise," Valerie replied.

"She's not wrong. This guy... I've heard stories," Angel said with a shudder. "He's a ghost."

"He's not a ghost. He's a man, just like every other killer we catch. And we will catch him," I said through gritted teeth. Then I turned to Jeff. "Anything else?"

"We found his laptop, which the tech guys are going over, and a safe with a lot of cash and some jewels in it, as well as a stash of what looks to be heroin in Black Cat packaging. We're testing it now."

I was slightly irked that he hadn't done as I asked, and my eyes flashed to him. "You found what?"

Jeff's cheeks turned pink, and he winced. "Well, yes, I know you said you wanted to be called, Detective, but it was after midnight and—"

I held up a hand to stop his spiel. Taking several deep breaths, I said, "It may have been late, Jeff, but I would still have appreciated the call. Next time, please do as I ask."

"Yes, of course, I will." He stumbled over his words.

Nodding, I asked, "How much of the drug did you find?"

"About three hundred and fifty-six grams. It was already portioned out in glassine baggies, ready for distribution."

I glanced up from the file to him. "That quantity carries a minimum fifteen-year sentence and a two-hundred-fifty-thousand-dollar fine."

"How did you know that?" Valerie asked.

I shrugged. "I know the law."

"Maybe you should be in Vice," she muttered.

"I'm happy where I am, thanks," I replied.

"So maybe Samson was killed because he was hoarding the drugs for himself instead of selling them for El Gato?" Angel speculated.

"Doesn't explain Ruby, though," I added.

"Right, didn't consider that. And if that were the case, wouldn't his killer have taken the drugs back to El Gato?" he continued.

"Not necessarily," Valerie interjected.

"What do you mean?" I frowned at her.

"Samson was never on our radar as a dealer. Maybe that was what he bought for a party or something."

"Hmmm," I murmured noncommittally. With as sloppy as she was, I wouldn't put it past her to have missed it. Which reminded me, I needed to get her to pay me back for the drinks from last night; however, now was not the time to bring it up. I'd need to do that soon though.

"Oh good, you're all here," Damien said, poking his head through the open doorway. "I'm ready for you when you finish up here."

"Jeff, do you have anything else for us?" I asked.

"Not right now. I'll let you know what's in the baggies as soon as the tests are finished."

"Thanks." I turned and headed through the door to go down the hall to the morgue. "Okay, Damien, what did you find?"

Angel and Valerie followed me into the room. Valerie made a face at the smell, but I'd grown fairly used to it over the years. I only needed Vicks in really smelly cases. Damien offered Valerie the jar, but she seemed confused.

"Put some under your nose; it helps with the smell," I offered.

"No, thanks, can we just get on with this?" She set the jar on the counter behind us by the door.

"Not a lot to tell. He wasn't an addict; I'd say more an occasional user if anything. No track marks on his body." He moved toward Samson's head and tilted it to show a small, raised spot on the neck that had some bruising. "This is where the injection went in. It was a mix of Rohypnol, pancuronium bromide and potassium chloride."

"So he knew he was dying, unlike Ruby," Angel said.

Damien nodded. "Yes, most likely. He probably dropped to the ground after the injection and was maybe aware of what was going on for about five minutes, maybe less, before he died."

I frowned. "Why would the killer want him aware, unlike what he did to Ruby?" I looked to Valerie. "You're our resident expert on El Gato; you have any ideas?"

She shrugged. "I've no idea. Maybe he just pissed him off, and El Gato wanted him to know it."

"Other than that, I can tell you he had a burger and fries for lunch, and a Coke. Not much beyond that. He was pretty healthy overall."

None of that helped me. "Okay, thanks, Damien."

"No problem. See you later."

We trudged back upstairs. As I flipped through the file, I could hear Angel and Valerie murmuring behind me, discussing where to go eat, but I wasn't really listening. I was trying to figure out why El Gato would go after two low-level drug users, or maybe not exactly users in Samson's case, but purchasers. Had he somehow bought the drugs on credit? Why not just take them back if that was the case? Why kill him?

I had to be missing something, and I had a feeling that Valerie was the one who had the information I was missing. In order to get it, I'd have to go with her to eat. When we reached the detective pool, I slapped the file down on my desk and said, "You know what, let's go eat. I'm craving Mexican food; let's go to Alebrijes."

Angel lifted a brow. "It's early; are they even open?"

"Yep, they serve breakfast." I reached in my desk drawer and pulled out my purse. "I'll drive."

We reached the restaurant and got a table.

Valerie immediately ordered a Coors before the waitress could even greet us. "And for you?" She looked at me and Angel.

"Water for me," I said.

"Same," Angel replied. "Can we get some nachos as an appetizer?"

"Sure, I'll get those and be right back to take your orders."

"So, Valerie, you've been after this guy for a long time. Surely you know stuff about him, right?"

"Well, yeah, of course I do." She had her gaze on the waitress, who was on her way back with our drinks. "Thanks," she murmured, taking the beer and downing it before our glasses even touched the table. "Can you bring me a couple more?" she asked, setting the now empty bottle on the table.

"Um, sure?" the waitress seemed hesitant. I couldn't blame her; it was barely ten in the morning.

"You were saying?" I prompted Valerie once the waitress scurried away.

"Just a sec, she's coming right back."

I flashed my gaze to Angel, who just shook his head.

"Here you are, ma'am; are you all ready to order?"

I placed my order for my usual fajitas, while the others added theirs, but I wasn't paying attention to that. I wanted to know what Valerie knew of El Gato, so once the waitress walked away, and after Valerie guzzled her second beer, I said, "So?"

"Right. Right, El Gato. I mean, I don't know who he is. I've gotten close a couple of times. I was at this one party, it was at the Four Seasons in Beverly Hills. Lots of celebrities and the like, you know? And others who were really rich, they were all flashing their money around, and someone said El Gato was there. I tried to get them to point him out, but the closest I got was the back of a head." She shrugged and finished off her third beer.

There were so many things I wanted to ask, but the one on the tip of my tongue was, "How did you get into that party? Were you undercover or something?"

"Oh, yeah, I was a guest of one of his lower-level thugs. They're dead now. El Gato found out they were skimming." She said it like it was an everyday occurrence.

"And they pointed out El Gato to you?"

"Well, yeah, but he had his back to me, and he was leaving, so I couldn't go chase him down or anything." She raised the beer bottle and shook it for the waitress.

"What did he look like from behind, then?"

She looked startled by my question, as though she hadn't expected me to ask. "Um, I don't know. He was in a suit, had darkish hair. That's all I could tell because the lights were dimmed."

The waitress brought Valerie another beer along with the nachos and set them on the table.

"Thank you," Angel said quietly to the waitress.

"So that's the closest you've gotten to him? And nobody said this guy's real name?"

Valerie shook her head. "That's a secret. Nobody shares that out loud. Not with me, not with anybody."

"So what else can you tell me about this guy?" I asked, picking at the nachos.

She drank down her fourth beer. "He's rich. Connected. Secretive. I don't even know if he's here in California anymore. I mean, his operation is, but I don't know if he personally is."

"Did you happen to take pictures at this party?"

"No, no cameras were allowed. You know how these people are. They don't want stuff getting out that shouldn't."

I sighed. This was getting us nowhere fast. When the waitress brought us our food, we began to eat, and I thought about the case. I looked over at Valerie, who was now on her sixth beer, if I was counting the empty bottles correctly. "Valerie, why do you think El Gato would kill Ruby and Samson?"

"I don't know, honestly," she whispered. "The only thing I can think of is that they owed him a lot of money."

That still didn't make sense to me, but the haunted look in her eyes told me she knew more than she was telling, and she was running scared.

15

DRINKS WITH THE BOSS

EL VIBORA

I stood before the mirror in my bathroom and adjusted the brown and gray wig I was wearing. I'd had it touched up recently, adding a bit more silver around the temples. It was a look that I had cultivated to seem natural to my boss. I never revealed my real face or person to him. To anyone, really. There might only be one person in the world who knew what I really looked like, and she wanted nothing to do with me.

I pushed thoughts of Sofia out of my mind. This wasn't the time to think about my regrets. I had a meeting to get to with Alejandro. He liked to pretend he was the big man, the big bad drug lord who squashed all his dissenters and competition; however, he never lifted a finger to do his dirty work. He put that off on men like me. It hadn't bothered me at first. Being the hammer he used to take out anyone who went against him, but lately, he seemed to have gone around the bend. Ordering deaths that didn't make sense and leaving his calling card. He was going to get himself caught eventually, and I didn't want to be around to get caught up in his shit.

Still, I was under contract and couldn't just back out right now. I still had a few years to go before I had enough to retire to Tahiti and live out my golden years. If I screwed El Gato over, word would get around, and my reputation would be void. Nobody would hire me. So for now, I was stuck.

I put the last touches on the prosthetic nose on my face to make sure it looked right. It was different than the one I'd worn when I took out Samson. I had a number of fake facial features, but this was the one I used when meeting with Alejandro. I put in the deep brown contacts that completed the look and then left my apartment. It wasn't in the best part of town, but it was cheap, and nobody paid any attention to me. My neighbors were all elderly. Several were half-blind and mostly deaf, which worked in my favor. I was neighborly to them, courteous, never caused them trouble, helped to bring in grocery bags or open a door. None of them would suspect that I was an assassin, or hitman for hire. None of them knew the real me. And that was the way it had to be.

I headed for the bus stop and got on the crosstown bus to the airport, where I picked up the rental car I'd reserved under the name Michael Landry. It was a black SUV with tinted black windows. The front windows were darker than normal but not as dark as the back, so my features were somewhat obscured in it. I got on the 405 and headed north toward Beverly Hills. Alejandro lived on the edge of Beverly Hills and West Hollywood on Sierra Drive. It was a seven-bedroom multimillion-dollar home that sat on a corner lot. Everything about the place was extravagant, from the high ceilings and French doors to the manicured lawn and in-ground pool and tennis courts. It spelled excess and opulence.

I pulled up to the gate and pushed the button. I gave the same name I always used, the one Alejandro had contracted me under and the one I'd rented the car under. "It's Michael."

The gate opened, and I pulled up the circular driveway and parked. At the door, one of Alejandro's men greeted me and led me through the house to the backyard. Alejandro was seated at the patio table, and a scantily clad woman was swimming in the pool.

Alejandro gestured to one of the seats as he called, "Maria, get out."

The woman in the pool stopped her laps and pulled herself up to the edge of the pool. Her golden tan glistened under the beads of water that slid down her body. She gave me an assessing look and then picked up her towel and wrapped it around herself before she moved toward Alejandro. "I'm going shopping," she said as she leaned down and kissed him.

"Javier will drive you." Alejandro's expression didn't change. He just waved a hand and dismissed her.

She huffed and turned toward the house with one of Alejandro's men following her. I assumed it was Javier, but I didn't care enough to ask.

One of his men set a brandy down in front of me and one in front of Alejandro, then backed off to the perimeter of the patio.

"*Déjanos ahora.*" Alejandro told him and the other men who were hanging around to leave.

I supposed it showed that he trusted me, but it wasn't the wisest move on his part. I could take him out easily and get out of here before his men were ever the wiser. They'd never find me. I didn't, of course. I wasn't ready to burn this bridge. I picked up my brandy and took a sip.

Once the men were gone, Alejandro picked up his drink and gulped it, then set it down. "Good work with those two losers."

I didn't say anything. Just tilted my head and gave a slight nod.

"I've got at least one more I need taken care of before you head back to Mexico."

I arched a brow. It was curious that he thought I would return to Mexico; that wasn't where I'd been when he'd called me in a few weeks ago. He didn't need to know where I was nor where I was going when he was finished with me for the time being. "Who?" I asked, wondering about my next target. If he set me on another woman, I might just act on my instinct to take him out and leave.

"A problem with an encroaching wannabe. Deon thinks he can move into my territory. *Quiero que se haga un ejemplo de él.*"

So he wanted an example made out of another drug lord. That wasn't a problem. "When?"

"I'll let you know when I've got solid information on him for you."

"What about the police problem?" I asked. It wasn't really a problem for me, but for him.

"For now we've got eyes on the issue. Should have it handled, but if this busybody becomes a problem, you might have to take out the lady cop."

Every instinct in me told me it was a bad idea, but I didn't voice that opinion. I'd have to be sure to have everything I needed in place to get out of the country if it came to that. I hoped it didn't, but I would have plans set up for every contingency.

"Let me know if you find it necessary," I said blandly.

"If she becomes more trouble, then I will. For now, stick by your phone. I'll give you a call when it's time to act."

I gave him a nod and took that as my dismissal. Rising, I started back toward the house.

"El Vibora," Alejandro called.

I paused and looked back at him, but didn't say a word.

"*Quiero que sufra*," he said, telling me he wanted Deon to suffer.

"Got it," I called back.

16

BBQ AND BITTERNESS
MARCY

Friday had been a day of boring activity, digging into Samson's background, trying to find connections that would lead us to who El Gato was, but we were getting nowhere fast. Because we were pretty much in a holding pattern, Captain Robinson told me and Angel to take the weekend off to recharge our batteries.

I was grateful because that meant I could actually spend Saturday with Frank, and then on Sunday we'd have the barbeque I had tentatively planned. I woke up early Saturday and cleaned the house. Stephen had called and said he had the exercise equipment ordered and that it would be delivered that morning as well, and he'd be over to set it up.

A knock at the door sounded as I shut the vacuum off. I pulled it open to see the delivery driver and his assistant. "I have a delivery for a Marcy Kendrick?"

"Yes, that's me, come on in."

The men picked up a large box, and the driver asked, "Where do you want this?"

"I'll show you." I led them to the bedroom I was turning into my exercise studio. "Here is fine. Thanks."

"We've got two more large boxes for you. You want them in here as well?"

"Yes, thanks."

Fifteen minutes later they had all three large boxes in the room and had left.

I sent a text to Stephen to let him know. I wasn't about to touch any of it when this was something he wanted to do, but I was anxious to see what he'd bought.

My phone rang, and hearing my brother's ringtone, I answered it. "Hey, are you headed over?"

"Yeah, be there in ten. I've got the weights, dumbbell and barbell in my car for the bench."

"So you did pick up one; is there going to be room in here to use all of this?"

"I measured it the other day while you were at work, before I ordered everything."

A chime sounded, and I looked at my phone to see Frank's number. "Hey, Frank's calling. I'll see you when you get here."

"See you."

He hung up, and I answered Frank's call. "Hey, what time are you coming over?"

"I'm picking up the meat right now. Figured we should get it in the marinade this afternoon so it's ready for the grill tomorrow. Wanted to know if there was anything else you wanted me to get?"

"Can you pick up some cases of beer and chips too?"

"Babe, that's a given," he said with a chuckle. "I meant anything else, condiments? Buns for the burgers? Potato salad?"

"Oh, potato salad might be nice. Let me see what I've got on condiments," I answered as I headed for the fridge. Opening it, I realized most of the bottles were full. "I think we're good."

"Once we get this all set up for tomorrow, do you want to go out?"

A grin spread across my lips. "Sounds fun; you got something in mind?"

"It's a surprise."

"Hmmm, not sure I'm dressed for a surprise." I laughed.

"Jeans and a T-shirt should be fine, and tennis shoes."

"Good thing that's what I've got on, then." I glanced down at my clothes. I'd probably end up changing anyway since I'd spent the morning cleaning. "Oh, Stephen's heading over to set up this equipment he ordered."

"I should be there soon. I can help him set it up while you get this ready."

"Sounds good. See you in a while?"

"Absolutely."

I finished up cleaning and was in my room changing when I heard the front door open. I'd given Stephen a key, so I knew it had to be him. "I'm in the bedroom; be out in a minute," I called out.

"No worries," Stephen called back. "I've gotta make a couple of trips anyway."

By the time I got out to the main part of the house, Stephen had made three trips already, and Frank was there helping him get the rest of the weights into the house. Frank set down the stack of circular disc weights for the barbell he was carrying, then walked over to me and pulled me into his arms, kissing me.

"Hi," he murmured against my lips.

I grinned. "Hi to you too. Did you get the food in the house before you started helping Stephen?"

"It's in the kitchen. Brought that in first; figured you'd want to get started on it."

"Sounds good. You boys have fun putting all that stuff together." I laughed. "I'll get the beer in the fridge so you can have one when you're done."

"Perfect," Stephen said as he came out of the exercise room. "Frank, come see what we've got. This is going to be better than going to the gym."

Frank let me go and went off with my brother while I headed to the kitchen. I washed my hands and then got out the pan to get the steaks all set up in the marinade. I put the hamburger in the fridge, along with the beer and potato salad Frank had brought. Once I had the steaks marinating and the pan covered in cling wrap, I slid that pan into the fridge as well.

I cleaned up the mess from the marinade and made sure my kitchen was tidy before going to see what they were up to. I walked into my exercise room to see they'd set up the weight bench and free weights on one side of the room, a treadmill in the center, and a Peloton bike in the back. On one wall they'd hung a large-screen TV that hadn't been there before. It was set to ESPN, and some baseball game was on the screen.

"Wow, you two have been busy. This looks great, but where is my yoga mat going to go?" I asked, my hands on my hips.

"Plenty of room right here." Stephen pointed to the center of the room in front of the treadmill.

"Well, let's hope I don't fall over and hit my head on that thing."

Stephen rolled his eyes. "You'll be fine."

"So are you guys finished?"

"Yep, and I think I'll hold off on that beer and take advantage of all this equipment, if you don't mind, sis?"

I shook my head and laughed. "Go ahead. Just lock up the house when you're done."

"Sure thing. You two heading out somewhere?"

"I'm taking her out," Frank replied. "Between our schedules, we haven't had a lot of time together this week."

"I'll be sure to be out of here before you get back. Have fun," Stephen said.

"We will," Frank answered and escorted me out of the room. "Need anything?"

"Let me grab my purse and my keys." I headed for the table in the living room where I'd put them earlier. "Okay, let's go."

IT WAS dark by the time we returned home. Frank had taken me to the Botanical Gardens and the Los Angeles Zoo. I hadn't been there in years, and I couldn't recall a better day. We'd seen all the animals, and my favorites had been the large cats. They were so majestic. Frank had enjoyed the gorilla reserve the most. When we left there, we went to Mambo's Café, which served Cuban and Latin American food. I'd never been there and found it to be really good.

"Today has been amazing," I murmured in his arms as we lay in my bed together.

His fingers trailed up and down my side leisurely, and he

kissed my temple. "I'm glad you enjoyed it. I did too. It was nice just getting out and enjoying the day with you."

I snuggled deeper into his side, loving the way my body fit with his. "It really was. Tomorrow should be good too," I said sleepily.

"I'm looking forward to meeting your brother's girlfriend and catching up with Angel."

"He's bringing Callie, so you'll get to meet her too."

"I'm actually surprised they're still together from what you've said."

I frowned. "What did I say?"

"I just recall you saying she had a little bit of a problem with him being a cop in the beginning."

"Oh, that. Yeah, but I think that had more to do with the whole Selene issue and her clientele not being happy with her for seeing a cop."

"Still, if she's swayed by people like that, I don't see it boding well for a future together for them."

He had a good point. I liked Callie, but she did tend to listen to other people's opinions quite a bit and not make her own decisions when it involved anything other than her business. But from everything Angel had said, I thought she was getting better about it. Maybe things would be alright between them. Either way, if she made him happy, then I was happy for him. He was my best friend, and I wanted only good things for him.

THE NEXT MORNING, Frank and I got up and started getting things ready for the BBQ. He mowed the lawn, which it didn't really need, but he did it anyway so we could play croquet. This was the first time I'd had a backyard to do this sort of thing, and I was kind of excited about it.

Together we set up the course and then got all the other stuff ready. Stephen and Yazmine were the first to arrive, with Angel and Callie showing up five minutes later.

"Angel, Callie, this is Yazmine, Stephen's girlfriend," I said, introducing them. "Yazmine, this is my partner, Angel, and his girlfriend, Callie."

"So you're a detective too?" she asked.

Angel nodded and looked at Frank. "So is Frank." He held his hand out to Frank. "How're you doing?"

"Doin' pretty good. Enjoying havin' a weekend with my tiny tornado," he said with a laugh. "How about you?"

"Not bad." Angel's voice sounded slightly off, but I dismissed it.

"You guys wanna help me get the meat on the grill?" Frank asked.

"Sure thing."

While the guys stood around the grill, I chatted with Callie and Yazmine. I told Callie that I was thinking of getting my hair cut and that I'd probably be making an appointment soon, probably after this case was over. Callie asked about the case, knowing we were investigating the deaths of Ruby and Samson. I couldn't really give them any information other than what the news had covered, but they seemed to take that in stride.

"I'm going to go in and get the cheese for the burgers. I'll be right back," I said, giving Frank a smile before heading in to the kitchen from the patio door.

As I opened the fridge, I felt hands slide around my waist, and I turned in Frank's arms. "Did you think I needed help carrying the cheese?" I laughed.

"I couldn't resist coming in and stealing a kiss." He grinned and leaned down, pressing his lips to mine.

A throat cleared, and I pulled back to see Angel in the doorway, a strange look on his face. It almost seemed like betrayal and maybe hurt or bitterness in his eyes, but he quickly masked it. "You two were taking a while; figured I'd better come in and get that cheese before the burgers burned."

My cheeks heated, and I turned back to the fridge, pulling the cheese out and handing it to him. "Well, we wouldn't want that," I said, keeping my voice light. I didn't know what was going on with him, but I didn't want to bring it up here and now.

Angel met my gaze for a moment, but then looked away as he took the cheese. "Coming?" he called over his shoulder to Frank.

"Sure, be there in a second." Frank nodded, but didn't take his hands from my waist. He waited for Angel to leave before pulling me back to him and kissing me again. "Everything okay?" he asked, looking into my eyes, studying me. "Between you and Angel, I mean."

"Yeah. I'm not sure what's up with him, but as far as I know, we're good."

He raised his hand and traced his fingers along my hairline, tucking a stray hair that escaped my ponytail behind my ear. "You know I really like you."

I grinned. "I really like you too," I replied. He was growing more and more important to me every day. I hoped he knew that and could hear it in my voice.

He smiled and pressed another quick kiss to my lips. "Let's get out there before our guests decide we've abandoned them, and they eat all the steaks."

Laughing, I followed him out of the house, feeling happier than I could ever remember being in my entire life.

But in the back of my mind, the expression on Angel's face when he'd walked into the kitchen had me second-guessing things. Was there something about Frank I didn't know?

17

SMASHED WINDOWS

MARCY

T he rest of the afternoon and evening went really well. We ate, we drank, we played croquet and cards, then we decided to extend the day and ordered pizza so we could all watch the Angels play the Guardians in Cleveland. Everyone left around eight, and Frank and I cleaned up the remains of the party.

"I think it went well," Frank said as he put the pillows back on my couch.

I nodded, but I had to admit I was a bit tired and ready to just relax with him for a while. "I'd call it a success."

He wrapped his arms around me and pulled me close. "Why don't you take a nice hot bath and relax for a bit, and I'll finish putting everything away?"

His thoughtfulness was one of the things I lov—*liked* about him. I wasn't ready to think in love terms yet. I knew I was close, but I wasn't ready. With everything that had happened with Jordan, and then me jumping head-first in with Henry, where I was ready to fall in love, I was now hesitant to do the same with Frank. I wanted this to last. I wanted him to last, and I was scared that saying or even thinking about the love word would break us up. I didn't want that.

"You sure?"

He kissed me and then nodded. "Go ahead. I'll be in there in a few."

It was a nice feeling, having someone I could depend on. I ran the water and got undressed, then slipped into the steaming bath. I leaned my head back along the edge and closed my eyes. Using my toes, I turned the water off and just relaxed.

There was a knock on the door, and I startled awake. I must have fallen asleep because the water was much cooler than it had been a moment ago. "Come in," I called, sitting up in the water.

"Did you fall asleep?" Frank asked, grinning as he poked his head in the doorway.

"Must have," I murmured, looking up at him. "Wanna wash my back?" I held up the soap scrubber.

"Thought you'd never ask." He took it from me and squatted down next to the tub. Once he finished making me really clean, he leaned in and said, "Now let's go make you all dirty again." His voice was husky and deep and made heat pool in my stomach.

I stood up, and he wrapped me in a towel, then lifted me from the tub and carried me into my bedroom. Laying me on the bed, he kissed my neck and down my body, loving me. He was tender and passionate and did everything to turn me on. I was flying high as we reached our peak, and we crashed over the edge together, sweaty and exhausted.

I laughed. "You weren't lying about making me dirty again," I murmured against his chest.

His chest rumbled as he laughed too. "I'd say we could

clean you up and do that again, but I'm dead. You wore me out, TT."

I grinned and kissed his chest. "How about just a quick shower; then we can get some sleep and maybe have a repeat before we have to get up for work in the morning?"

"Now that's a plan I can get behind," he replied, kissing the top of my head.

The shower took a little longer than I'd anticipated because Frank got a second wind, but eventually we made it back to bed, clean and thoroughly spent.

I woke to the sound of shattering glass and someone yelling. "What the hell?" I muttered, reaching toward my nightstand for my gun. Since I now had Frank's well-being to think about, I tended to rest it next to the lamp rather than under my pillow to avoid any kind of accidents with it.

"Stay here; call dispatch," Frank murmured softly. "I'll check it out." I could see he already had his weapon in his hand as he reached for the light.

"Wait," I said, not wanting to turn the light on for anyone to see us. "I've got a flashlight."

"Whoever this is already knows we're in here." He went on and turned the light on.

As he did, I noticed my bedroom window was shattered, and there was a brick on the floor surrounded by the glass. Outside, I could hear someone ranting, and after a moment, I recognized Jordan's voice.

"You bitch! You're the reason I lost my job! It's your fucking fault!" he screamed.

"It's Jordan," I said with a sigh. "How the hell did he find my house?"

"Your ex?"

I nodded as I phoned dispatch to send an officer.

Frank got out of the bed, slid his feet into his pair of slippers, and cautiously moved toward the window. "Brasswell! Marcy's calling the cops, but if you don't get out of here before they arrive, I'm going to come out there and beat your dumb ass!"

"Frank," I said, shaking my head at him, but I couldn't help the grin that touched my lips.

He looked back at me, and my smile fell. He was serious.

"Who the fuck are you? Why are you with my wife?" Jordan screamed.

"She's not your wife, and if I have to come out there, you're going to regret it! Leave now, Brasswell. Go home and sleep whatever the hell this is off!"

In the distance I could hear the sirens as they raced toward us. Hell, I never anticipated being on the other side of a domestic violence call. My face heated at the idea of it. Jordan wasn't just embarrassing himself; he was embarrassing me now. I didn't like it one bit. It was one thing for him to berate me in front of our colleagues because he didn't like the way I took down perps, but to make me look weak like this, that pissed me off.

I got out of bed and started getting dressed. I tossed Frank his jeans, and he put them on.

"I think he's gone. At least he's stopped yelling," Frank said.

"He probably ran when he heard the sirens." I was still angry.

The patrol car pulled up at the house, and I went to the front door, opening it to find Officers Liz Allen and Sarah

Jenkins standing on my porch. "Hey, come on in," I said, gesturing for them to enter.

"Ma'am, we got a call about a domestic disturbance? Is it him?" Officer Allen's eyes went to Frank, taking in his disheveled appearance.

"No, Liz, this is my boyfriend, Detective Frank Maldon from Santa Monica PD."

Her mouth dropped open slightly, and she seemed surprised, but she quickly recovered. "Okay, then?"

"My ex-husband threw a brick through my bedroom window and was shouting profanities at me. Frank got him to leave, but I'd like to file a report for the vandalism."

"Yes, of course, ma'am. You should probably consider a restraining order as well."

"She's not wrong. Have you filed one yet?" Frank asked, concern lacing his voice.

I shook my head. It had been on my agenda, but I just hadn't gotten around to it. "Not yet."

"Babe, considering Jordan has access to firearms, and he's acting so erratically, I really think you need to get it sooner rather than later." Frank slipped his arms around my waist and then tilted my chin up. "I know you're completely capable of taking care of yourself, but he sounded unhinged and dangerous tonight. I can't help thinking what might have happened if I weren't here."

I nodded. He wasn't wrong. "I'll file for one tomorrow."

He gave me a wry smile. "You mean today; it's already four in the morning."

"Oh, right. Damn. We have to get up in two hours."

Frank chuckled. "I doubt we'll be getting back to sleep, TT."

I glanced from him to Liz and Sarah, who were standing

awkwardly in my living room. "Right. Sorry, I'm still half asleep. Let me show you the damage so you can get the report filed."

I led them back to my bedroom and the mess that Jordan had made of my window.

"Did you touch anything?" Sarah Jenkins asked.

"No, you should be able to get his prints off the brick."

She nodded and bagged it. "We'll drive through the neighborhood, and if we see him, we'll haul him in. And we'll get the report filed so you can have it as evidence for your protection order."

"Thanks, Sarah. And I would appreciate it if you kept this quiet."

Liz grinned. "Which part? The hot detective in your bed part, or the crazy ex-husband, our ex-lieutenant, vandalizing your house?"

My cheeks heated, and Frank laughed.

"All of it," I choked out. I didn't need my sex life to become fodder for the gossip mill around the precinct. It was nobody's business about me and Frank but our own.

Frank grinned and kissed the top of my head. "That might be asking too much, TT. They know you're human now."

Liz and Sarah both laughed.

"Don't worry, ma'am, we won't gossip about you and Detective Maldon. I was only teasing you," Liz replied, then she looked at Frank. "If Santa Monica has a bunch of single detectives who look like you, I might have to move precincts."

"I'm sure they'd be happy to have you," Frank said, laughing along.

"You two have a good rest of your night. What's left of it anyway."

I walked them out and then turned back to see Frank carrying the broom and dustpan to the bedroom. I followed him and wondered what I was going to do about the shattered window. I stood there frowning at it while he swept up the glass.

"I don't think you scowling at the window is going to fix it, TT, unless you have some secret superpower that I don't know about." He grinned at me.

Sighing, I shook my head. "None that I know of. Just don't know what to do about the window now."

"Don't worry, babe. I don't have any cases I'm currently working on, and I can take the morning off to get it handled."

I moved toward him and wrapped my arms around his torso, then kissed his chest and looked up at him. "Thank you."

"My pleasure," he murmured. "Let me dump this, and then I can kiss you properly."

I smiled and let him go. He headed to the kitchen, and I heard him dump the broken glass in the garbage and put away the broom before returning to me. He wrapped me in his arms and kissed me. Whether it was proper or not would be for my nonexistent great-aunt Fanny to decide. I was pretty sure there was nothing proper about that kiss, and I was pretty glad about that.

18

PROGRESS AND A PERSISTENT PURSUIT

MARCY

"You sure you don't mind waiting for the window repair guy?" I asked, as I stood on my front stoop with Frank.

"Not at all. I know you've got this case, and I can take some time to be here." He smiled and pulled me close. "How about you come out to mine tonight?"

The thought of going to his place was soothing in a way. I figured, since Jordan had found my house now, Frank's place might be more relaxing, and I had to admit he made me feel safe too. Yeah, I knew I could protect myself, but sometimes it was nice to share that burden. "Yeah, I think that sounds good; it might be late though. Is that okay?"

"Babe, you can come over at two a.m. and I wouldn't care. I just want you with me."

I felt warm at his words, and I smiled. "Okay. In that case, pack me a bag and take it to your place?"

He chuckled. "You gonna trust me to go through your clothes?"

Rolling my eyes, I nodded. "Sure. Just make sure you put

some work clothes in there for tomorrow. And don't forget my toothbrush and makeup bag."

"I won't." He leaned down and kissed me. "It will all be there ready for you. Go get 'em, TT. Have a great day."

"You too." I reluctantly left his embrace and walked down the path to my car.

As I backed out of my driveway, I waved to him and headed to the precinct. I had no qualms about leaving him in my house; it felt natural. My thoughts shifted from Frank to my upcoming day. I'd had a text from Angel a bit ago telling me that Howard had found something. Not only on the photos we'd found, but also on Samson's laptop. So that was our first task for the day.

Driving, I decided I should call Valerie and see if she wanted to join our meeting with tech. Maybe she'd recognize something in what we were about to see. "Call Detective Burnett," I told my Bluetooth.

"Calling Detective Burnett," the robotic voice repeated.

I heard the phone ring several times before she answered. "This is Burnett."

"Hey, it's Kendrick. I just wanted to give you a heads-up. Reyes and I are meeting with tech this morning, if you want to join us?"

"What time?"

I glanced at my dashboard clock; it was nearly seven. "Probably around seven thirty."

"Sure, I'll be there."

"Great, see you then." I hung up and stared out at the traffic on the 110.

I thought about pulling off and grabbing coffee, but I'd already had two cups this morning. The problem was I was still tired. Jordan had screwed with my sleep, and now I was lagging. Still, getting off the 110 and going to the coffee shop would put me about fifteen minutes behind. Would it be better for me to keep going and hope that either Angel had grabbed me one, or that the beignet truck was there?

My fingers were crossed for the beignet truck. The food truck spots were generally first come, first serve, so if they made it out early, then I'd be in luck. I took the ramp off the 110, and a few minutes later I was pulling into the parking lot. Unfortunately, my luck wasn't with me. The only food trucks in sight were Holy Grill and Armando's. Both had really good food, but they weren't the beignet truck.

I put the thought of coffee from my mind and headed into the precinct. Angel wasn't around as I put my purse in my desk. I wondered where he was, but I wasn't worried about it. I turned on my computer and started going through my email and frowned as I saw another four emails from Jordan. I forwarded them to my brother without opening them. I thought about filing the restraining order, but before I could pull anything up on doing that, Angel showed up.

"Hey, we ready to head over to tech?" he asked.

It was nearly seven thirty. "Sure. Burnett is meeting us over there."

"Sounds good." He nodded. "Good game last night."

"It was. Yesterday was fun. We'll have to do it again," I said and then yawned.

"Did we leave such a mess that you didn't get enough sleep?" Angel asked, sounding concerned.

"Oh, no. It wasn't that. Jordan showed up drunk off his head at, like, four a.m. and threw a brick through my window."

"What?" Angel looked shocked. "Marce—"

"It's fine, Frank ran him off, and he's taking care of the window for me."

"Frank stayed the night?" His voice sounded strained, but when I looked over at him, his expression was neutral, and I thought maybe I imagined it.

"Yeah, and thank goodness he did and offered to take care of things today for me, or I'd still be at home dealing with it."

"That is good of him. Doesn't he have to be on the job today?"

"He's going in late. Cleared it with Captain Stafford to take the morning off."

"Must be nice."

I stopped and looked at Angel. "Hey, are you mad at Frank or something?"

Angel looked startled. "What? No."

"Then what is it?" I asked. "You seem to have a problem with him, or with me and him..."

He sighed. "No, I don't. I just... I see how happy he makes you, Marce, and I guess I'm just having a hard time sharing you."

Arching a brow at him, I asked, "What do you mean sharing me?"

He shook his head and pursed his lips like he was trying to come up with the words to explain what he meant. I waited patiently, knowing he would get there, but I wasn't going to let him off the hook.

"Since we became partners, and you left Jordan, we've been there for each other pretty much exclusively. I know you had Stephen, but he's been going through his own stuff for a long time now, and I feel like it's been you and me against the world. You're my best friend, and I'd do anything for you, and I guess I miss having you rely on me in that way." He looked away.

He wasn't wrong. Looking back, I really had relied on him for a lot. And I could see that over the last month or so I'd started to rely less on him and more on Frank.

"Angel, you're my best friend too. That's not going to change. I still count on you to have my back in all situations, but you aren't the only one to have it now. Look at it as a shared burden. Frank's not going to take me away from you as a friend. He's not replacing you, just like Callie's not replacing me in your life."

He nodded. "I know. I've been telling myself that for the last several weeks. I like Frank. I think he's good for you. I didn't mean to make you think I didn't. Just know that if I seem upset or standoffish, it's not you, it's not him, it's me. I'm working on it. You'll just have to be patient with me."

I grinned. "Always. Hey, did you ever get a hold of all those celebrities Ruby was possibly blackmailing?"

"Not so far. All I get is voicemails for some of them, so I've left messages."

"Okay, sounds good. Now, we ready to go see Howard?" Glancing down the hall, I could see Valerie standing outside the door. She hadn't noticed us yet; she was on her phone, typing.

"Yep. Let's go." He seemed lighter and more comfortable than he had five minutes earlier.

When we reached Valerie and the doorway to tech, I greeted her. "Hey, glad you're here. Shall we?" I gestured to the door.

"Sure," she agreed and went in.

"Howard, what have you got for us?" Angel asked, shaking his hand.

"Quite a bit, actually. Come on over here."

We stepped deeper into the room and over to a large computer setup. Samson's laptop was on the table next to another keyboard and the huge monitors.

"First, you were right about those photos. They match the Cascade Rise penthouse that belonged to Samson Martinez."

"So he did throw the party they were taken at," I muttered, regretting once more not getting to interview Samson before he was murdered.

"That's what it looks like. Now, on to the laptop. We recovered a number of emails between him and Ruby, as well as him and another person connected to El Gato. That's where it gets good. I've got them pulled up for you to read." He tapped a button, and the large monitor showed the first email.

*Ruby, he wants a payment asap, he's threatening to take you out. You wouldn't even be where you are without me. You have a debt you need to take care of before we both pay for it. You've got to pay up. Please take care of it. –
Samson*

Howard scrolled to show Ruby's reply.

Samson, El Gato is a pig, and I've got the proof now, so he can suck it. He can't touch me, and I can get all the smack I want from him. Stop worrying about it. – Ruby

"What did she think she had on him?" I asked. "Do either of them mention it?"

"It's pretty vague, but from what I gather, Ruby knew

who El Gato was and was attempting to blackmail him into giving her free drugs," Howard replied as he showed us the rest of the emails.

"Wow, that's probably why she's dead, but what about Samson? Doesn't look like he was in on the blackmail from the sound of those emails," Angel added.

"That's where these others come in." Howard switched email threads and pulled up a new one.

Sam, El Gato isn't happy with you. You opened your big mouth and told that harlot his business. You better find a way to make this right, or he's going to hold you accountable too. – J

"Who is this J?" I asked, looking from Howard to Valerie.

"Javier Suarez is the name linked to the email account," Howard replied.

Valerie nodded slowly. "I've heard that name before. At least the first name."

"What do you know about him?" I questioned, keeping my eyes on Valerie.

"Not a lot. He's a low-level guy in the organization. One of El Gato's distributors. He's the one who gets the drugs to the dealers, but he's not super high up or close enough to El Gato to bother with."

That seemed off. If it were me, I would be all over this guy, following him, seeing whom he reported to. Then trace that guy to the next. All the way to whoever El Gato was. But I didn't work Vice, so maybe I was missing something, and they had another plan for going after drug dealers. I'd give her the benefit of the doubt for now.

"Still, he's the closest we've got to El Gato for now. We

should look into him, run some surveillance, see if we can connect him to El Vibora too. We should get a warrant for his emails, don't you think?" I said, looking at Angel.

"That's a good idea. I'll talk to the captain, see if he can get the ball rolling on that," Angel offered.

"Good idea."

"Do you need me for anything else? I've got another case I'm working on, and I need to get back to it," Valerie murmured a moment later, backing toward the door.

"Sure, go ahead. If you come across anything in your notes or whatever we could use, send it on down to us," I said, but I had no hope she would.

Nodding, Valerie scurried out of the room.

As I watched her leave, it reminded me that I still needed to get her to pay me back for the drinks we'd had the other night. I supposed it would have to wait.

Angel and I spent the rest of the day digging into Javier Suarez, Samson Martinez, and Ruby Gold, trying to identify every person linked to them who linked to each other. We were trying to create a web of social connections that might lead us to who El Gato was. It was a time-consuming activity, but it felt like we were getting closer.

That evening, as I left the precinct, I was glad to be heading out to Santa Monica and getting out of the city. Between this case and Jordan, I was stressed. Halfway there, I realized I never did get around to filing that restraining order. I should have taken the time to do it, but I'd just been so caught up in the case that I hadn't given it a second thought today.

I switched lanes on Santa Monica Boulevard to let the vehicle behind me pass, but then noticed that they switched lanes as well so they could stay behind me. That started to set off warning bells in my head. The sun was setting, so the sky was full of pinks and oranges and purples, and the light was dim, but I could tell that the vehicle was a van. I wasn't sure what color it was though, as the headlights were bright in my rearview mirror.

I pressed harder on the gas, and my car jumped forward a little, pulling away from the van.

It didn't last. The van increased their speed as well.

That was the second warning bell that went off in my head, and now my gut was telling me that someone was following me purposefully. I shifted lanes again and slowed my speed. The van followed suit, but this time as I moved, I made a note that the van was white. I couldn't get a tag number though.

The 405 was coming up, and I pressed on the gas harder again. I shifted lanes once more, this time so I'd be in the right lane to go south on the 405. I hoped I could lose whoever this was because I didn't want to lead them directly to Frank. I didn't know if it had to do with the case, or if this was some creeper who was trying to scare a woman driving alone, or if it was Jordan. He drove a sedan normally, but that didn't mean he couldn't have gotten a hold of a van.

My actual fear was that it wasn't Jordan, but El Vibora. If he thought we were getting too close, he could be after me to take me out like other cops had been taken out. I wasn't going to go out like that. I had a plan in mind if I couldn't lose them soon.

I made the left onto the 405, pressed the gas and then wove through traffic, trying to put space and cars between me and the van, but the van was right on my bumper. It was almost as though we were connected. The other cars I attempted to put between us slowed and honked and screamed at us. I didn't blame them. What we were doing was incredibly dangerous.

I wasn't on the 405 long. I took the ramp to the 10 and sped down the road toward the ocean. I was heading for the Santa Monica Police Headquarters on Fourth Street. So far, the van had stuck with me, but I figured if I went straight to the police station, they'd leave me be. In an attempt to lose them, I got off the 10 and made a right onto Lincoln Boulevard, but again the van stuck with me. They didn't try to ram me, just stayed maybe a foot behind me. It was almost like our vehicles were connected with a tow chain they were so close.

Getting frustrated, I made a quick right onto Pico Boulevard, hoping they'd be going too fast to follow, but no luck; they continued staying on my tail. Instead of paying attention to the road, like I should have been, I was watching them in my rearview mirror, hoping I could catch a glimpse of whoever this was, but in doing so, I missed my turn onto Fourth Street.

Frustration filled me. I could circle around and get there, but I could also head for the station on the Santa Monica Pier. At this point they'd be about equal distance. I decided to opt for the Santa Monica Pier. I made another right, turning onto Ocean Avenue, going well above the speed limit. I half hoped I'd catch the eye of a patrol officer and they'd pull me over, but my luck was bad tonight.

I swung onto the Santa Monica Pier and honked excessively as I raced down it toward the police station on the pier so that the people walking would get out of my way. I was calling major attention to myself, and the van started to pull back, but it was still following me.

Finally I reached the station, and I pulled as close to the

building as I could, threw my car into park, turned it off, yanked the keys from the ignition, grabbed my purse and pushed open my car door. I didn't even bother to close it. I just ran for the station's door.

I probably looked like a lunatic as I reached Desk Sergeant Glenn. My heart was racing, and I couldn't quite catch my breath for a moment as I waved my hand at him.

"Detective Kendrick, everything okay?"

I shook my head. "Followed," I choked out between gasps of breath. I sucked in some air and willed my heart to calm down.

"You were followed?"

I nodded. "Yes, sorry, just a little out of breath." It dawned on me that I hadn't been running in a while, and I probably needed to get back to it. This was completely unacceptable, not to mention embarrassing.

"Were you on foot?"

"No," I started, finally feeling my breath come back to normal. "I was driving down from LA. I couldn't lose them, so I thought I'd come here, and maybe then they'd leave. It was a white van. I didn't get a plate number."

"I can send an officer out to check the lot, see if they're out there waiting?"

"Please, that would be helpful," I agreed.

"Of course." He picked up the phone and spoke to someone; then a couple of officers came from a back room and headed out the front doors. "They'll go check around, see if they can see anything."

"Thanks." I pulled my phone out and dialed Frank.

"Babe, you on your way?" he answered.

"Sort of. I'm at the station on the pier. I was followed." I explained everything to him, this time a little more coherently than I had to DS Glenn.

"I'm coming to you. You can leave your car at the station and ride with me. Whoever that is might be parked somewhere and waiting for you to leave the pier."

"You think so?" I was still so shaken I obviously wasn't thinking clearly, because, of course, they probably were.

"Babe, if they followed you all the way from LA, then yeah, I think that's a definite possibility."

"Okay, I'll wait inside."

"See you in a few."

I hung up and slid my phone back in my purse. The shakiness was wearing off and was quickly being replaced with anger. I wanted to march outside and confront whoever was in that van.

A moment later, the two officers returned.

"We didn't see any kind of van parked anywhere or driving around, ma'am, but we did close your car door. Did you leave it open?"

I paused and then glanced toward the door, recalling my sprint into the building. "I think I did. Thanks for closing it. I'm just waiting for Detective Maldon to get here, and then I'll move my car. I'm going to leave it here overnight if that's okay?"

"Should be fine," DS Glenn replied. "Why don't you give your keys to Officer Delcourt, and he can move your car for you?"

I did as he asked, giving my keys to the patrol officer, who headed back outside to move my car. Frank walked in a few minutes later with Officer Delcourt at his side.

"Thanks," I said, taking my keys back.

Frank reached for me, taking my hands in his. "Are you okay?"

"I'm fine. More pissed off than anything. And I really need to start running again."

He gave me a wry look. "Okay?"

"Never mind," I murmured, not wanting to explain about why I'd said that. I knew I needed to do it, and that was enough.

"So do you know who it was?" Frank asked as we headed back out of the station.

"Not sure, but I'm leaning toward Jordan." I had this eerie feeling that if it had been anyone else, they would have stopped me long before I reached the SMPD station.

The question was, if it was Jordan, why was he following me?

19

OH VALERIE

MARCY

"I don't like it, TT." Frank handed me a cup of coffee the next morning. "I don't like Jordan being out there somewhere trying to hurt you and me not around to help."

I loved how protective Frank was over me; it made me feel good to have him backing me. "If it was Jordan, he's basically harmless. Sure, he followed me, scared me a little bit, but he wouldn't hurt me. Not really. It's Jordan."

Frank set his mug down and moved toward me, taking me in his arms. "Look, I know you've known the man for a long time, but even you have to admit he's never been this unstable. You don't know what he's going to do. He blames you for losing his job and his standing in the community. Men have killed for less. I just want you to be very careful. His behavior is erratic and violent; he needs to be taken off the street."

Sighing, I knew Frank was right. I was making excuses for Jordan, but over the last few days... well, he wasn't the man I'd known before. I'd blocked his number on my phone because he wouldn't stop leaving me insane voicemails, and he'd started calling from other numbers. I kept blocking, but it was getting tiring. He was also sending me emails that were incoherent and insulting, not to mention threatening. I really did need to get that restraining order because I was starting to think that Jordan needed to be admitted for a psych eval.

"I'll be careful. I promise."

"You coming back here tonight, or do you want me to come stay with you?" Frank asked.

"I think it might be better if I stay in LA. The less I'm on the road, the better."

"Then I'll come to you after my shift. Do you want me to pick something up?"

"I'll get some steaks, and we can grill, does that work?" I suggested.

"Perfect." He smiled and kissed my temple. "You about ready? We need to get your car so you can head in."

I glanced at the clock on the stove; it was nearly six thirty. For the first time in a long time, I wasn't actually looking forward to going to work. I loved my job, but right now I was feeling stressed out, and I really wanted to just spend the day with Frank, maybe sitting on the beach, and just relaxing. Unfortunately, that wasn't an option.

"Yeah, okay." I picked up the overnight bag he'd packed for me and my purse, but he took the bag from my hand. I smiled at him, and we headed for his truck.

Fifteen minutes later, he slid my bag in the back seat, pulled me to him and kissed me, then said goodbye. "Be safe," he said with a wave.

"You too." I backed out of the parking spot and headed back to LA as I kept an eye out for that van.

. . .

"Do you have anything new on El Gato?" Valerie asked. She was standing behind me at my desk, looking over my shoulder to see what I was working on.

I turned and stood up, partially blocking her view. "Not really. We're trying to see who else connects Javier, Ruby, and Samson. There's quite a number of people both Samson and Ruby knew, but as far as I can tell, there's no connections between Javier and Ruby."

She nodded. "Is there anyone standing out to you that you might think is El Gato?"

Angel walked up carrying two containers of food; he'd gone to the Lobsta truck to get us lunch. "Oh, hey, Burnett, I didn't know you were going to be joining us, or I'd have gotten you lunch too."

"I'm not. I just wanted to know if you'd found anything on El Gato."

I turned and tapped my keyboard, closing my computer. I didn't need her snooping while I ate. "There are any number of celebrities who stand out, but as far as them being El Gato? I have my doubts." Even if there was one I suspected, I didn't think I'd share that with her, not right now.

"Hmm, well, keep me informed, yeah?"

"Sure," I said, but didn't really mean it. I was still feeling as though there was something off about her. She seemed hyper-focused one minute and scattered the next. She was interested in the case and then not. And mostly it seemed she was more concerned with whether or not we'd identified El Gato. Like she couldn't stand it if we were able to figure it out when she couldn't. I supposed she just didn't want us to make her look bad.

Valerie stood there for another few moments as though she was waiting for more, but then turned and walked away. I watched her go down the hall and to the elevator, texting on her phone.

"Shoot," I muttered, thinking I should have asked her to pay me back before she left.

"What's wrong?" Angel asked, his brow furrowed.

"I meant to get her to pay me back. I keep forgetting."

"Yeah, she's probably forgotten all about that. You'd better eat before it gets cold," Angel said, nodding to my lunch.

"Right." I smiled at him. "Thanks for grabbing it for us."

I opened my Styrofoam box and began to eat. I was still preoccupied with Valerie and what was going on with her. I decided I needed to take my worries to the captain and see what he had to say. I'd seen him head into his office about thirty minutes ago, and he hadn't left, so now might be a good time. I closed the lid on what was left of my lunch and put it aside.

"I'll be back," I murmured as I got up and headed for Jason. "Hey, is the captain available for a few minutes?" I asked when I reached him.

"Let me find out, one moment." Jason picked up the phone and spoke to the captain for a minute and then looked up at me. "He says go on in, but he doesn't have too long before he has to go meet the deputy mayor and chief of police for lunch."

"I'll make it quick, thanks, Jason." I headed for the door and knocked before poking my head in the doorway. "Sir?"

"Come in, Kendrick. Do you have an update on the case?"

"A minor one, sir," I said as I took a seat and then explained where we were on the case before delving into my concerns. "I wanted to talk to you about Burnett."

He stopped writing and put his pen down. He looked at me and sighed. "Is she causing you trouble? Not being a team player?"

"Not exactly, sir, it's just—" I tried to gather my thoughts about how to explain this nagging feeling I was having. "I'm concerned. She's been after El Gato for a decade and still has no idea who he might be. She knows next to nothing about him, who his associates are, why he would go after Ruby or Samson, but when we came across Javier, she knew the name and then said he's just a low-level thug. I don't know what she's been up to for the last ten years, but it seems to me she's dropping the ball on this."

Robinson dragged a hand over his face. "What I'm about to say needs to be kept quiet, understand me, Kendrick?"

My stomach tightened. "Yes, sir, but may I share with Angel?"

"Reyes is fine, but keep it between you. Burnett was a fantastic Vice cop for years. She busted some high-level drug lords and made a name for herself. Then El Gato showed up, and she caught the case. Unfortunately, about six years ago, she lost her dad, and then her mother became seriously ill. Cancer. She's been struggling for the past five years trying to care for her, do her job and pay for it all. She's still doing her job to the best of her ability, but El Gato has been the albatross around her neck. She can't seem to make any headway on him. Whenever she gets close, or one of the undercover operatives do, something happens to them, or Valerie's inroads into his operation get shut down. It's got the team a bit spooked, and to be honest, with everything that's been going on in Vice over the past year and a half with the Selene Webb issue, well, Valerie's been left to her own devices for too long."

I felt a wave of sympathy for her over her mother, and then I recalled she'd said she'd recently lost her aunt as well. I could understand her trying to do it all and coming up short. Didn't excuse her drinking on the job, but I did understand her a little better.

"The mayor and chief both thought having you work with her might get her back on her feet with the El Gato case. You've got a great track record for catching perps, and they thought you might be able to help her bring him in. If it's not working though, maybe we'll have to look at changing things—"

"No. No, it's fine. I didn't know she was going through that. I'll try to be more patient and understanding with her, sir." I decided then that I wouldn't bring up the money she owed me. She probably needed it more than I did. Continuing, I said, "I get that there aren't a lot of people who look at things the same as I do, sir. Maybe I can help Valerie get El Gato. I'm going to do my best. You know I don't like leaving cases open-ended."

"I know, Kendrick. You still looking for the woman who helped the Broken Badge Killer?"

"Every chance I get, which hasn't been a lot lately."

"You'll find her," Robinson assured me, though I was afraid he was more optimistic than I was on the topic.

"In the meantime, Angel and I are still waiting on the warrant to get into Javier's email."

"I'm meeting the chief for lunch. I'll see if he can expedite that for you."

"Thanks, enjoy your lunch."

He gave me a wry look. "I don't know how enjoyable it will be, but thanks for the sentiment. If I'm not back this afternoon, I just wanted to remind you and Angel, no overtime right now. And stay focused on the El Gato case. Jason knows to direct all incoming calls to the others."

"Yes, sir." I stood, and with a nod, I headed back to my desk.

"What was that about?" Angel asked.

I glanced around the room to see if anyone was paying attention to us. Considering the captain had asked me to keep it quiet, I didn't really want to say it here in the detective pool. "Let's take a drive over to Samson's place."

Angel frowned, but nodded. He knew I had something to say, but obviously didn't want to say it here. "I'll grab my keys."

I flipped open the lid on my lunch and ate a couple more bites before putting the box in the trash bin. I'd eaten most of it, but now it was cold and didn't taste as good. I grabbed my purse and followed Angel out of the precinct to his car.

Once we were on the road, he said, "Okay, what gives?"

"I talked to Robinson about Burnett. Found out a few things, but the captain doesn't want her business bandied about the station."

"What did he tell you?" He tossed a glance my way as we headed toward West Hollywood and Beverly Hills.

"Robinson said that Burnett lost her dad about six years ago, and then her mom got sick with cancer. She's been taking care of her ever since and has been struggling."

"Wow, that's tough. I guess I can understand the stress

she's under, why she's drinking. Don't like that she's doing it on the job, but yeah." He nodded.

"Robinson also said that a lot of Vice is spooked about El Gato. They've had several undercover operatives made and killed, and anytime Burnett gets close to locking in on who El Gato is, who's at the top of the operation with him, the avenue to it gets shut down." I got quiet as I considered the implications of that. "Then there was the whole Selene thing and Vice... so they've been reeling a bit down there."

"Sounds to me like we've got a leak," Angel muttered. "At least Vice does."

I nodded. "I was thinking the same. What if the drugs Grant was running were from El Gato's operation?" I was referring to Grant Weaver, a detective from Vice who'd been taken down several months ago for human trafficking and drug running.

Angel gave me a surprised look, but then nodded slowly. "Yeah, could be. Maybe he was the leak that got the operatives killed. Should we go see him?"

The idea of driving up to Pelican Bay State Prison where Weaver was doing time didn't strike me as a great idea, especially since I knew he'd probably lie. He wasn't the most trustworthy person I'd ever met. Besides, the captain would never approve it. "No, Robinson also mentioned we can't take overtime right now anyway, and that would be a lot of overtime."

"Weaver probably wouldn't admit it, even if he was sharing information with El Gato."

I snickered. "That was my thought as well. El Gato would likely have him killed in prison if he even suspected Weaver might talk."

"True." Angel pulled up to Cascade Rise and parked. "So

what are we doing here?" he asked, looking up at the luxury apartment building.

I shrugged. I didn't really have a reason for being here. "I thought maybe we could go look for more connections. Maybe Samson had an address book CSI missed, or something physical that he used to contact El Gato."

"Wouldn't hurt to look." Angel pushed open the driver's door and got out. "Let's see what we can find."

AN HOUR LATER, we had come up empty-handed and returned to the lobby of the building.

As we were about to leave, the woman at reception stopped me. "Excuse me, ma'am? Detective?"

I turned around and saw her half out of her seat, trying to get our attention. "Yes, what can I do for you?"

"Oh, well, it's just Mr. Martinez's cousin has been by asking about cleaning out his apartment. He wants to put it back on the market and, well... we weren't sure what to tell him."

His cousin? Had we come across a cousin in our research of Samson? I wasn't sure. I glanced at Angel, and he seemed confused as well. "The investigation is still ongoing, so it may be a few weeks yet before he can gain access. Do you by chance have this cousin's name?"

"Sure thing, one second." The woman sat back down and shifted a few things on her desk, then came up with a card. "This is what he gave me."

I took it from her and looked at the card.

Alejandro Gómez, G & G Imports/Exports.

I'd seen that name before. I showed the card to Angel, and he nodded. "Thank you, we'll get in touch with Mr. Gómez. However, if he contacts you before we do, you might let him know it may be a while before he can take possession of his cousin's things."

"Okay, thank you."

"My pleasure," I replied and then left with Angel. When we reached the car, I said, "Wasn't this guy's name in some of Samson's social media posts?"

Angel nodded. "Yes, I think there were a couple where he was mentioned. And he was in a couple of the pictures Ruby took at one of the parties."

"Why didn't he come up as next of kin on Samson? I thought all his relatives were down in Mexico?"

"His parents definitely are. I made that call. I'm not sure where this Alejandro Gómez fits in as far as Samson's family goes."

"Maybe I should give him a call and find out."

"Let me do some digging into him before we do that. See what I can find," Angel suggested.

"All right. I need to look into filing a restraining order anyway."

Angel flashed his eyes toward me. "What did he do now?"

I told him about being followed all the way out to Santa Monica the night before. "And I'm pretty sure it was Jordan. He's getting more and more unstable, Angel."

"Damn, I thought I'd gotten through to him," he muttered. "He'd seemed okay and said he'd back off when I talked to him a few days ago."

I shook my head. "He hasn't. He's calling me from random numbers. I think he's gotten some kind of number-spoofing app or something because every time I block him, he comes back with another. And the emails have gotten pretty disturbing as well." I'd caught a few words in a couple of them before forwarding them to Stephen.

"Shit. I'm sorry, Marce."

"Not your fault. This is all on Jordan. Anyway, I need to look into that order. At this point I'm getting concerned for Katie."

"You don't even like his wife."

"I know. Tells you how concerned I am." I bit the inside of my lip as I thought about it. "Should I call her, do you think?"

"I could do it if you don't feel comfortable."

"No, I think it needs to come from me. I'll call her." I pulled out my phone and dialed her cell. It wasn't a number I often called, almost never, but I had it just in case.

The phone rang and rang, then went to voicemail.

"Katie, it's Marcy. I just wanted to make sure you're okay. Jordan has been acting odd. He threw a brick through my window the other night, and last night he followed me all the way to Santa Monica, trying to scare me. I just wanted to check on you. Call me if you need help or anything." I hung up and looked over at Angel. "Think she'll call me back?"

Angel shrugged. "Maybe? She's not your biggest fan."

I snorted. "No, she's not." But then I wasn't hers either.

20

LATE NIGHT GUEST

MARCY

As I pulled into the grocery store parking lot, my phone rang, playing "Adore You." I parked and answered. "Hey, I just got to the store," I said, smiling even though Frank couldn't see me.

"Babe, I'm sorry, I can't make it over there tonight. My mom had a breakdown, and my dad and I are getting her into a facility. I just—" He sounded broken, and his voice cracked.

"It's okay, go take care of your mom. I'll be fine."

"You sure? I can try to come later..."

"No, you need to be there for your dad too. Go be with them, it's okay. I promise I'm fine."

"Thanks, I'll text you later, make sure you're okay. And I'll call you in the morning."

I couldn't believe he was still worrying about me with his mom going through what she was. It had to be so hard on her losing a son the way she had. Frank had been going to therapy after losing his brother, but being a mother, that had to be even worse.

"I'll look forward to it," I said softly.

"Me too, TT. Be safe." He hung up.

I sighed and looked up at the grocery store. I debated going in and buying something to fix for dinner, but now, since Frank wasn't coming over, I didn't have an appetite anymore, and I didn't want to cook for just me. I went in anyway and found a premade salad and some fajita chicken. After making my purchase, I returned to my car and headed home.

I doctored up the salad while the chicken heated in the microwave, and then I added the chicken to it too. I took the salad and a beer from my fridge to the living room and sat down on the sofa. Pulling up Prime, I began to stream *Marlowe*. Liam Neeson was good in everything, so I figured this detective movie was probably good too.

When it was over, I shut the TV down, tossed my salad container and beer bottle in the recycling bin, then headed to my bathroom for a shower. Afterwards, I sent Frank a quick text, just telling him I was thinking of him and that I hoped his mom was doing better.

A minute later he replied.

> She's stable now, feeling better after being admitted. Dad's handling it okay. Miss you, TT.

> Miss you too, Frank. Get some rest, okay?

> I will. Check your windows and doors. Make sure they're locked.

I smiled and laughed a little.

Already done. I'm safe inside with my Glock. I promise to shoot anything that tries to break in.

Good! Sweet dreams. I'll call in the morning.

Night Frank.

I set my phone on the night table and picked up my tablet as I snuggled under my blankets. I figured I'd read a little before going to sleep.

By the time I put the tablet down, it was after ten. I was just about to turn off the light when there was a knock on my front door.

A moment later my doorbell rang persistently, and then there was another rush of knocks. If it was Jordan, I was going to be pissed off. Still, I picked up my Glock and headed for the door, flicking on all the house lights along the way. I wanted as much light as possible in case this turned nasty.

I looked through the peephole and was shocked. Quickly, I set my weapon down, unlocked the door and opened it. "Katie, are you okay?"

Katie Brasswell, Jordan's current wife, stood on my porch, tears racing down her cheeks. Her left eye was bruised and slightly swollen. She looked lost and scared.

Katie and I had never been friends. She'd been a college student when she'd had an affair with Jordan and had been the reason for me getting out of the marriage. I didn't exactly blame her for my marriage to Jordan falling apart; he was the one I blamed. Looking back now, I'm glad things between us ended, and most days I wished I'd had the nerve to do it sooner. I'd been one of those who thought marriage was a forever thing, and that because of my vows, I needed to stick to them and try to make things work. However that affair had been just too far over the line for me.

"Can I come in?" she asked hesitantly as she looked back over her shoulder with worry.

"Of course." I gestured for her to enter. "How did you find me? What's going on? Do you need some ice for your eye? Did Jordan do that?" I asked, still flabbergasted that she'd come to me.

"I've left him." She sniffled and wiped her eyes on the edge of her T-shirt. "He's been drinking so much, and tonight he came home really drunk and hit me. I kicked him out. I found your address written down on a notepad on his desk."

"Damn, I knew he was getting worse, but I didn't expect him to hurt you," I murmured as I directed her to a chair in the kitchen while I made her an ice pack.

"I'm scared of him. He's not the same man I married." She sniffled again, her eyes getting teary.

I held the ice pack out to her. "I can relate to that, but he was never like this. This is a whole new level of crazy. I'm sorry you're going through this. Do you want to stay here?"

She shook her head and took the ice pack in one hand. "No, I'm going to go to my parents', but I got your voicemail, and I just... I thought you should know he was ranting about you too. When he hit me, he... he thought I was you." Her voice was barely a whisper.

Now that made sense in a weird way. Katie wasn't the one he was putting the blame on. "I appreciate you letting me know."

"I got a call from the station. Jordan's in jail."

"If you don't mind me asking, what happened?" I asked, curious. "Did you press charges against him?"

"He was drunk driving, and when he got pulled over, he assaulted the officer. That's what they told me. The officer recognized him and said he wasn't going to press charges, but they've put him in the drunk tank overnight, and he's going to be charged for the drunk driving and disorderly conduct. I'm going to use this time to get away from him."

"Good plan." I nodded. Though I thought it was wrong for the officer not to press charges. Jordan needed to be held accountable for his actions. "Are you filing charges for that?" I nodded toward the bruise on her face.

Katie looked down at her lap and shook her head. "No," she whispered, "I couldn't do that to him. I don't want to be with him anymore, but I don't want him in jail either."

I sighed, knowing I couldn't force her to press charges. "Would you like me to drive you to your parents' place?"

She looked up at me, tears spilling from her eyes. "Would you do that? They live in Lakewood."

It wouldn't be too long a drive, especially at this time of night. Only about thirty minutes. "Sure."

"Thank you," she murmured. "I've got stuff in my car … oh, my car… what about it?"

"You can leave it here in my driveway. Have your dad come and get it tomorrow; that way you don't have to worry about Jordan messing with you."

"You're being very kind to me, after everything…"

"I don't blame you for what happened between me and Jordan."

Ten minutes later, I'd transferred her things from her car to the trunk of mine. I opened the passenger door for Katie, who was still holding the ice pack to her eye. I pulled out of the driveway and started down the dark street.

However a moment later, headlights flashed on behind me, and I grew concerned. I didn't want to worry Katie, but I was terribly afraid that they hadn't kept Jordan in the drunk tank as they'd said they were going to.

I made a turn, and the car followed. I made a second turn, and once again, the car followed. I glanced at Katie, who had her eyes closed and the ice pack pressed to her swollen one. I was glad she hadn't noticed what was going on. It was the last thing she needed.

I kept my speed steady and my eyes on the car behind me. Unlike the van the other night, this car stayed about three car lengths back. Something told me that because of that, this wasn't Jordan.

But if it wasn't him, who was it?

21

DEATH OF A DRUG DEALER
EL VIBORA

I was enjoying a quiet moment walking down Mill Street in the Arts District. It wasn't often that I had time to just be. To just relax and take in the beauty of the art all around me. It was soothing in a way. So different than what I normally dealt with.

Thoughts of Sofia invaded my mind as I strolled. This was where we'd met. Probably why I was here now. Reliving those memories. I could picture her here, laughing in the sunlight, her hazel eyes sparkling as she tossed her long dark hair over her shoulder. She was dressed in a colorful flowing top, tight jeans and a pair of Skechers.

I could see her walking in front of me, turning to toss me a grin over her shoulder as she pointed out something that caught her eye, her lips spread wide in an open grin. She was glorious. The most beautiful woman I'd ever met and the kindest as well. It was no wonder we didn't work out. She couldn't handle what I did for a living. Still, I didn't blame her for leaving. It was my fault for sharing too much.

It didn't stop me from wondering what she might be

doing now. Was she involved with someone new? Were they treating her well? Did she still think of me? I would never know the answers to those questions because I had promised her that I wouldn't try to find her. It was a promise I would never break.

My phone buzzed in my pocket, and I pulled it out. Alejandro. "*Si?*" I murmured, turning away from the groups of people enjoying the art and sunshine and retreating to the shadows.

"We've got a bead on Deon. He's holed up at his house near Venice Beach. I'll text you the address. You know what to do." Alejandro didn't say any more, just hung up.

I pocketed my phone again as it buzzed with the text for the address, and stared at the people walking by, enjoying the day. Not a care in the world. I envied them.

With a sigh, I headed back to the rental I'd picked up for the day. It was a nondescript black SUV and looked exactly like a million other cars on the road. I returned to my apartment and changed my appearance. Gone was the brown and gray hair, traded for a blond spikey wig. I wanted to look like just another surfer out catching waves. Not that I would be. I added blue contacts and veneers for my teeth, as well as a blond goatee.

Satisfied with my appearance, I grabbed my gear and headed toward Venice Beach. It was a nice drive, but I wasn't really paying attention to any of the sights. I was gearing myself up for what I needed to do. I'd already prepared the syringe with the lethal cocktail I would be injecting Dennis "Deon" Butler with.

This was actually a killing I could get behind. Deon wasn't a good guy. He was a violent gangbanger who'd made his way up the ranks by murdering Alejandro's men, stealing his product and selling it for himself. Not that Alejandro was much better. He wasn't, but I'd signed a contract with him. At the time I supposed I thought he was a lesser evil. When I'd first started working for him, it had been various other drug lords I'd been taking out. It had only been recently that he'd sent me to take out some people I wasn't sure deserved their deaths.

It didn't matter. It was my job, and I was good at it. Maybe even the best. They did sing songs about me down in Mexico; that was something.

It was nearing twilight as I reached the neighborhood Deon lived in. The homes were ostentatious, very lavish, and full of glass windows that looked out over the coast, with beautiful sandy beaches for backyards.

I grabbed my beach things, a towel, and a radio that I wouldn't be playing, along with a cooler that held a soda, a sandwich, and a book. I put my bag with what I needed for Deon in the cooler under the sandwich and drink, so they wouldn't be ruined, and started for the beach. There were plenty of people around; a bonfire was being built not too far away. It was drawing a lot of attention.

I set up camp where I could keep an eye on Deon's place. Luckily for me, he was outside, dressed in a pair of trunks and holding a beer. He was making it easy for me to track him. The overconfident fool obviously thought he was untouchable. There were two other men there as well, but they didn't look like guards, more like friends. They weren't my target though.

I spread out my towel and reached in the cooler, pulling out the soda and the book. Sitting down, I sipped at the soda and pretended to read as I kept an eye on Deon. He and his buddies headed down to the beach, toward the bonfire. I watched him as he hit on the women, manhandling them like he owned them.

An hour into my observation, the sun fully set, and I ate my sandwich. I couldn't pretend to read any more, so I headed for the bonfire, sticking to the outskirts of it as I kept my eye on him. Nobody paid me much attention.

Hours passed, and eventually, Deon made his way back to his house. I returned to my setup and opened the cooler, digging into my bag of tricks. I pocketed what I needed and then crept toward Deon's place. He'd returned to the house with a girl who looked about sixteen, but I doubted she'd be staying long after I made my entrance.

I put on my latex gloves, slid the glass door open slightly and entered the home silently. I could hear Deon and the girl in one of the bedrooms. I kept to the shadows as I moved toward them. The door was cracked to the bedroom. Deon was standing naked in the center of the room, the girl on her knees in front of him. Both were too occupied to notice me.

I pulled the syringe from my pocket and uncapped it, then swiftly moved behind Deon. Before he knew what hit him, I injected him with the lethal dose of laced heroin.

"What the fuck?" Deon shouted. His hand went to his neck. He started to sway.

I looked at the girl, my expression cruel. "Get your shit and get out. You tell anyone I'm here, I will find you and kill you too. Do you understand?"

She looked terrified, her eyes blurring with tears, but nodded as she grabbed her swimsuit and booked it out of the house.

I wasn't sure I trusted her to keep her mouth shut, so I needed to take care of this quickly. I glanced back at Deon, who was now on his knees and falling backward toward the bed.

"Wha... you... do... to me?" he stuttered.

"No less than you deserve. El Gato sends his best wishes for a painful death. By now you can probably feel the fire in your veins. You should have left his men and his product alone." I flicked the ace of spades card at him, and it landed on his chest as he cried out in agony. He was scratching at his arms, digging into his skin like he could get the toxic concoction out of his veins. He wouldn't.

I glanced at the clock on the bedside table. It wouldn't be much longer. I waited for the light in his eyes to go out and then checked his pulse to be sure he wouldn't be able to be revived.

Sure he was dead, I turned off the light, walked out of the room, closing the door slightly. I promptly left the house and returned to the beach. Only fifteen minutes had passed.

I waited on the beach for an hour to make sure the girl had kept her mouth shut. Eventually Deon's two buddies headed for the house with a couple of girls. They didn't seem to be in any kind of hurry. They knew nothing. Good. That was the way I wanted it.

I packed up my things, taking my time. I was in no hurry. I didn't want to draw attention to myself, which rushing would do. Then I strolled down the beach and back to my car, nobody the wiser.

22

A TRIP TO THE BEACH

MARCY

"Hey, I think we've got one of yours out here on Venice Beach."

That was not what I expected to hear when I answered Frank's call. "One of mine?" I asked, suddenly back in work mode.

"Dead body with a Black Cat playing card. Ace of spades."

"Got an ID?"

"Dennis Butler, better known as Deon on the streets, from what I'm told. Drug dealer, I think."

"Can you hold the scene until Angel, Burnett, and I get there?"

"That's why I called, TT. I knew you'd want to be here. I'll text you the address."

"Thanks. I'll call Burnett and grab Angel, and we'll be on our way."

"Be safe."

As I hung up the phone, Angel asked, "What's up?" He stood up and grabbed his keys.

"We've got another dead body, this time in Santa Monica over on Venice Beach."

"Let's go. Did I hear you say you were calling Burnett?"

I nodded and dialed her number as we headed for the door.

Her line rang several times before she eventually answered. "S'up?" she said, but it sounded strange to my ear.

"There's been another hit. Out on Venice Beach. I'll send you the address; meet us there."

"'Kay." The line went dead.

I shrugged. "I guess she's coming. She didn't say much."

"Does it really matter if she does or doesn't? She hasn't really been that much help so far," Angel said snarkily.

"I know, but she might know our victim. I want to get her take on his murder."

Angel nodded. "Makes sense. She does know this world better than us. Who is the vic, anyway?"

"Frank said his name is Dennis Butler, better known as Deon. Also said he thinks he's a drug dealer."

We arrived at the scene thirty-eight minutes later. Angel parked in front of the lavish home, and we walked past the yellow crime scene tape, waving our badges at the SMPD who were on the scene. I pushed open the front door and found Frank in the hallway.

I glanced into the living room and saw a couple of men and two younger girls seated on the couch, three officers standing in the room around them. "I take it they found the victim?"

Frank nodded. "Two of Deon's boys, and the women they brought home last night." His voice lowered as he added, "If you can call them women; their IDs say they're both seventeen."

I shook my head. The men had to be at least ten years older than them. The age of consent was eighteen in the state of California. If I had my way, they'd be brought up on sexual assault charges. I narrowed my eyes at them. "Why aren't they cuffed?"

"Calm down, TT. They will be. That's why the officers are in there, and the girls' parents are on their way."

Usually, someone telling me to calm down would immediately have me seeing red, but the rest of what he said did what those two words didn't. I gave him a nod. "Okay, where's the body?"

"Through here. He's been dead for a while. The coroner is with him now."

"Who's the coroner on duty?" Angel asked.

"Daphne Maple," Frank replied as we entered the large bedroom.

I took in the short redhead bent over the body in blue scrubs and a white lab coat. When she looked up, I noticed her eyes were a bright blue, and she had a dusting of freckles across her nose. She had a serious look on her face, and her lips were pressed together in a line of concentration.

"He's been dead between eight and ten hours. Closer to ten, if I had to guess." She stood up. "I'm Dr. Maple, and you are?" She held her hand out to me.

I shook her hand. "Detective Marcy Kendrick, LAPD HSS. This is Detective Angel Reyes, my partner—" As I said that Valerie showed up behind Angel, looking a little bit of a mess. Her hair was wild, her eyes a little too bright, and her blouse was buttoned incorrectly. "And Detective Valerie Burnett from LAPD Vice," I added hesitantly as I looked at Valerie.

"Pleasure," Daphne said. "I take it this victim is part of your case? Should I have the body sent to Dr. Black?"

"If you wouldn't mind. I'd appreciate it."

She nodded. "I can tell you that he's got an injection mark in his neck. There's saliva on his penis, so I think he was engaged in sexual activity either just before or during the attack."

That surprised me, considering who our killer was. El Vibora didn't leave evidence behind, so it couldn't have been him. But then if Deon had been with someone else, where were they?

I glanced at Frank. "Do we have another victim somewhere?"

"Not that I've been made aware of. I'll check with the precinct, see if we have any other bodies from last night."

"If we don't, then that person is a witness. We need to find out who they are."

"Do you want to question his boys? Maybe they'll know?" Frank suggested.

"Good idea," Angel added.

I looked over at Valerie. "Burnett, you know him?"

She nodded. "Deon." She shook her head a little and added, "Dennis Butler. Drug dealer. From what I've discovered, he's pretty much a thorn in El Gato's side. Always stealing from El Gato... has a reputation for killing El Gato's dealers and stealing his product."

"And you didn't bust him?"

"Yes, I did. He just finds his way out of it," she said, sounding high strung and breathy, her voice almost panicky.

"Can I speak to you in the hallway, Detective Burnett?" I said suspiciously.

Valerie's eyes widened, and she looked like a deer caught in the headlights. "I-I have to go," she muttered and nearly ran from the room.

"That wasn't weird at all," Frank said, his eyes on the door Valerie had just rushed through.

"I don't know what's going on with her, but yeah, that was strange," I replied.

"She smelled like weed," Angel added.

"You think she was high?" I asked.

"Higher than a kite." Angel nodded.

"Great." I shook my head and glanced at Frank. "Let's go talk to these thugs."

"Are you done viewing the scene?" Daphne asked before we could leave the room.

"If you want, you can go ahead and send the body to Dr. Black. And thanks again for doing that."

"Sure, no problem," she answered and turned back to the body.

We went into the living room, and the two men now had handcuffs on, their hands behind their backs, while the girls had been moved to the other side of the room with their parents. I didn't give them much of a look, as I was focused on the men.

"You were Deon's boys?" I asked.

"Ain't sayin' nothin'," one of them muttered.

"Lawyer," the other added.

I sighed and pressed the bridge of my nose. "Look, I just need to know Deon's movements last night and who he was with. Can you answer that?"

The two men looked at each other and shrugged.

The first one said, "We were just chillin', hangin' with the crew down on the beach. Deon and some chick took off 'round ten or eleven. We didn't see 'em after that."

"So he was with a woman?" Angel questioned.

"Yeah, he ain't no dick eater," the second guy said with a snort.

"Do either of you know the woman he was with?" Angel questioned.

"Naw, just some bitch. They hang out on the beach, lookin' to ride big dicks and do some blow," the first guy said, laughing like he'd said something witty instead of disgusting and sexist.

"Okay, thanks." I turned to Frank and glanced toward the girls on the other side of the room. "Maybe they know her?"

"Worth a shot. If their parents will allow them to answer."

I walked across the room, which was pretty big, double the size of my own living room, and stopped in front of the two families. "Good morning, I'm Detective Kendrick; this is Detective Reyes and Detective Maldon. I'd like to ask your daughters a couple of questions if you wouldn't mind?"

"Jonathon Cameron," one of the fathers said, holding out his hand, which I shook, "this is my wife, Samantha"—he nodded toward his wife—"and Amber will answer whatever questions you have, Detectives."

I could see he was livid, but the grip he had on his daughter's arm wasn't tight or abusive in any way. "Thank you." I flashed my gaze to the other set of parents and arched a brow.

"Thomas Brink, my wife, Melody, and our daughter, Laura. She'll answer your questions too."

"Thank you. Ladies, I understand you were on the beach last night when you met up with those men over there?"

Amber's lip trembled as she said, "Yes. We were just having a fun day at the beach when we got invited to the bonfire. Seth and Vince were there. That's them." Her eyes flashed to the two men across the room. "We didn't know they were part of a gang—"

"Or nearly thirty," Laura added; her gaze turned pleading as she looked at her parents.

"So you didn't know who they were before you joined them at the bonfire?"

"They weren't there when we were invited to stay and hang out. There was a huge group of people, but they came later with... with the guy..." Amber's eyes watered, and tears spilled down her cheeks.

"With Deon?" I said, trying to get her past what she'd seen.

She nodded. "Yes." The word was barely more than a breath.

"And did you see Deon leave the party with someone?"

"No, not really. Seth said he'd taken some girl up to the house. I asked whose house it was, and he said Deon's. That he was one of those really rich party guys and would we like to see the house... so we said yeah."

"Did you know the woman Deon was with?"

Laura shook her head. "No, and they weren't here when we came up. I mean, I guess Deon was in—" She stopped, her eyes got very wide, and then she turned and threw up in the plant pot she was standing next to.

Amber pulled free from her dad and went to Laura, pulling her hair back and soothing her. She glanced over her shoulder at us. "We didn't know Deon was dead in there. We never looked in that room until Seth went to get him this morning."

I sighed. "Okay, thank you. If we have any further questions, we'll be in touch. Please make sure the officers have your information."

"Oh, believe me, they will have our information, and we want those men charged," Laura's dad seethed.

Frank assured the families that the two men would be charged for sexual assault of a minor, corruption of a minor and anything else they could throw at them and make stick.

I turned away and walked with Angel back to the hallway. I very much doubted that we were going to find the girl, if she was even alive.

"What are you thinking?" Angel asked.

"That I'd really like to find this missing witness. Think that saliva could lead to her?"

"Maybe. Stranger things have happened. We should also put a notice out that we're looking for anyone who was at the bonfire last night."

"That's a good idea."

Frank walked up and put his hand on my lower back. "What is?" he asked.

I explained Angel's idea. "What do you think?"

"Worth a shot. Why don't I handle that, since you two have your hands full with the rest?"

"You don't mind?" Angel asked.

"Nope. Happy to help."

"Great. You ready?" Angel looked at me.

"Give me a minute?"

He gave me a nod and headed for the front door.

I waited with Frank until we were alone in the hall. "How's your mom?"

He dragged a hand through his hair and sighed. "She's

better. She's going to stay and get some therapy, but she seemed in good spirits when I talked to her this morning."

"I'm glad. So why don't I come here tonight. That way you'll be close to your dad if he needs anything?"

Frank smiled. "Sounds like a good plan."

"Then I'll see you tonight." I smiled and headed for the door.

23

THE VIPER OF DEATH

MARCY

It was almost seven when I made it back to Santa Monica. I pulled into Frank's driveway and felt my shoulders untense. Like all the worries I had about Jordan, about the case, about everything, just melted away. I shut off my car, grabbed my overnight bag and headed for the front door.

Frank was waiting for me and opened the door before I even reached the stoop. "Hey, you," he said, a huge smile lighting his face.

"Hey, yourself," I replied, stepping into his embrace with a smile.

"Let me take that." He reached for the bag and brought it inside, setting it on the sofa in the living room. "I was thinking, why don't we go down to the pier, get dinner, and then we can come back and relax?"

"I like that idea. Let me change clothes first, though?"

"I figured you'd want to. Take your time." He kissed me and added, "I'm glad you're here."

"Me too." I really was. I loved the time I spent with Frank.

Thirty minutes later we were walking on the pier, heading to Bubba Gump Shrimp. I loved the peel-and-eat shrimp, which they steamed in beer. We got a table and gave the waitress our orders. Along with the shrimp appetizer, I ordered the Dixie-style baby-back ribs, and Frank chose the Bourbon St. mahi-mahi and shrimp, and we both ordered beer to go with it.

"Do you want to talk about the case?" Frank asked.

"Not really, but I want to know if you got a lead on our missing witness," I replied, picking at my napkin.

He shook his head. "Not so far, but we've identified a group of kids who were at that bonfire. We're going to talk to them tomorrow, and hopefully one of them will know the girl."

I smiled. "I'm glad about that. Maybe we'll catch a break."

Frank reached across the table and took my hand in his. "I have no doubt that you can catch this guy, TT." He entwined our fingers and squeezed, giving me a smile. "I just worry about you and wish it was me who had your back on the daily."

I smiled. "Maybe it's not the way you want, but you do have my back on the daily. And I have yours."

"Not the same, babe. I trust Angel, but in a way I'm jealous of him." He gave me a wry look.

I laughed. "Funny, recently he said the same of you."

His smile fell. "What?"

I suddenly realized I needed to explain. I didn't want him to worry he was going to lose me to Angel. "Since divorce, Angel has had my back. He's my best friend, and I guess I'm his. I relied on him, and he has always been there for me. Now I have you, and I don't depend on him as much, and he's a little jealous of that."

"Okay, I can understand that, I guess." He nodded, and he grew thoughtful. "I guess being your partner, you two would be close, almost like siblings. I had that kind of relationship with Daniel... we always had each other's backs until—" He stopped talking and looked down, his fingers tightening around mine. "Sorry, didn't mean to bring the evening down."

"You didn't. It's good to talk about your brother. To remember the good times, the good things about him."

"I know. It's just hard."

"I have the same trouble with remembering my mom," I admitted.

Frank knew all about my mom, her life and death and what she'd done to Stephen, and also how conflicted I was because she'd been a great mom to me. I was a kid; I hadn't known the heinous things she'd done to my brother until just this last year. It was a lot to deal with, so at times I missed her, and others I was so angry I wanted to bring her back from the dead just so I could kill her.

"I know, and you handle it so much better than I do."

"I've had more time than you," I replied. "It will get better."

"I know. And I have you." He smiled.

The waitress brought our food, and we changed the topic of conversation to something lighter. When we were done, we walked along the pier for a bit, took a ride on the Pacific Wheel and then headed back to his place.

That night, after making love, I snuggled into Frank's chest and attempted to sleep, but I couldn't get my mind to settle down. Facts about the case kept playing through my head. Despite my track record, I was actually worried about being able to bring El Gato and his henchman El Vibora to justice.

"What's going on in that beautiful head of yours?" Frank asked, kissing the top of my head.

I sighed. "Thinking about the case. I'm more frustrated than anything and feeling a little out of my element. I guess I'm just afraid I won't catch El Vibora or El Gato, because they've got a lot of money backing them."

Frank held me tighter. "You're great at your job. If anyone can catch them, it's you, TT."

"I'm used to chasing serial killers. And yeah, El Vibora is a serial killer, but he's not like the psychos I normally go after. He's a different animal. More dangerous in a way."

"You're right, they aren't the regular mentally ill killers you are normally chasing. Those guys make mistakes, but this guy is trained for this. It scares me because I can't be there to keep you safe. I'm terrified he's going to see you as an obstacle and attempt to take you out of the equation."

I pushed up on his chest to look into his face. "You know I'll be careful, right? I don't take chances," I said, and then I recalled a few times in the recent past where I actually had taken chances, and he knew about them. "Okay, let me retract that. I have taken chances, but I am working to be more careful now." I winced at how that sounded.

He sighed. "I trust you, Marcy. I do. It's just... I care about you. A lot. It's just hard knowing I'm so far away and I have to trust someone else, even a good cop like Angel, to have your back. I know I keep telling you I wish I were the one who could be there, but what I'm really trying to say is you're *important* to me."

It wasn't a declaration of love, exactly, but it was close.

I reached up and touched his face, staring into his eyes. "Frank, you're *important* to me too. I promise that I will be very cautious on this case. I know these men aren't the typical kind of bad guys I go after. It's like I'm chasing Jason Bourne and El Chapo. I swear I will take that into account as I pursue them."

He nodded. "Thank you. I'm working on not being so overprotective, but you'll need to be patient with me." He tilted his head forward and kissed me on the forehead.

I smiled. "Overall, I like that you're protective. It makes me feel safe and allows me to relax. But you have to trust that I can also protect myself and do this job. If you can't, then this will never work."

"I do trust that you can do your job. Better than most. Just know that I'm going to do my damnedest to be there anytime you need me."

I laid my head on his chest and held on to him tighter. "You know I would do the same for you, right?" I turned my face up toward his, to catch his gaze.

"I do." He sighed. "We'd better get some sleep, or we'll be dragging tomorrow."

LATER THE NEXT DAY, I replayed that conversation in my head. It hadn't been a fight or even an argument exactly, but an intense discussion that I wanted to reflect on. It was the kind of conversation that Jordan and I should have had prior to getting married. Only if we had, we never would have gotten married because Jordan wouldn't have been so open and honest about how he was feeling. He'd have told me I needed to stop doing what I did best and leave this case to Vice. He wouldn't have trusted me to do my job right. He would have done everything he could have to get me to give up the case.

It was amazing how different Frank was from Jordan. From anyone I'd ever met, really. Telling him he was important to me was about as close as I could get to telling him that I loved him. My thoughts then turned to Henry, who had been an amazing man too, but much different to Frank as well. Henry had been gentle and kind and smart and funny. I'd seen the potential in having him as a life partner, and when that had been ripped away from me, I'd mourned him and the lost relationship as though it had been my last chance at love.

Frank was some of those things as well, but I had to admit he and I were probably better suited to each other than Henry and I had been. Frank understood the job, and I knew he could protect himself. We both had trauma in our past that created a bond in a way and strengthened our connection to each other. We were both a mess, but our individual messy lives were very compatible. We probably understood each other better than anyone else ever could understand us.

"What are you thinking about so hard over there?" Angel asked from the driver's seat as we headed out to dinner.

We had spent the day working the case and getting nowhere. We'd skipped lunch and were both starving by the time the shift ended. Since neither of us had plans for the night, we decided to go out to eat.

I glanced over at him and smiled. "Life," I answered, "and how messy it is."

He chuckled. "You sure you don't mind trying El Patron Cantina? I know you prefer Alebrijes."

"I just know what to expect at Alebrijes, and I'm comfortable there. Doesn't mean I won't try something new." I grinned at him.

"I promise their food is fantastic, and the live music is great." He pulled into the parking lot and found a spot not too far from the door.

"Have you brought Callie here?" I asked, thinking maybe Frank might like it.

"Yeah, she loves it."

"I take it she's working late?"

Angel nodded. "Client wanted a balayage, and Callie said because her hair is so long, it's going to take about three hours, so she won't be home till after ten tonight."

"I have no idea what that is. Do you?" I asked, completely lost.

As we headed for the door, he shook his head. "Not really, some special kind of highlights or something, from what she said."

We entered the building and waited for the hostess to seat us. A moment later we had a table near the wall with a mural of Day of the Dead masks. We could see the band from where we sat, but we weren't so close we couldn't hear ourselves think. The atmosphere was festive and friendly.

I looked over the menu and decided on their El Patron Baja burrito with the beer-battered fish. It was something different, and tonight it sounded good. Angel went with a steak-filled California burrito.

After we ordered, he asked, "So no plans with Frank tonight?"

"He's coming by later. He's having dinner with his dad, then meeting me at my place."

"Things good with you two?" Angel asked.

"Yes, we're good."

The band began a new song. Suddenly his face paled, and he turned to look at the band.

"What's the matter?" I asked.

"Listen."

I did as he asked, and suddenly I understood. Well, not exactly understood; they were singing in Spanish. But I caught the words *"El Vibora de los muertos."* A shudder went through me, and I had to ask Angel to explain.

"Why are they singing about El Vibora?" I murmured, trying to keep anyone from overhearing me. "I get *muertos* is death... but what are they saying?"

"To some, especially in Mexico, El Vibora is a folk hero. He liberated a town from a really bad guy, a drug lord who had basically enslaved them. That's what the song is about. Him bringing death to the drug lord and freeing them from his tyranny."

"So they revere this killer?"

Angel shrugged. "It's complicated."

"No, it's not. The man is a killer. He's not a hero."

"Don't look at me. I didn't write the song, Marce. I agree with you."

I sighed. "Sorry. I know."

The rest of the meal went well, and the music was pretty good, aside from the El Vibora song, and soon we were headed back to the precinct so I could pick up my car.

I glanced in the sideview mirror and noticed a car following us.

"We've got a tail," I murmured, watching the car drifting into oncoming traffic and overcorrecting. "I think they may be drunk, they're swerving all over the place, but they've been with us since we left the restaurant."

"Call it in, and I'll try to lose them. Can you tell who it is?"

"Looks like a woman, but it's hard to tell, could just be a dude with longer hair."

"Can you get the plate number?"

"Yeah." I pulled my phone out and called dispatch. I gave them a description of the car and the plate number as Angel made a quick right turn, getting us away from her. I watched as the person's car tires screeched on the street as they passed by the turn. Whoever they were, they were going to cause an accident.

Angel took the next left and then a right, and I couldn't see them anymore. "Why are they following us?"

I didn't know the answer to that, but I was going to find out.

24

HIDDEN FILES AND DISTURBING ENCOUNTERS

MARCY

W hen I walked into the detective pool the next morning, I ran into Howard. He seemed excited and was bouncing on his toes. "Morning, Howard, what's up?"

"So you know how Lindsey's crew went over the Martinez place?"

I nodded, waiting for him to get to the point. "Yes?"

"Well, they found a hard drive duct-taped to the back of the entertainment center. I was able to get into it."

This was news to me. How had I missed that in the CSI report? I frowned and turned to my desk, looking for the file as Angel walked in.

"Don't you want to know what I found?" he asked; his voice almost squeaked with his uncontained excitement.

"I do—" I started.

"What's going on?" Angel asked, joining us.

"Howard found something on a hard drive from Samson's place. I'm looking for the report from CSI because I don't recall that being on the list of things found, do you?"

Angel moved to his desk and grabbed the file I was looking for and opened it. "Yeah, it's here," he said, pointing to one line in the report.

I was more distracted than I'd thought. "I missed it," I murmured, suddenly glad there were others who were working the case and more on top of it than me.

"It happens. There's been a lot going on," Angel replied. "So what did you find, Howard?"

"Finally! Come with me, and I'll show you." He turned and practically sprinted back to the tech department.

Angel and I followed at a slightly more reasonable pace. I was anxious to see what he'd found too, but still mad at myself for missing the piece of evidence.

Howard pulled up the large screen in front of us and hit a button. "Okay, so this is the hard drive. See these files? I've been able to get into four of them."

"What about the others?" I asked, seeing there were nine in all.

"No luck so far; they're encrypted pretty heavily. They'll take some time to break."

"So what's in the four you could get into?"

"Watch." He hit a button, and a video popped up.

I watched and listened to a Hispanic man in an Armani suit talking to some other men in Spanish. He turned and opened a silver briefcase. The camera zoomed in on the case, and in it, I could see, were probably thousands of little glassine baggies with the Black Cat label. The man said something else and then handed one of the baggies to the man, who investigated it and nodded, then gestured for another man to come forward. The man opened a black case, and inside was a great deal of money.

"Is that who I think it is?" I asked, my eyes wide.

"Depends, if you think it's El Gato, you'd be correct." Howard smirked.

"I want facial recognition run on that immediately. I want to know exactly who each of them are."

"Already being done. Should have an answer soon."

This was the break we needed. "Okay, you said there were four files you got into; what else is there?"

"Well, two of them were just business folders, mostly contracts and prospects for Ruby about future work. But the other one had a treasure trove of information." Howard's grin widened.

"You going to share with the class?" Angel asked, amused.

"Right." He opened the folder, and it was full of Word documents. He clicked one of them. "Take a look at this."

I scanned the document, and suddenly Samson's death made a whole lot more sense. "He was blackmailing El Gato."

"Looks that way. And he was using that video to do it."

"Wow, good job, Howard."

"Thanks. We'll keep working on the others."

"I have an expert I could take it to if your commander will allow it," I suggested, thinking of Stephen.

"Let me keep working on it today. If I can't break it, I'll talk to the commander and see what he says. If we do let you take it, it will be a copy, not the original, because we don't want it corrupted."

"Sure, I get that. Let me know either way." I was suddenly in a great mood. "And get on the facial recognition. I want everything on those guys."

"You got it."

Angel and I headed back to the detective pool and ran into Captain Robinson. "Morning, Captain," I greeted him.

"Kendrick, Reyes, where are we on the case?"

"Just had a bit of a breakthrough, sir. Howard found a video file of El Gato and is running facial recognition on it. We should have an answer to who this guy is soon. Maybe from there we'll be able to identify El Vibora as well."

"Great news." He nodded, looking thoughtful. "So what are you working on right now?"

"We're kind of in a holding pattern, sir. We haven't had a lot to work with up to this point, so we're catching up on some old case work."

"I may put you in the rotation today, then. I don't want your man-hours going to waste. If something comes up with the facial recognition, let me know, and we'll revisit it."

"Yes, sir."

Angel and I headed for our desks, but we weren't there long. Jason called us up and sent us out on a domestic violence case.

We spent the rest of the day taking on various small cases, and by the time the shift ended, we still didn't have an answer on who the men were. Sometimes facial recognition was fast, and other times it was as slow as pouring molasses. Apparently, we were going with molasses on this one.

I waved to Angel as I drove out of the parking lot to head home. I could feel the tension in my neck and shoulders. I really needed to go on a run. So when I got home, I changed my clothes, put my belly holster on and then slid my tank top on over it. Of course, I could use the treadmill in my exercise room, but I really wanted to be out enjoying the nice weather.

I locked up the house and then stretched before

heading out. I started slow, heading out of the neighborhood and a few blocks over to a more urban area. There were a lot of people shopping and walking and just taking in the day, but my neck started to itch, like I was being followed.

I wasn't sure where the feeling was coming from, but it had me agitated. Part of me thought maybe it was Jordan, but then he was never really a runner, and I could easily outpace him unless he was in a car. I glanced to my right without turning my head. I wanted to see if there were any cars driving slowly, tracking me.

Nobody seemed to be driving slowly on the street though. The feeling was still there, so I decided to pick up my pace and sprint across the street. As I did, I tried to see if anyone followed, but there was a crowd of people on the walkways. It was hard to tell if any of them were just going in this direction or actually following me.

Frustrated, I ducked into an alley on my right and then moved to stand between two large dumpsters. Maybe it wasn't the smartest move, but I pulled my gun as I worked to slow my breathing. My back was to the wall, so I knew any threat would be in front of me now, and with my gun, I felt pretty confident I would be okay.

A moment later, a man with graying brown hair, hazel eyes and a large nose entered the alley, looking around.

I stepped out, keeping my gun lowered, but ready to be used. "Why are you following me?"

He looked amused and said, "I was simply curious. You intrigued me."

The way he said it creeped me out, even though his words weren't really all that inciting. "Look, this is Los Angeles; if you want to meet women, go to a bar, don't freaking follow them and scare the shit out of them. They might be armed like I am, and shoot you."

He grinned and nodded. "I like you." He then shook his head and looked almost regretful. "I hope we don't meet again." With that, he turned and left the alley, disappearing into the crowd.

I leaned back against the wall and wondered what the hell that was all about. Some men were just insane was the only thing I could come up with, because who said, "I like you," after being told they could be shot for doing what he was doing?

Blowing out a breath, I reholstered my weapon and walked back out to the street, turned in the opposite direction he had gone, and started back home. But it was a long while before I could get the incident out of my head.

25

STRANGE BEHAVIOR

MARCY

"Do we have a name yet?" I asked Angel as I sat down.

"Nope. Whoever this guy is, he's pretty private would be my guess."

I sighed, and my lips twisted mulishly. It had been nearly twenty-four hours since Howard had shown us the video, and I wanted answers. "I wonder if Valerie might recognize him."

"That's an idea. Where is she? Have you seen her lately?" Angel asked, turning in his chair.

"I haven't seen her in a few days. Do we even know who it was that was following us the other night?"

"Patrol didn't find the car, the plate was stolen off a Ford Escape, so they can't even trace it."

"Well, great." I pressed my lips flat as my thoughts returned to the man in the video. I tried to decide what to do. "Should I call Valerie? See if she can come take a look at what Howard found?"

"Might be worth a shot," he agreed.

I grabbed the landline phone from the cradle and dialed the number for Valerie's desk.

She answered after three rings. "This is Burnett."

"Hey, it's Kendrick. Howard over in tech discovered something; can you come take a look?"

"What, on his laptop?" Valerie asked. "I thought he already went through it."

"No, this was something different. I'll explain when you get here."

"Okay, just... give me a few minutes."

I hung up. "Says she'll be here in a few minutes."

"How did she seem?"

"Normal, I guess, why?"

Angel's lips twitched, like he couldn't decide how to answer. He sighed and replied, "After the other day, I'm wondering if she's sober enough to give us the information we need."

"You make a good point. Hopefully so." I pulled up my email and started forwarding the six emails Jordan had sent to me over to Stephen. I really needed to get that restraining order filed, I thought with a sigh.

"What's up?" Angel asked, looking at me curiously.

"Just more shit from Jordan."

"Marce, have you gotten that order yet?"

"I was just remembering I need to do that, but every time I start to pull the file up, I get interrupted."

"You need to do it. He's gone off the deep. You know he was arrested the other night? Drunk driving and disorderly conduct, as well as assaulting an officer; however, the officer dropped those charges as a favor to him. Though, the drunk driving and disorderly conduct charges are still in play. He's damn lucky he didn't hurt anyone."

"Yeah, well, he did hurt someone. He hit Katie."

"He what?" Angel's jaw dropped. "How do you know that?"

"She came by my place and told me she's leaving him. She had a black eye. I took her to her parents' house."

"What the hell is he thinking?" Angel muttered. He glanced back at me and said, "File that order, Marce. I mean it. He's going to blame you for Katie leaving. Don't take any chances."

"I know, I know. I'll do it now." I pulled up the order on my computer and started it, but before I could even get the first line typed in, Valerie showed up. I glanced over at Angel as if to say, *See, I told you! Interrupted again.*

"So what's this evidence you want me to see?"

I turned off my monitor again. I didn't need anyone seeing what I was doing while I was away from my desk. "Come with us to tech," I said, rising from my seat.

"End of day, Marce, you need to get it done," Angel murmured.

I gave him a nod. "Yeah, I know."

"What are you talking about?" Valerie asked, looking curiously between us.

"Sorry, it's another case, not connected to this one." I gave her a tight smile. "Shall we?"

Valerie nodded and followed us to tech.

"Hey, Howard, can you pull up that video you showed us yesterday? I want Detective Burnett to have a look. She may know these men."

"Sure thing, Detectives. Give me one second. Still no luck on the facial recognition, though."

"What video?" Valerie looked startled. "What facial recognition?"

"So, the CSI team found a hidden hard drive, and it had several files on it. Howard was able to break the encryption on several of the files, and one of them was this video we're about to show you."

Valerie nodded and swallowed hard. "Where did they find this hard drive? How do we know it's legit?"

I glanced at her, arching a brow. "It was in Samson's apartment. And one of the files shows that Samson was blackmailing El Gato with this video. We just want to know if you recognize any of the men in it."

"Oh, yeah. Sure, I can take a look."

I gave Howard a nod, and he hit play. As Valerie watched the screen, I watched her. Her eyes widened, and an expression of fear crossed her face before she quickly masked it.

"Is that El Gato?" she asked, seeing the Hispanic man with the briefcase full of glassine bags. "Who are the others?"

I narrowed my eyes at her. "So you don't recognize him?"

"No, why would I?" she asked.

"Well, you did say he was pointed out to you at that one party..." Angel interjected.

"Yes, but it was from behind. I guess it could be him, but I don't *know* him."

The way she was acting had me wondering if she was really telling the truth. "So in the last ten years of chasing El Gato, you've never seen this man?"

Valerie pursed her lips. "No."

I sighed. "Okay. Well, that sucks. I guess we'll just have to wait for the facial recognition to work."

Valerie sucked in a breath. "Will that work? I mean, if he's not in the system..."

"Widen the search," I told Howard. "Send it over to the

DEA, maybe they'll have some file on this guy, or any of them for that matter. See if we can get Interpol in on it. If they've got this guy on file, I want to know it."

"Yes, ma'am. Oh, and I talked to the commander. We couldn't get the files opened, so he approved me making copies for your expert."

"Expert? Who are you taking it to?" Valerie asked.

Something in me told me not to tell her exactly who or where I would be taking the files. "Someone I've worked with before, but they're very private and like to remain anonymous. Angel doesn't even know them, right, Angel?"

Angel gave Valerie a bland look. "Nope, they'll only speak to Marcy."

"The captain is okay with that?" Valerie asked suspiciously.

"The captain is the one person who does know my source, seeing as he had to approve them being used. He's seen all of their credentials and gave me the authorization to use them," I assured her. "Why? Is that a problem?"

"Of course not," she replied. "Well, if that's all you needed me for, I've got another case I need to get back to."

"Sure, thanks for looking at it for us." I didn't take my eyes off her as she practically sprinted out of the tech room. I glanced at Angel. "That was weird, right?"

"Very weird. I got the feeling she did know him and is now spooked. How about you?"

"Same." It bothered me that she was holding back. I had to wonder if she was afraid of this guy, now knowing he was El Gato. Was she afraid she would be next on his hit list? If that was it, then I couldn't blame her, but I still wanted to know what she knew. I needed to find a way to get her to talk.

"Here's the copy of the drive, it's a new drive, so your expert shouldn't have any problems with it, just with the encryptions."

"Thanks, Howard." I took the drive and carried it back to the detective pool and locked it up in my desk.

"Think it'll be safe in there?" Angel murmured.

"Not sure, maybe?" I sighed. "We need to get it to Stephen as soon as possible."

He nodded. "Does he even know you want him to try to crack it?"

"No. I should probably call him."

"Ya think?" He chuckled. "Go ahead and do that and then get the file finished."

"Yeah, okay." I nodded and picked up my cell phone. I dialed my brother's number and waited.

"Hey, sis. What's up?"

"Hey, so I have a hard drive that I need you to take a look at. Our tech guys haven't had any luck, and I thought you might be able to break through the encryption."

"Oh, sure, I can do that. I'm going to be busy most of today though. I'm on a job. Can you bring it by tomorrow?"

"That'll be perfect."

"Okay, I'll see you then. Oh, and I should have some information for you on your other task for me soon."

"You've found out some things?"

"Yes, but I don't want to discuss it over the phone. I'll tell you when I see you tomorrow. It should hold."

I was slightly disappointed, but I understood it was sensitive information, and he needed to tell me in person. "Okay. See you tomorrow."

"Bye," Stephen said before hanging up.

"Tomorrow?" Angel asked.

"Yeah, he's on a job right now. I guess it can wait another day. In the meantime Howard's on the rest. Maybe we'll get lucky."

The rest of the workday passed in a blur. I finished the protective order and got it filed, but then Angel and I were sent out on an active-shooter case at a Dollar Store on Whittier Boulevard. It had been a disgruntled employee who'd decided to try to take out the manager and anyone who got in their way. Luckily, no one had died, but three of the victims and the shooter were in intensive care with multiple gunshot wounds. I'd had to turn my gun over to the captain when I returned to the precinct, just as a formality, but thankfully IA wasn't getting involved.

Before I left the station, I pulled my secondary Glock from the lockbox in my desk. I wasn't about to go home without a service weapon. Especially with Jordan acting so unstable. "I'll see you tomorrow," I said as I slid the weapon into the holster on my hip.

"See you," Angel replied, looking up from his phone.

I headed out to the parking lot and started toward my car. I looked about the parking lot and then focused on my car. A moment later a head popped up near the backside of my car, and I realized it was Valerie. She looked straight at me, gave me a small wave, and then turned on her heel and hurried away in the other direction. It was very odd behavior, even for her.

That was strange, I thought as I got closer to my car. *Did she mess with my car?*

I walked all around my car, but didn't find anything off. I even checked the wheel wells and tires to see if she had done something to them, but they looked fine. She'd probably just been tying her shoelaces or something. Maybe she dropped her purse and bent to pick it up. I could think of a bunch of reasons for her to be there, but they didn't relieve the tension I felt between my shoulder blades. Apprehensively, I got in and took a breath, half afraid that it was going to explode the minute I turned it on, but as it turned over and nothing happened, I expelled a relieved breath. I was being absurd. My instincts were off. Valerie hadn't planted a bomb in my car. I was overtired and imagining things.

"Go home, Kendrick, you're tired, and Frank's waiting for you," I muttered and pulled out of the parking lot, but in the back of my mind, I still wondered what exactly she had been doing.

26

AMBUSHED

ANGEL

I was really worried about Marcy. I cared about her, loved her actually, and I hated seeing her stressed and frustrated by Jordan. The man had never treated her well, but this was a whole new level of abuse that he was inflicting on her. I wanted to be the one to solve this for her, but Jordan wasn't cooperating. He was so full of anger and wrath for being fired, and he one hundred percent blamed it on Marcy.

After Marcy finished the paperwork to file the restraining order, and had gone home for the day, I'd called Jordan and attempted to talk to him like a reasonable adult. The problem was that I was the only one being reasonable and acting like an adult. He'd shrugged me off and scoffed when I said that he'd be getting paperwork informing him of the protective order.

Maybe that was the wrong move because the next day I watched Marcy glance at her phone every time it rang, and then swipe the screen to send the call to voicemail. When she listened to them later, it had been at least six calls in a row of someone screaming so loudly that I could hear it from my desk. "Block it," I said, rolling my chair over to her.

She rolled her eyes. "I have. I've blocked it after each call. He's got some sort of number spoofer, so he just changes phone numbers. They should be illegal."

I couldn't help but think she was right, they should be.

Her phone rang again, and she sighed as she picked it up again, ready to send the call to voicemail.

"Wait, let me," I said, holding my hand out for her phone.

"You sure you want to deal with him?" she asked, arching a brow.

"Give it to me." I bounced my hand up and down, waiting for her to put her phone in it. When she did, I answered. "Jordan, it's Angel—"

"You motherfucker! Put the fucking bitch on the phone! She's ruined my life, and now Katie's gone, and I don't know where the fuck she is!"

"Marcy hasn't done a damn thing to you; you did this all to yourself! Why would Marcy know anything about where Katie is?"

"I just fucking know! You think I don't know my fucking wife? She interfered in my marriage to Katie and fucked with her head, made her leave me!"

"Which wife are you talking about? Because Marcy isn't your wife anymore, Jordan."

"She's mine! She's always been mine and will always be mine! I own her, and if I want to beat the shit out of her, I have that fucking right!"

"Except it wasn't Marcy you beat, was it?" I pushed. "It was Katie. And you wonder why she ran away! You've lost your damn mind, Jordan. You need help. You're drunk off your ass and not making sense."

"I don't give a fuck! Put my fucking wife on the phone, Angel, or so help me, I will fuck you up!"

"Look, like I told you last night, Marcy's filed a restraining order against you. You need to stay away from her, Jordan. You need to get some help and get your head back on straight. If you decide you want my help, you know my number." I hung up and hit block on the number.

"Thanks for trying," Marcy said with a sigh. "Let me guess, he blames me for Katie leaving?"

"Looks that way."

"I'll just turn my phone off." She took it back and clicked a few buttons. "I'm going to go talk to the captain; then maybe we can head over to Stephen's and get him the hard drive."

"Sounds good. I'll be ready when you are."

Twenty minutes later, Marcy handed me the hard drive as she put her seat belt on. She turned the car on and pulled out of the parking lot. I'd offered to drive, but she said she wanted to, and I didn't mind.

"So what are you thinking for lunch?" I asked, my stomach rumbling. I'd skipped breakfast and was starving.

"Something quick? Maybe In and Out?" she said as she glanced over at me.

At that moment I saw a car barreling toward us and screamed, "Look out!"

The black SUV rammed into Marcy's door, sending us sliding sideways and spinning into the fire hydrant on the edge of the street. The rear of the car was half into the sidewalk while the front of the car was crossways in the road.

My head was reeling, and I couldn't be sure if I'd blacked out or not.

A moment later my door was yanked open, and something was sprayed into my face.

I gasped, sputtering, my eyes burning. "Fucking hell!"

I heard Marcy screaming too but was too blinded to do anything. Then I felt someone grab the hard drive out of my hands.

"Stop!" I shouted and tried to push my way out of the car. "Marce, you okay?"

"Yeah, go! Get after them!" she urged.

Everything was super blurry, and my eyes were watering so bad from the pepper spray. I couldn't see hardly anything, but I heard a car, the one I was pretty sure hit us, squealing its tires as it spun and raced away.

"This is Detective Kendrick," I heard her say. "There's been an officer-involved accident..."

She went on, but I didn't focus on that. I was busy pulling off my jacket and shirt so I could attempt to get the residue of the spray off me. I used the back of my shirt to wipe my face.

"Sir, are you okay?" a man came up to me.

"I was pepper-sprayed. I need water. Do you see a place I can get some?" I asked, since I still couldn't make out much.

"Here, I've got a bottle with me."

I felt it pressed into my hand, and I immediately unscrewed it and tilted my face up to the sky as I poured the water directly into my eyes. A sink would have worked better, but this was the best I had at the moment. The water helped, and the stinging lessened some. I was able to blink, and though things remained slightly blurry, I could see a little better. I would have to flush them again, but I'd need more water for that.

I heard the sirens heading in our direction and felt a wave of relief, knowing the medics would be here in a minute. "Thanks, I appreciate your help," I said to the man. "Did you happen to see the accident? Did you get a look at whoever hit us?"

"No, sorry, I just saw the guy steal something from you and take off in the car that hit you. Didn't see his face, but he looked Hispanic. He was dressed in jeans and a T-shirt."

"That's something at least. Can you stick around? We might need you to look at some mug shots."

"Sure," he said and then added, "Is she okay? The driver?"

I turned to the car and noticed Marcy's head lolling against the back of the seat. There was blood on her face. "Damn it," I muttered as I stumbled toward the car.

"Let me," the guy said, moving past me.

A wave of jealous frustration swept over me, and I suddenly felt extremely protective of her. "No! I've got her." I willed my feet to move quickly and jutted myself back into the car on the passenger side. "Marcy!" I reached for her face; my palm touched her warm cheek and came away sticky. I tapped her cheek a little. "Marcy, wake up. Marce, come on, you've got to wake up."

"Frank?" she mumbled.

My heart constricted at her words. "Marce, it's Angel; come on, stay with me."

Her eyes blinked. "My head hurts," she slurred.

"Detective Reyes, are you okay? Can you get out of the car on your own?" a woman asked from Marcy's shattered window. She was wearing scrubs, so I assumed she was one of the medics.

"Yes, but Detective Kendrick is injured."

"Let's get you out first; then we'll see about getting her taken care of."

I nodded. "Marcy, I'll be right here; just stay awake, okay?"

She started to nod, but then moaned. "Call Frank for me?"

There was that pinch to my heart again, but I said, "Yeah, I'll call him."

I backed out of the car, my jaw clenched. The last thing I wanted was Frank coming to her rescue. But I knew that he'd kick my ass if I didn't call him. Hell, Marcy would kick my ass if I didn't call him. Knowing all of that didn't make calling him any easier. I wanted to hate him. I wanted to keep Marcy to myself.

Suddenly, Jordan's words flashed through my mind. *She's mine. She's always been mine and will always be mine.* The thought that I was behaving like Jordan jarred me. Marcy wasn't mine. Not in that way. She was Frank's. I was her friend, nothing more. I would always be her friend, nothing more. I needed to get myself under control and deal with this stupid protective, possessive feeling I had for her before I ruined our friendship and my relationship with Callie.

Callie.

Damn.

I pulled my phone from my pocket, scrolled until I found Frank's number, it took me a minute because my vision was blurry, and then called him.

"Angel?" Frank answered, mild concern lacing his voice.

"Marcy is okay, but we've been in an accident—"

"Where is she? What hospital?"

"She's being seen by the paramedics right now; let me ask," I said, putting my hand over the receiver of the phone, and looked at one of the medics. "Hey, what hospital are you taking her to?"

"LA Community," the medic answered.

I relayed that to Frank. "She's asking for you."

"I'm already on my way. I'll be there as soon as possible," he said and hung up.

I'd heard the fear and concern in his voice, and I knew he cared about Marcy at least as much as I did. I was glad about that. I really was. I hated that I was envious of him for being with her. I needed to figure out a way to get my head back on straight. Maybe I needed therapy? Marcy had been going to therapy for a while now, and she really seemed to be doing better. She was definitely happier. *Probably because of Frank,* my mind added, and I sighed.

I thought about calling Callie, but didn't want to worry her. I'd tell her about the accident later. For now, I needed to see one of the medics and get my eyes flushed out more.

"Detective Reyes, let me help you," one of the medics said, approaching me. "You've got a laceration on your cheek that's bleeding freely, so I don't think there's any glass in it, but let me take a look."

"I was pepper-sprayed too. I was able to get some water and flush my eyes, but they still sting."

"I was wondering why you were missing your shirt and jacket. I take it you pulled them off to get the spray away from you?"

I nodded. "And to wipe my face with the back of my shirt, until someone gave me the water."

"Yes, the gentleman is with one of the patrol officers now. There were a number of witnesses to the hit-and-run."

I hadn't even realized that. Maybe I was more out of it than I thought? "How's Marcy?"

"She took the brunt of the glass shattering, hit her head pretty hard on the steering wheel, and dislocated her shoulder. We're a little worried about a concussion. She'll be going to get X-rays and some stitches," he said as he flushed out my eyes again. "Might be a good idea to bring you in for the same; this cut is deeper than I thought. And it wouldn't hurt to check you for a concussion as well."

A HALF AN HOUR LATER, Marcy and I were both in the ER, in adjoining curtained rooms.

Frank burst through the curtain and rushed over to Marcy, scooping her into his arms and holding her tightly. "TT. God, I've been so worried."

"Frank," she squeaked.

"Careful, her shoulder was dislocated," I murmured, trying to tamp down the jealousy I felt.

"Shit, I'm so sorry, babe." He released his hold on her somewhat. "What happened?" he asked, his eyes roving over Marcy as though looking for every injury.

I couldn't help but trace my eyes over her too, taking in the numerous stitches she had on her face, the ones above her left brow, the group of ten that went down her cheek, the five along her hairline. She didn't seem too bothered by them, but I could see how upset Frank was as his thumb traced gently over her face.

"Some asshole T-boned us. I think we were ambushed, and I need to get back to my car and check it, because I have a feeling there was a tracker on it. The ambush was too perfect for it to have just been coincidence."

I moved my gaze from Frank's hand on her cheek to her face. "What?"

She nodded and then winced. "Last night, before I left the station, I saw Valerie near my car. I looked it over, but I wasn't looking for a tracker. I thought she'd sabotaged it."

"You thought Detective Burnett did something to your car, and you didn't say anything?" I asked, incredulous.

"I didn't find anything at the time, but I want it inspected more thoroughly because I think she did put a tracker on it, and if she did..."

"Then she's compromised," Frank said, finishing her sentence.

I gritted my teeth. I willed myself to calm down. "I'll call CSI, have them look it over."

I pulled my phone out and turned away as Marcy and Frank started whispering to each other. I tried to ignore them as I made the call. When I finished, I looked back over, and they were kissing. Fire burned in my chest at the sight, and I wanted to rip him away from her.

I cleared my throat three times before they broke apart. "They're on it," I muttered.

"Thanks, Angel."

"When can I take you home?" Frank asked.

"They want to keep us both for a bit, make sure our concussions aren't problematic. They said mine is worse than Angel's, but I feel okay."

"Can I get you anything?" Frank asked her, tucking her hair behind her ear.

I felt like I was a peeping Tom watching them, and it bothered me. "You know, I think I'm going to get out of here."

Marcy's brow furrowed. "You sure?"

"Yeah, Frank's got you. I don't really need to stay. I feel fine other than burning retinas from the pepper spray."

"You're not going to drive, are you?" she asked, concerned.

"I'll call Callie." *Or an Uber,* I added in my head. "See you later," I muttered as I hightailed it out of the small room and over to the nurses' station. I had to get out of there before I did something I regretted.

27

FEELING BEATEN, BLOODY AND BRUISED

MARCY

Anger over the loss of my car surged through me as I watched Angel leave the room. Not just my car, the hard drive too. I wasn't mad at him, but at whoever did this. I had a very bad suspicion that Valerie was involved, and I couldn't wait to find out if I was right. Just as thoughts of her passed through my mind, she came running in as though I'd conjured her up myself. It was all I could do to keep from blurting out my suspicions.

"Oh my God, are you okay?" she slurred, tears falling down her cheeks.

That was highly suspicious to me too. Why was she crying if she wasn't guilty for doing this? Still, I held my tongue. I didn't have the proof yet that she was involved. "I'll be fine," I replied.

Angel re-entered the room in a huff. He seemed irritated for some reason. "What are you doing here?" he asked Valerie, his tone short.

"It's all over the station what happened to you. I've been so worried," Valerie replied on a half-sob.

Angel frowned.

Frank moved his arm from around me and held his hand out toward her. "I'm Frank Maldon, and you are?"

I blinked, realizing I'd never introduced him. "Sorry, Frank, this is Detective Burnett. Burnett, this is Detective Frank Maldon from SMPD."

Valerie looked startled as she shook his hand and then suddenly yanked it back quickly. "You... your brother—" She slammed her lips together, and her eyes flew to his. "Sorry. I just... I'm sorry." She started backing toward the door, glancing at me and Angel. "I'm glad you're both okay. I need to go." She turned and fled the room as quickly as she'd entered it.

"Well, that was not suspicious at all," I murmured softly.

"Was it me?" Frank asked, pain filling his eyes.

"I don't think so, I think there's more going on with her than we know."

Frank nodded, but I knew he was going to be hurting over thoughts of Daniel. I leaned into his side, and he wrapped his arm around me again. It hurt to move my left shoulder, but I wished I could hug him properly. Instead, I used my right hand to pull his hand tighter around my waist. Did his weight against my injured shoulder hurt? Yes, but I didn't care.

"The doctor cleared me to leave, so I'm going to head out," Angel interjected.

"Did you hear back from CSI?" I asked before he could make it out the door.

"Not yet. I'll call you when I do."

"My phone got busted in the accident. I'll have to get a new one on the way home."

"Then call me when you get one. Maybe get a new

number while you're at it. That way Jordan can't keep harassing you," he tossed over his shoulder as he paused at the curtain before leaving the room.

"Now there's a good thought," Frank agreed.

They were right. I should have thought of doing that before. "Can we stop at the phone store on the way home?"

"Of course, babe." Frank smiled. "As long as you get out of here before they close, that is."

"Right. Hopefully it won't be too much longer."

THREE HOURS later I was home, fussing with my new phone, getting everything important transferred over. Frank wasn't letting me do anything strenuous, though I'd offered to cook dinner. Instead, he had me tucked under a blanket on the couch, my left arm in a sling to keep it immobile, while he decided what to fix.

As I messed with my new phone, Frank brought me some painkillers and a bottle of water that he had opened for me. "I decided to call for pizza, figured that would be fairly easy for you to eat, and it would be better than anything I could make. Should be here pretty soon. Did you get your phone fixed up?"

"Just adding my apps now. I'll need to call Angel and everyone to give them my new number."

"Why don't you send out a mass text to everyone; then he can call when he's heard from CSI?"

"That's a good idea." My head must still be fuzzy because I should have thought of that. I pulled up my text messages and clicked to include everyone in my contact list, then sent them a message telling them it was me and that this was my new number. "Done." I set my phone down and smiled up at him as the doorbell rang.

"Perfect timing," he replied, leaning down to kiss me before going to answer the door. He returned a few minutes later carrying two boxes that smelled heavenly. "Let me get us some sodas." He put the boxes on the coffee table and then headed to my kitchen.

By the time he returned, I was sitting up and had made room for him next to me.

He set the drinks on the table next to the boxes and put the plates he'd also grabbed on his lap. "What kind do you want?" he asked, opening the first box. "Got a meat lovers with mushrooms and tomatoes added, and a four cheese."

"Can I have one of each?"

He fixed my plate and then handed it to me.

Just as I was about to take my first bite, my phone sprang to life playing the song "Calling All Angels" by Train. I put the pizza back on the plate and picked up my phone. "Hey, Angel," I answered.

"How are you feeling?"

"Beaten, battered, and bruised, you?"

"Same, but probably not as bad as you."

I chuckled. "So did you hear from CSI? Did they find something?"

"Just like you suspected. They found a tracker under your back bumper."

"Damn it." I had really hoped I'd be wrong. "We'll need to confront her."

"Let's play it by ear. Now that we know she may be compromised, let's do some digging."

That reminded me. "I've actually already got Stephen

digging into her. You know I've thought there was something off about her for a while, so I had him start looking."

"Excellent. Let's wait and see what he finds. Maybe we can use that to force her to confess, and we can finally get somewhere real on this case."

"Sounds like a good plan. I'll check in with him tomorrow. I haven't told him about the accident, just that we couldn't make it over today with the hard drive. I didn't want him to worry."

"Okay. Do you need anything?" Angel asked.

"Other than a new car? Nope." I sighed. "I really loved that car."

"I know how you feel," he replied, and I knew he was thinking back to the accident he'd had almost a year ago that had him on the injured list for a while.

"Yeah, I'm sure you do. I'll have to get a rental, I guess."

"I can pick you up tomorrow if you need me to," he offered.

I glanced at Frank and then said, "I think I have it covered, but if I need you to, I'll give you a call in the morning."

He didn't say anything for a moment but, eventually, said, "Okay, well, then I'll see you tomorrow."

"Bye, Angel." I hung up and put my phone on the table.

"Everything okay?"

I nodded, glad my head wasn't hurting too much when I did that anymore. "Yep. I was hoping you'd drop me at the station tomorrow morning on your way back to Santa Monica," I said before picking up my pizza and taking a bite.

"Be happy to, babe. Though if I had my druthers, I'd keep you here tomorrow, and we'd both call in for a sick day."

I laughed. "Your druthers, hmmm?"

He nodded. "Yep." He grinned and picked up the TV remote, turning on the preshow to the baseball game. "You wanna watch, or are you tired? Do you want me to turn it off?"

"I'm fine, and no, don't turn it off. I probably won't watch all of it, but I'm happy to sit in here with you." I leaned into him, and he wrapped his arm around me.

It was a good way to spend the evening, especially after the day I'd had.

THE NEXT MORNING, Frank drove me to the precinct and dropped me off with a kiss and a promise to see me later that night. He'd offered to pick me up from work, but I told him I was calling for a rental this morning. I couldn't be without a car. He fussed over me driving with the sling, but seeing as it was my left arm that was immobile and not my right, I told him I'd be fine.

"Bad news," Angel said, the moment he saw me.

My brow furrowed. "What now?"

"You know that hard drive we were taking to Stephen?"

"Yeah?"

"Tech screwed up. The files were all corrupted on it."

"What? How do you know?" I set my purse down and sank into my chair.

"They made another copy, thinking we could try again, but this time decided to check the actual files. They were copy-protected. So they stole it for nothing."

I pressed the spot between my eyes and then pinched the bridge of my nose. "So I lost my car and dislocated my shoulder for nothing."

"Yeah, Howard's very apologetic about that. He said the commander read them the riot act over not checking and just assuming it was all good."

I sighed. "I guess it's just as well. At least they won't know exactly what we have on them."

"True." Angel nodded.

I glanced at the box of evidence sitting on his desk. "You know, considering what we now know regarding a certain detective, we should get this evidence locked up properly. I don't want any of it to go missing."

"Good point," Angel agreed. "I'll take it down to the evidence room."

"Thanks, Angel." I smiled as he stood and picked up the box. "I'm going to call my insurance and arrange for a rental, and then call Stephen so we can go see what he's got on you-know-who." I didn't want to say her name and have someone overhear.

"Sounds like a plan." He strode away with the box.

I picked up the phone and started making the necessary calls.

28

GETTING THE DIRT
MARCY

"I could have driven," Angel said, glancing at me with a frown. "And I could have picked you up this morning."

"I know, and I appreciate it, but Frank drove me in."

"Oh." He turned and stared out the window.

"Angel, what is going on with you?" I sighed. "I feel like you're angry with me because of Frank."

"I'm not," Angel immediately denied. "Mad at myself, not you and Frank. Look, we've already talked about this, but I'm still working on it. In my head, I know we're partners and best friends and that's all there can be, but sometimes I wish there were more."

I glanced at him and realized we needed to have a real conversation, so I pulled into the parking lot of the gas station I was closest to and parked the car. I turned to him and really looked at him. "Angel, you know there can't be, right?"

He nodded. "I do. That's why I'm angry at myself. I start playing this 'what-if' game in my head, thinking up all the ways it could work, but all of them end with you or me quitting the force or transferring, and I don't want that. Then I think about Callie, and I really like her. Might even love her, but I'm all twisted up about you, and I feel her pulling away, or maybe it's me pushing her away, I don't know."

I sighed. "You have to get over this. You're going to lose Callie if you don't."

"I know. And I don't want that. How do you deal with this?" He waved his hand between us, bringing up the attraction we both knew was there between us.

"I acknowledge the fact you're a very attractive man, and under other circumstances there might have been a chance for us to pursue something, but, Angel, those other circumstances aren't going to happen. I'm not quitting my job, and I'm not transferring to another precinct. You're not quitting yours either. We work really well together, and you're my best friend. I don't want to lose what we have for something that probably wouldn't work out anyway. I'm a mess. I have a lot of trauma in my life, and it makes my personal life chaotic and complicated."

"I know that. I understand that—" He broke off and sighed, then looked at me with sad eyes.

"But you can't relate to it," I said softly. "You'd want to fix me, or fix it for me. And when you finally realize you can't, it would break you and then break us."

"Can Frank?" he murmured.

"Frank's different. Frank has had a similar trauma in his life. He knows how messy my life is and gets it because his is messy in the same kind of way. We're broken in the same way, and he doesn't try to fix me, and I don't try to fix him. Now will my relationship with him last? I can't say. But I want to try. I want it to work. However, if you're going to get mad at me every time he's around or I bring him up, eventually, I'll break up with him because of you, and then I'll end up resenting you, or I'll have to distance myself from you and lose you as a friend anyway. I really don't want to do that because you're important to me, and I need you in my life."

"I don't want that either. Frank is a good guy. He's a great detective, and I've seen how protective he is of you, but he lets you be you. You're good together," he admitted.

"So are we good?" I asked.

"Yeah. We're good. I needed this conversation, I think. It helps to get rid of those what-if questions with real answers." Angel smiled, but it was melancholy. "I think I *am* going to take Callie down to Mexico, to meet my family."

"It will be good for you to spend some more time with her away from LA."

"I think so too," he agreed. "While we're here, do you want anything?" He gestured to the gas station convenience store. "I'm gonna grab a soda."

"Sure, bring me a Dr. Pepper." I figured he needed a few minutes away from me to get his head sorted.

"Be right back." He shoved the door open and got out.

While I waited, I sent Frank a text, just telling him that I was thinking about him and to have a good day. A moment later, he replied.

> Thinking about you too, TT. I'll see you tonight. Thought I'd pick up some steaks, and we could grill?

> Sounds great. Be safe!

> You too!

I put my phone away as Angel returned to the car with two fountain drinks. He handed me one and put on his seat belt. After taking a sip, I put it in the cup holder and then started the car. "Ready to go?"

"Yep. Let's go get the dirt on Valerie." He smiled.

I pulled out of the parking lot and headed for Stephen's apartment.

As soon as we knocked on the door, Stephen yanked it open, took one look at me and pulled me into a hug.

"Ow." I winced as he squeezed me. "Good to see you too, bro."

"Are you okay? You didn't tell me you were hurt and that was why you couldn't be here yesterday."

"I didn't want you to worry. We were T-boned on our way here. I'm fine. Angel's fine. The bad news is that the hard drive was stolen. The upside is it was a copy, and turns out the files were copy-protected and ended up being corrupted, so you wouldn't have been able to access it anyway."

"Do you still have the original?"

"At the station. And maybe if you want to come work with the tech department, you could break into it there, but they aren't going to let it out of their hands for now."

"Makes sense. I could come see what I can do that would be legal to get into them, but you know I tend to use alternative methods..." He let his words trail off as he closed the door behind us. "Speaking of alternative methods, I've got a slew of shit on Detective Burnett for you, but yeah, not exactly legal or useful in court."

"That's okay, I'm looking for leverage to get her to talk, not to jam her up in court if it's not warranted."

"Great, so let me show you." He gestured toward the desk with the computer set up in the corner of the room. He sat down and started pulling up documents. "So these are her financials. I started with ten years ago and worked my way forward. As you can see, about six years ago, there was a minor drain on her account, that was a payment to the funeral home for her dad, then the burial costs. Good chunk of money. But then within the next year, there were medical bills coming in, and she began struggling. Had a bunch of overdrafts and the like."

"That would be her mom's cancer."

"Right, but take a look at this." He zoomed in and widened the screen on a deposit of thirty-five thousand dollars. "And then this one." He moved to the next month in the document, and there was another direct deposit of thirty-five thousand. "And this goes on almost every month up until last month. She hasn't gotten one this month yet."

My jaw dropped. "All direct deposits? Where are they coming from?"

"Now that's tricky. It's from an off-shore account in the Cayman Islands. An import/export business. So I can't say she's not working for them, but it does seem highly suspicious, right?"

"Right. Do you have the name of the company?" I asked because something about it being import/export was ringing bells in my head, and I couldn't say why.

"It's G & G Imports/Exports. It looks like they mostly deal in art. It's owned by the Gómez family and run by Alejandro Gómez."

"Angel, why is that name familiar?" I questioned. I'd seen it or heard it somewhere, but I couldn't place it.

"Remember the receptionist at Samson's place? She mentioned Samson's cousin who wanted to clean the place out and get it ready for sale. Didn't she say his name was Gómez?"

"That's it." I snapped my fingers. "Did we ever follow up on that?"

"I did. When I spoke to Samson's mother, she said Gómez is her nephew, and he was taking care of Samson's things here for them. I left a message for the man at his business number about when he'd be able to get into the apartment, but he never called back."

I found it odd that his name had come up again, but this time in regard to Valerie. "So if Valerie was accepting payments from this G & G Imports/Exports, then she had to know Samson, right?"

"Well, not necessarily. Just because Samson is the owner's cousin doesn't mean he had anything to do with the business," Angel replied.

"Okay, maybe, but it's a pretty big coincidence if she didn't."

"True. And we can use it to put pressure on her." Angel grinned.

"So I also found that prior to her financial trouble, she was very much into the party scene. Not sure if that helps or not, but there's all kinds of incriminating photos of her doing drugs and stuff."

"Wow. Okay, can you make me a copy of everything?" I asked.

"Sure. Just give me a second, and remember, this can't be used in any legal capacity, sis."

"Yeah, I'm aware." I shook my head at him.

"Here you go," Stephen said, handing me a thumb drive.

"Thanks. Wanna grab lunch with us?" I asked as we headed for the door.

"Naw, not today. I'm meeting Yazmine later this afternoon, and I have some work to get done first."

"Okay, we'll have dinner soon, yeah?"

"Sounds good." He hugged me. "Be safe."

"Do my best." I smiled, and Angel and I headed down the stairs to my rental car.

"So what now?" Angel asked, clicking his seat belt.

"Lunch and then we confront Valerie with what Stephen found."

I was so done with this woman. I wanted answers, and I was going to get them, come hell or high water.

29

BREAKING VALERIE
MARCY

I t was close to eleven now, so most places were open for lunch. I wanted to go somewhere I could sit down to eat and get my anger at Valerie tamped down before I confronted her. I needed her to talk, and my showing my anger probably wouldn't do either of us any good.

"Astro Burger or Gina's Pizzeria?" I asked with a glance at Angel.

"Let's go to Astro Burger. I'm not in the mood for pizza."

I continued driving and took the E. Third Street exit and then turned onto West Beverly Boulevard. Once I was parked, we headed into the restaurant, which had a retro vibe to it. We sat down in a booth, and I ordered the bacon avocado cheeseburger, while Angel had a steak sandwich.

"So what's the plan?" Angel asked as we ate.

I finished chewing my bite of burger and took a drink of my soda. "I want to go see Lindsey and get the tracker Valerie put on my car before we confront her. I want to show her that I know what she did."

"I wonder if her showing up at the hospital was her guilty conscience making her check on us," Angel suggested.

"You're probably right, and I think that's going to be what eventually gets her to break."

He took another bite and chewed, looking thoughtful. "I get that she was drowning in debt, but to accept this kind of bribe money... I don't know how she's lasted this long without being caught."

I had my own thoughts about that, but I didn't want to voice them right now. "I could never. I don't care how deep in debt I am—I could never do what she's done," I murmured.

"Me either," Angel agreed. "I'd rather get a second job, moonlighting as a security guard or something."

"Same." I shook my head. "I couldn't compromise myself that way."

"Still, maybe we shouldn't judge."

I arched a brow at him. "I can empathize with her situation, and I understand the temptation to do what she did, I'm not judging her exactly, but I know I wouldn't make the same choices she has. And I think it's wrong that she's profited off the deaths of others. Not just Ruby and Samson and who knows who else, but also all those kids who've overdosed over the years because they became hooked on El Gato's product when she could have busted him." The more I thought about it, I realized I was actually judging her, and I was okay with it. "You know what? I think I am going to judge her. She doesn't deserve to wear the badge, and I hope IA takes her down when we get her to confess."

Angel sighed. "You make a good point. She does have a lot of blood on her hands if she really is working with El Gato."

I finished my burger and fries, but my anger at Valerie

was still simmering just below the surface. Eating hadn't done much to tamp it down, but I was a little calmer. "You ready?" I asked, gathering my trash.

"Yeah, let's go."

We headed back to the station, but instead of going to our desks, we headed to the CSI lab. I knocked on the door and stuck my head in Lindsey's office.

"Hey, girl," she said, looking up from her computer. "How's the shoulder?"

"It's doing okay. Just sore."

"Probably will be for a few weeks." Lindsey pursed her lips. "What brings you down here?"

"I wanted to see if you had the tracker you found on my car," I answered.

She turned to a pile of things on the file cabinets behind her. "I've got it here somewhere. I put it with some of the other stuff for your case, figuring it was part of it. What do you need it for? We didn't find any prints on it."

"I know where it came from, and I'm going to confront the person with it."

Lindsey handed me the evidence bag, her brows raised. "You know who put it on your car?"

"Pretty sure. If I'm right, I'll fill you in later. Maybe lunch sometime?" I suggested.

"Sounds good. Send me a text, and we'll figure it out."

"Perfect. Thanks for this," I said, lifting the evidence bag. "See ya," I added.

"Bye." Lindsey waved and turned back to her computer.

Angel and I headed for the elevators, and he pushed the button. "To Vice?" he asked as we entered the car.

I nodded, and he pushed the button for the right floor. I tapped my foot impatiently, unable to be still. Angel, on the other hand, was the picture of calm. I could feel my ire bubbling just below my skin, heating my flesh. I knew I couldn't lose my temper with her, but I wanted to. I was keyed up, and it was almost the same feeling I had facing down a killer. My mind was clear—focused, but I was like a grenade with the pin already pulled. Ready to explode.

"You good?" Angel murmured, giving me a side eye.

I nodded.

The doors opened, and as we stepped off the elevator, a wave of serenity washed through me. I didn't need to go in hot. The evidence would get her to talk. And if it didn't, well, then I could let my anger out.

I pasted a smile on my lips and headed for Valerie, who was seated at her desk, her head down over her phone as she texted someone. When we stopped at her desk, she looked up, startled, like a rabbit facing off with a snake. My smile widened.

"Hey, so we've got some great evidence we wanted to share with you, figured we'd come to you," I said, keeping my voice pleasant since there were several other detectives around us. I didn't need to air all of this in front of them.

"Oh? What do you have?"

I glanced over my shoulder and toward the rooms with the glass windows. Like our office in HSS, Vice had incident rooms too. "Why don't we take it into one of the incident rooms. There's quite a bit to go over, and we don't need to disturb anyone else while they're working on their own cases."

Her brow furrowed, but she nodded. "Sure, okay," she agreed, her voice hesitant.

She stood up and straightened her skirt before moving between me and Angel, heading for one of the rooms. She opened the door, and we followed her in. I nodded to Angel, and he moved to close the white blinds that covered the windows while I closed and locked the door. Glancing at Valerie's face, I could see the fright in her eyes, but she quickly tried to mask it with defiance.

"What's this all about? Why are you locking us in here?" Her voice shook as she spoke, and her breathing picked up as she exuded a nervous energy.

"Have a seat." I directed her toward the table. "Angel, can you boot up the computer?"

"Yep. Got the thumb drive?"

I handed it to him as Valerie sank down in a seat, perching on the edge like she'd flee at any moment, but I wouldn't let her get away. I folded my arms and kept myself between her and the door. "You see, we've been doing some digging."

"What have you been digging into?" She once again looked like a scared rabbit.

"You."

"Me? Why? That's ridiculous. I'm not going to sit here and let you try to gaslight me," she started, getting defensive as she stood up and started toward the door.

"Sit your ass back down, or I will take every bit of this to IA, including this," I said, removing the magnetic tracker from the evidence bag. It was a bluff, sort of. I couldn't take the thumb drive to them, considering how I'd gotten the information was at best in the gray area but most probably illegally obtained.

Valerie gaped at the tracker as she backed up until her legs hit the chair, and she sank down. "I don't—what is that?"

"Really? It's the tracker you put on my car. And don't

even try to deny it. I saw you by my car. And then shortly after that, Angel and I were ambushed. Is this what you've done to all of your partners? Did Angel and I screw up your plans by surviving? Is there some other plan in place to get rid of us now? Or was it just for them to steal the hard drive? Do they know it was only a copy?"

Her mouth worked open and closed like a fish blowing bubbles. Her eyes filled with tears. "I'm sorry, but you were going to ruin everything! I can't let you identify him. He'll kill me," she started sobbing.

And there it was.

"Angel, pull up the files. Show her what we have."

Angel clicked on the file and pulled up her financials. "We've got all the bribes you took, Burnett. We know you were being paid by Alejandro Gómez from G & G Imports/Exports. Is he El Gato?"

Valerie's face turned pink and splotchy as tears poured down her cheeks. "He'll kill me. I'm as good as dead," she kept murmuring through her sobs.

I squatted down, getting on her level. "We can protect you, Valerie, but you have to confess to what you've done. You know the DA will set you up in a safehouse. They've been after El Gato for ten years. You can hand him over on a silver platter. If you're lucky, they won't prosecute you, and you'll get set up somewhere with a new life." I had no idea if that would happen, but it was the best-case scenario, and it was her best chance at not being murdered by this guy.

She put her head down on her arms on the table and cried for a few minutes before finally looking up and giving me a nod. "Okay. I'll tell you everything," she said as she took the tissues I offered to clean her face.

I waited patiently for her to start as Angel and I took

seats at the table. This was just her first step. She'd have to go to the captain and say it all again, but this was a good start.

"I used to be a great detective," she began. "But I was undercover about seven years ago, trying to bust this mid-level dealer on the party scene. I wanted a big bust, and I thought I'd have to do stuff to get him. It started with weed, then coke. I didn't know it, but there were pictures. It would have ruined my career, but at the time I thought I could just write it off as me being undercover, and it would be okay. I made excuses. Then Dad died, and Mom got sick and there were suddenly all these bills. They were stacking up, and I was drowning in debt."

I knew most of this, but it was good hearing it directly from her.

"One day, I was near the end of my rope, and a package arrived at my house. It had pictures of me doing drugs and other incriminating things, and there was a note with a meeting time. I was told to be there, or those pictures would go to the press."

"So you went?"

Valerie nodded. "It was with Alejandro Gómez. El Gato. He wanted me to work for him. He said he'd save me. He'd fix my money problems, and in return all I had to do was feed him information." She raised her gaze to me, and her lips trembled. "If I hadn't agreed, he was prepared to kill me right then and there, and he told me that. He couldn't risk his identity being exposed."

I got it. She felt caught between a rock and a hard place. Didn't excuse what she'd done, but I understood how she'd made that choice. "So you took him up on his offer?"

Silent tears now slid down her cheeks, but she gave a

single nod. "At first it was just little stuff. Telling him when there would be a bust coming so he could get his key people out of the way. Then... well, it got worse."

"Your partners. Did they know you were compromised?" I asked.

Her shoulders shuddered as she closed her eyes and wept. "When they figured it out, El Gato killed them because he couldn't turn them dirty. That's why I stopped working with anyone. I told the brass it was too dangerous, and I could do this on my own. I was busting a lot of lower- and mid-level dealers, El Gato's competitors mostly, but I made it look like they were all working for him. Then with all the other stuff going down in Vice, well, they finally agreed they were spread too thin to give me a new partner anyway."

I wanted to shake my head, but I kept still. I needed her to keep going. "What about Ruby and Samson?"

Her lips trembled again, and her watery gaze met mine. "It's my fault. Ruby told me about the blackmail. We were friends. I'd met her a couple of years ago on the party scene, and she was always the life of the party. I figured getting to know her would help me get into the bigger parties, with more celebrities. She told me that Samson was Alejandro's cousin, and he had dirt on him. They were anonymously blackmailing him. Alejandro had been trying to figure out who could have filmed him, and he'd been taking out anyone and everyone he could think of who might have done it, but he hadn't considered it being Samson."

"So the others in the video? Are they dead too?" I asked. We hadn't been able to identify them yet either.

"Yes. The video was from a location in Mexico. The men in the video were criminals from other countries. One was Venezuelan; another was from Argentina. The third was from Ecuador. El Gato had El Vibora kill them all, but the blackmail didn't stop. When I told him about Ruby and Samson, he went ballistic. He'd already called El Vibora up to LA because he wanted him to take out Deon, so he ordered him to take out Ruby and Samson as well."

She had so much blood on her hands. It made me sick to look at her, but I needed to know everything, so I kept at it. "Do you know who El Vibora is?"

She shook her head. "I think he used to be CIA or Mossad or something. The rumors about him are vast, but they say he went rogue and turned merc, working for various factions, then went into assassin for hire. That's when he accepted the contract with Alejandro."

"And nobody knows exactly who he is?" Angel asked.

"Nobody. Not even Alejandro. The guy is like a ghost. He changes disguises, and he's meticulous about it. Nobody knows what he really looks like."

"Where can we find Alejandro Gómez?" I asked.

"He has a home in West Hollywood," she said quietly.

"There's something I don't get," Angel interjected. "How did Samson get a hold of video of Alejandro doing that drug deal?"

"Samson used to be a legit agent to the stars, but he wasn't very good at it. Ruby was his biggest client. He saw how successful Alejandro was and decided to try to make himself useful to him. He got Ruby and a lot of other stars hooked on the Black Cat drugs, and became their connection. Alejandro trusted him because they were family. But Samson was resentful of the wealth Alejandro had amassed. He wanted it for himself, so he came up with the blackmail scheme. Samson talked Alejandro into using him as an enforcer, and he would travel with him all over the world.

That video you've got is just one of several Samson had on his cousin."

"Is that what's in those other encrypted files?"

"Probably. Or it could be video of El Gato at the site of someone being murdered. I know Alejandro didn't want them seen. I'm supposed to be trying to get my hands on the original hard drive and corrupt it, but tech hasn't put it in the evidence room yet." She sighed and looked down at her hands. She was shredding the tissue she was holding as she spoke.

I sighed and thought over everything she'd said. I had one more question for her, but it was more just to satisfy my own curiosity. "Valerie, were you under orders to follow me?"

Biting her lip, she looked down and then nodded. "Yeah, El Gato had me keep tabs on you and Angel before I got the tracker. And I followed you with that woman who showed up at your house, but that was really because I wanted to talk to you, and I just didn't know how without El Gato finding out."

"What about to Santa Monica? Did you follow me there and try to run me off the road?"

She seemed surprised at that. "No, I didn't do that. Someone tried to run you off the road?"

"Never mind," I murmured. I was pretty sure that had been Jordan anyway, even if it was a van. It just felt right. I gave Valerie a hard look. "You'll have to share all of this with the captain and the DA. It's the only way to save you."

Sniffling, Valerie nodded. "I know. I'm ready." She glanced up at me and added, "Will you go with me?"

"Absolutely," I agreed. "Let's go."

30

DIRTY COPS TO THE LEFT OF ME, DIRTY COPS TO THE RIGHT OF ME

MARCY

The captain was understandably livid upon hearing Valerie's confession. He let his tongue loose on her, and from the looks we got as we left his office later that afternoon, I knew that practically the entire detective pool had heard what he'd shouted at Valerie.

While I trusted most of the detectives I worked with, there were some that I found questionable. Valerie must have too, because as we walked out, she was shaking and looking around, meeting various gazes with terror in her eyes. She kept mumbling about him killing her. I tried to assure her that she'd be okay as she followed the DA to the elevators, but as I looked around, even I felt uncomfortable.

"Well, that was something," Angel murmured as we sat down at our desks.

"I don't know what we could have done differently," I replied, keeping my voice low. "Maybe I could have spoken to the captain alone? Reminded him to keep calm, that we don't want this made public, but—"

"Little too late for that." Angel frowned and turned his phone toward me.

"What the hell?" I muttered, taking his phone and reading the newest headline.

Breaking News, LAPD Vice Cop Valerie Burnett Under Indictment for Accepting Bribes

"Robinson is going to have somebody's head. Who the hell leaked this?" I scrolled through the article and saw that they'd labeled it a "developing story" with details to come. We had a mole. I looked around the office, trying to figure out who it was.

"I don't know, but we need to let Robinson know before he hears about it from someone else."

Sighing, I rose from my seat and handed him back his phone. Together we returned to Robinson's office. Jason didn't even stop us; he was too busy fielding the numerous calls that had started coming in. I knocked on the door, and before he could even tell us to come in, I opened the door. "Sir, we've got a big problem."

"What is it, Kendrick?"

"Angel, show him."

Angel handed him the phone, and Robinson's face went from red to purple. "Son of a bitch. Who?"

"I don't know, sir, but I figured you'd want to know."

He clenched his teeth as he breathed hard through his nose. "I want the leak plugged. Find them."

"Yes, sir." How I was going to do that, I didn't know. I hated thinking badly of the people I worked around, but if I'd learned one thing after the last scandal that rocked the department, it was there were a lot of dirty cops, and some in more ways than others, but still, to sell out to the media, that was a specific kind of dirty. Especially in this situation.

"No, you know what. I've got this." He slammed his hands down on his desk and stood up before storming out of his office. He stared out at the detectives currently in the detective pool. "Nobody is leaving this office until I know who had the balls to leak sensitive information to the press. I mean *nobody*. I don't care if the building is on fire. I want to know right now." His voice carried across the room and rattled the glass of the incident rooms.

There were startled and ashamed looks coming from some of the detectives.

"Vance?" I questioned, seeing him looking particularly ashamed. "You got something to say?"

"She's a dirty cop; she deserves all the shit coming her way," he answered, lifting his chin defiantly.

"What about you, Miguel?" Angel said, speaking to Detective Miguel Álvarez.

I didn't know him well; he was fairly new to our department, having switched over from Vice about three months ago.

"Vance is right. If she was working with that drug lord and taking bribes, getting good cops killed, then she deserves what she's getting."

"Did either of you leak this to the press?" Robinson seethed.

Álvarez looked away, then gave a nod. "I'd do it again too. She got my brother killed. I've always suspected."

"My office. Now!" Robinson pointed toward his office, his chest heaving as he tried to restrain himself as he started back toward his office behind Álvarez.

I gave Vance a disgusted look. "Did you call them too?" I'd never really liked him.

"No, but maybe I should have," he snarked. "What's the matter, Kendrick, you friends with that dirty cop? You were probably in on it with her—"

Angel got in his face. "Fucking shut your mouth right now," Angel said, grabbing Vance's suit jacket and shaking him.

I grabbed Angel's flexed bicep with my good hand. "Angel, he's not worth an assault charge; let him go."

Angel looked around the room, his narrowed gaze moving from face to face. "Anyone else think Kendrick's dirty? Because if she is, then so am I. I'm her partner, after all. You gonna paint us with that brush?"

There were a bunch of heads shaking in denial, and then Hummel said, "Look, Vance is just pissed off about Burnett bringing more shit down on the department, and he was blowing smoke up Kendrick's skirt to piss her off like normal. You didn't mean it, right, Vance?"

Vance shrugged. "Yeah, that's right. Just a dig, Kendrick."

"Sure, Vance. Sure." I gave him a disgusted look. He'd always been a dick to me, and he'd been one of Jordan's toady friends back in the day.

I was so done with this day. I needed to get out of here and take a shower. I hated the feeling that there were cops around me who were on the take, or would sell me out to the media just for a payday. "Tell the captain I'm taking an hour of PTO."

Angel nodded and watched me leave. I could feel his protective gaze on me as I left the office, but I didn't acknowledge it. I just headed straight for my car. Once I was in, I sent Frank a text.

> Left early, headed home. You coming by? I'd really like to see you.

I hit send, wishing I could have told him I needed him. I needed his arms around me. I needed him to console me. I needed his reassuring presence and the comfort of his closeness. Before I could even turn the car on, he answered.

> Absolutely. Be there around six thirty, have to stop for the steaks and beer.

I'd forgotten that we'd made plans to grill tonight, but remembering now, I felt my shoulders relax, because I knew I'd be seeing him soon.

> See you then, be safe.

You too, TT.

I got home and decided to do a workout in my exercise room. I changed into yoga pants and a sports bra, then clicked the TV on, turning it to YouTube, and found a yoga channel. I followed along, doing the poses as my body began to shed the stress from the day. My shoulder was still a little bit sore from the accident, but it felt good to do some of the stretches.

Once I was loosened up from the yoga, I switched the station to Britbox and put on a British comedy. I stepped onto the treadmill and set the pace for a jog to start. By the end of the half-hour show, I was running full out. When I couldn't go any further, I slowed the speed and cooled down, then turned the TV off. I'd watched three episodes of the half-hour comedy as I'd run. Glancing at the digital display, I noticed I'd run eight and a quarter miles.

I wiped down the treadmill and turned everything off before heading to the shower. The hot water on my shoulders felt good as it sluiced over me. A lot of the tension and stress from the day melted away. I'd needed that run and this shower.

By the time Frank arrived, I had the cut-up potatoes in the air fryer, a salad made, and some asparagus skewered with some mushrooms and ready to go on the grill with the steaks. I'd brushed them with olive oil and dusted them with garlic powder too, which was making my mouth water. I was starving.

As soon as he walked in the door, I rushed into his arms before he could even put anything down. I wrapped myself around him, just holding on to him and breathing him in. His arms came around me, and I felt at peace.

"Babe, you okay?"

I nodded against his chest, but didn't say anything.

"Did something happen?" he asked softly, just standing there holding me.

I nodded again and then took a deep breath and stepped back, taking the beer from him. "Did you see the headline of the *LA Times* website?"

"No…" He dragged the word out.

I picked up my phone from the counter and handed it to him after he put the steaks down and dropped his overnight bag to the floor by the kitchen table. I put the beer in the fridge and washed my hands before getting the steaks ready for the grill.

"Damn, who leaked this? Is Burnett okay?"

"Álvarez, he used to be Vice, but transferred to IISS a few months ago."

"I know him. Worked a few cases with him; didn't really like him. His brother was Vice also, right?"

"Yeah, he was killed in action a couple of years ago. According to Álvarez, Burnett is the reason he was killed."

"Shit. Was he on the take too?"

"I don't know," I said softly. "Just feel like we've got a lot of dirty cops in the LAPD, and we haven't even scratched the surface to getting rid of them."

Frank sighed and wrapped his arms around me, holding me tight. "That may be true, but there are good cops like you and Angel too."

"Like you," I murmured against his chest.

"Yes, like me too." He tightened his arms a bit, as though he were trying to merge my body with his. "IA will find them and weed them out. It will take time, but they will get them."

"Is it bad that I want to find them and weed them out myself?"

He chuckled. "You gonna give up HSS to go work for IA?"

I wrinkled my nose. "No."

"Then I think you're going to have to let them do their job."

Sighing, I huffed, "Fine. But if they don't get on it soon, I might just have to do something about it myself." I grinned.

"And every LAPD officer would tremble in their boots," he teased. "My TT would wipe the floor with them and leave them begging for mercy."

"You're damn right I would." I winked, feeling better.

"Come on, let's get these steaks and vegetables on the grill."

31

BLOOD-LUSTING BOSS
EL VIBORA

"My place, one hour."

I stared at my phone and snorted. The man was getting more and more demanding of me, and I didn't like it. He wasn't paying me enough to be at his beck and call for every petty misdemeanor and transgression he found in his organization. Him calling and demanding that, then hanging up, just fueled my anger at him.

"One more year," I muttered. That was how much longer our contract was for. One more year and I was a free agent again. I could get away from him and his blood lust. I could go work for a dictator over in Azerbaijan, or down to Nicaragua, and have less headaches than I had working for Alejandro.

I returned to my apartment and, after a shower, put on my disguise, making sure it was perfect. I still had the rental car I'd picked up at the airport, so I headed for his house. I could feel the tension in the air as I entered and was escorted to Alejandro's office.

"Leave us," he said to his other men.

I watched them leave, still not having spoken a word.

"Sit," he directed, his voice short.

Gritting my teeth, I did as he asked. "Is there a problem?" I asked, keeping my voice calm.

"It's that fucking lady cop."

My thoughts turned to the intriguing woman I'd followed the other day while she jogged. I hated the thought that I might have to kill her. From everything I'd seen about her, she was very good at her job, and she wasn't corrupt. I had a good deal of admiration for her. Unfortunately, if she was becoming a thorn in Alejandro's side... I sighed. "What has she done?"

"She fucking turned on me. After everything I've done for her," Alejandro ranted as he paced the room, dragging his hand through his hair. "That bitch flipped the script. Gave them everything, according to my source. They know who I am, and I won't stand for it. She needs to be made an example of. I want her flayed alive and dismembered as a warning to others to keep their fucking mouths shut."

I blinked. That wasn't the kind of murder I did, and he knew it. "That is not how I operate," I said quietly. "If you want a monster, then maybe you need to get another assassin to take this one."

He turned on me, rage filling his face as he pulled a gun on me. "You are still under contract with me, and if you don't do as you're ordered, then I have no need for you anymore." He cocked his weapon and pointed it at my head.

"I didn't say I wouldn't do it. I merely questioned the method." I stayed calm, not moving as I met his gaze. "I'll kill her, but—"

"Do it your way, then mutilate her body. I want her made

an example of. Nobody, and I mean nobody goes against El Gato." He lowered the weapon and uncocked it.

"Very well. Anything else?" I asked, looking at him blandly.

"There might be more, might need to clean house out there at the LAPD. Depends on what they do with the information the bitch gave them," he seethed. "Still can't believe her nerve. I took care of her, gave her everything she asked for, and this is how she repays me."

"It wasn't out of the goodness of your heart. You were blackmailing her," I reminded him.

He snarled, and his eyes blazed. "Her mother is alive, isn't she? She's not suffering under the massive weight of medical debt, is she? She's got money in the bank now, doesn't she? And she got to stay working as a cop even as she got high on the drugs I comped her. The bitch owes me."

He wasn't wrong. He had done all of that for her, but it was all to protect himself and his business. Still, for her to turn on him, that took some cajónes. Ones I hadn't known she had. In a way I thought better of her for it, but that wouldn't stop me from doing my job.

"When do you want it done?" I asked.

"As soon as I know where she is. Be ready."

"Always." I stood, and when he didn't say anything else, I left.

32

VALERIE'S VIDEO TESTIMONY
MARCY

"Can you be there?"

It was an unusual request, but I wasn't about to deny her. "Okay, Valerie. I'll be there," I replied as I glanced at the clock. "Just me, or Angel too?"

Valerie was quiet for a moment, then said, "Just you. I don't think I can get through this alone, but I don't want a big audience."

I nodded, not that she could see me. "I understand. I'll see you soon." I hung up and glanced over at Angel. "Valerie wants me to sit in on her deposition."

"Why? It's not like you're friends, right?"

"Definitely not, but I don't think she really has any friends." To me that was sad. Maybe if she'd had friends, she wouldn't be in the mess she was in.

"What time do you need to be there?"

"In an hour. You want to grab lunch before I go?" I asked.

"Sure, you want to eat here or out?"

"Who's out there?" I questioned, thinking about it.

"Lobsta and Holy Grill were there when I came in."

"Let's have Holy Grill." I grabbed my purse from the drawer. "We can eat outside if you want?"

He stood up. "Sounds good. Might be good to get some fresh air."

We headed out of the station and down the street to the food truck. I ordered the house kabob, which was beef and lamb with garlic, onion, cilantro, and parsley. It came with rice, hummus, and a tahini dip, which was made from toasted ground hulled sesame, as well as an Israeli salad.

Angel ended up getting food from Lobsta, not wanting to have garlic breath when he went to see Callie later. I thought it was rather sweet. I hoped that meant he was making an effort to get over his feelings for me and focus on Callie and their relationship.

We carried our food to one of the outdoor picnic tables and sat down. It was a pretty day, which wasn't surprising, as most days were pretty here, but there was a slight breeze. I had to put my soda on top of my napkins so they wouldn't blow away.

After we ate and cleaned up, Angel returned to the station, and I headed over to the courthouse, where Valerie was meeting with the DA.

I saw Valerie and her lawyer standing in the hallway, and I went to join them.

Before I could even say hello, her lawyer moved in front of her and held a hand up to stop me. "You aren't welcome here."

I raised a brow and glanced at Valerie. "Are you sure? I've been invited by your client."

"It's okay, Silas. I did invite her. I just... I need her here, okay?" Valerie's voice was low, and she seemed nervous.

"She's the reason you're in this mess—"

"No, I'm the reason I'm in this mess. All Detective Kendrick has done is figure it out. She's a good detective, and I trust her to help keep me safe from El Gato and his henchmen."

Her lawyer looked like he was about to argue, but then gave a nod. "Fine, however, she cannot say anything or ask any questions."

"Wasn't planning to," I replied.

The DA, Anderson Caulder, walked up. "Good afternoon," he said, looking at all of us. "Detective Kendrick, I wasn't aware you were going to be here. I don't have any questions for you at this time."

"I know, Mr. Caulder. I'm here as a favor to Valerie. With El Gato's assassin still in play, I think she's a little worried."

"She's perfectly safe in my custody." He seemed slightly offended.

"Look, I trust Detective Kendrick to help keep me safe. El Vibora can be anywhere, and you won't expect him," Valerie explained.

"Very well. Come in." He gestured to the room we were going to be convening in. "I've got the camera ready to go."

We sat around the six-person wooden table, with me on the same side as the DA across from Valerie and her lawyer. I was closest to the door, so should anyone attempt to break in, I could act.

Anderson hit record on the camera's remote and began asking Valerie questions. I'd heard most of this before. But when Anderson asked her about El Gato's organization and if she knew of any other cops who were compromised, my ears perked up, and I turned my gaze back to Valerie.

Valerie's startled gaze met mine.

"Answer the question, Detective Burnett."

Her lawyer leaned in and whispered in her ear.

Valerie nodded and then said, "Alejandro has numerous government officials in his pocket, including several cops. Before his arrest, Grant Weaver was one of his informants. He would trade information for drugs, which he would then sell or give to the women he was trafficking. There are also a handful of patrol officers on his payroll, three other Vice Detectives, Hill, Watterson, and Rivera as well as"—she looked directly at me as her voice lowered to a whisper— "Detectives Ortiz and Flores from HSS."

My heart nearly stopped at that. I knew Ortiz and Flores and had thought them to be decent guys. I didn't work directly with them, since they were nightshift, but it was hard hearing confirmation that there were dirty cops in my department.

"I see. Which government officials, that you are aware of, are on his payroll?" the DA asked.

Valerie swallowed hard and looked down at her hands, which were folded in front of her. "The deputy mayor," she murmured, barely above a whisper.

I glanced at Anderson and saw the startled look in his eyes. I saw his finger hesitating over the stop button, but after a moment he moved it.

"You have proof of this?" he asked.

"No, not really. I've seen David Combs with Alejandro at a few parties. I mean he was part of his entourage, not just someone at the party."

At that he did push stop on the video. "I will quietly look into these allegations on the deputy mayor, but if you have no concrete proof, proving it will be difficult. Is there anything you can give me?"

Valerie thought about it for a moment. "Check the surveillance videos of Club Helix from about two months ago. The VIP section. I wasn't exactly sober while I was there, but I did see the deputy mayor partaking in some of the drugs."

"I'll check it out." He clicked the record button again. "Let's continue."

He went on to ask more about each of the patrol officers who were compromised so he could pass their names on to IA.

I was feeling sick hearing about how much corruption was in our precinct, and I wasn't sure how much longer I could stand sitting here without losing my lunch.

Eventually, the video testimony ended, and Anderson said, "Okay, so I'm going to have some officers out of Long Beach take you to the safehouse. They'll stay with you and keep you safe. We've got a rotation of officers from Santa Monica, Long Beach, and Huntington Beach on this because we didn't want to use anyone connected to the LAPD area who might be compromised or want to do you harm because you were one of them."

Valerie nodded. "Thank you," she whispered, looking solemn.

"I'm not going to say where the safehouse is, since there are others in the room."

I didn't take offense. That was the whole point of a safehouse. "I'm going to go, Valerie. It looks like you'll be in good hands now."

"Thank you, Marcy. I know you don't think much of me, but I appreciate you being here."

I gave her a smile and said, "Take care," then left the room. I didn't need to hang around and wait for her to be escorted out. She'd be okay with officers from other areas watching over her.

It was time for me to head back to the precinct and give Captain Robinson a heads-up that our department was about to be turned on its head. He might already know what happened before I got there, but the least I could do was tell him what Valerie had shared about the two HSS detectives she'd implicated.

I just hoped it didn't paint another target on my back.

33

KILLING THE QUEEN OF CLUBS
EL VIBORA

"My men have tracked her down," Alejandro said the moment I answered my phone.

"Where?"

"These *policía es estúpida*"—he chuckled—"got the bitch being guarded at a house in Santa Monica by a couple of my men."

"So why don't they just take care of her?" I questioned, not really wanting to do this particular killing.

"¿*Estás jodidamente loco*? I pay you to assassinate the ones I need killed. They don't get paid for that shit. Do what I said. I want it bloody."

"Where am I going, and how do I get in?"

"Do I have to explain your job to you?" He sounded pissed off. "I'll text you the address. One of my guys, Scott Schueller, will have a uniform waiting for you. You just make sure you look like him. He'll be on the door. I'll send you a photo of him. They go on shift at nine."

"Fine." I hung up and waited for the texts.

I had a couple of hours to prepare, which it sounded like I was going to need to make sure I had my disguise correct.

My phone buzzed with a picture of the officer I was supposed to look like. It wouldn't be too hard. He was young, mid-twenties, tanned, with spiky, ash blond hair and blue eyes. It looked as though he had a broken nose at some point because it was crooked. Luckily, he had a decent set of teeth, and I wouldn't have to fake a broken tooth or discolor mine.

I got to work making the prosthetic nose, and while it set, I went through my wigs, finding the right shade I could dye to match his, and then I cut it so that it replicated his cut. For now I put on a pair of sweats and a white T-shirt along with some dark running shoes. I grabbed my kit and headed out, driving to the house in Santa Monica.

The house sat at the end of a dead-end street. The house across the street looked vacant, and the one next door was dark, but it looked lived in. I sat in my car and watched for a few minutes to see if there was anyone coming or going from the area, but it seemed quiet.

Getting out of my car, I closed the door softly and strolled over to the man I was to impersonate. His eyes widened upon seeing me.

"Damn, you look just like me," he whispered. "I'm not going to go down for this, right?"

I shrugged. I had no idea if he would or not, but I doubted it. "Just get an alibi set up. Be somewhere else for a while."

"Where the hell am I supposed to go?" he asked, handing me the uniform he'd stashed in the bushes.

I took the uniform from him, intending to change in the trees off to the far side of the house. "Maybe ask the officers inside if they want pizza, offer to go get it."

"How does that help you?"

"Let me worry about that. Let me change. I'll be back in a moment." I strode off before he could say any more and got changed into the uniform. By the time I emerged, I looked like Scott Schueller's twin brother. I hung the sweats up on a tree branch, intending to return for them after I completed this job, then headed back to Scott.

"Damn, you do look just like me; that's freaky."

"How many inside, and where are they all located?"

"Three inside, two in the living room. One of them is cool, works for El Gato. The other is older and wears glasses. The third is a woman; she's probably in the hallway, guarding Valerie, who's in the master bedroom."

"What's her name?"

"Corrina Miller, why?" He suddenly looked nervous.

I didn't bother to answer his question. "Where is the master bedroom located? Where does the hallway go?"

He sighed and then used his finger on the side of the house to draw it out for me. "So if you enter through the front door, there's a small room to the left that connects to the living room, go straight from the door and you'll end up in the kitchen, but before the kitchen, if you take a right and go down the hallway, the master bedroom is on the right at the end."

"Is there a back door?"

"Yeah, in the kitchen, but the yard is fenced."

"There's a gate on the side, though." I'd seen it as I went to the wooded area on the side of the house.

"It's been padlocked shut."

I smirked. "That's not going to stop me. Where does the back door go?"

"To the kitchen."

Rolling my eyes, I said, "I know that; where in the kitchen does it go? Is there a line of sight to the living room?"

Scott frowned as if thinking about it. "Yeah, there's an open archway that leads from the breakfast nook in the kitchen to the living room, but they're facing the TV and will have their backs to you."

"Give it five minutes, and then go in and offer to get pizza. Don't let them ask Valerie or the guard on her door if they want some. Go to the hall and, when you see me, make the call, but then return to the living room and make sure they don't check on Miller."

"Right." He nodded. "Then what?"

I rolled my eyes. "When the pizza gets here, answer the door."

He frowned but then acquiesced. "Okay, if you think that will work."

I hoped he wouldn't screw this up. If he did, I might have to kill him and the other cops here. I didn't like relying on others. It got messy. I headed to the side of the yard, pulled on a pair of clear latex gloves, and got out my lock picks. It took me less than a minute to get the padlock on the gate off.

I eased the wooden gate open and crept close to the house, moving along the siding toward the back door. I continued toward the windows just past the door. I wanted to get a look inside to see where the two officers were. Seeing them seated on the sofa, their backs to the kitchen, focused on the baseball game on the TV, I was reassured.

I moved to the back door and got to work on the handle lock and dead bolt. With it unlocked, I put my lock picks away and returned them to my bag. I pulled out the two syringes, as well as the hunting knife and extra latex gloves. I slid the knife into the waistband of my pants on my left hip.

The syringes I put in my right pocket and my gloves in the left. They were different colors so I would be sure to use the correct one on the right person. The light blue one, which also had an indention on the top, was full of an anesthetic and sedative, and I'd be using it on the female guard. I didn't want to kill her. Just incapacitate her.

I set my bag down next to the door and turned the knob, gently easing the door open. I heard Scott come in the front door and waited for him to engage with the two guards in the living room.

"Hey, it's all quiet out there. I was thinking of ordering pizza. Do you guys want some?" Scott's voice carried into the kitchen.

"I'd like some. Pepperoni," one of the men answered.

"Yeah, pepperoni sounds good; should I go ask Miller what she wants?" the other man asked.

"She likes plain cheese. I already asked her," Scott said. "I'll go call it in."

I made my move. I saw Scott in the hallway and nodded at him, then turned and walked down the corridor toward the bedrooms. I could see a woman leaned against the wall, her eyes closed, her arms crossed. She was making it too easy. I fingered the syringe in my pocket, pushing the cap off the needle.

Her eyes opened, and she said, "Oh, hey—"

Quickly reaching for her, I covered her mouth and stuck the needle in her neck, then as she went under, I gently lowered her to the floor. I'd have thirty minutes or so to get this done and back out to my car before the pizza arrived. I slipped into the room and noticed Valerie on the bed, asleep. That was good for me.

She didn't move as I crept toward her, needle ready. I put

my hand over her mouth and injected her. She woke and struggled for a moment, but then the drugs kicked in; she'd be gone soon. I waited a moment for the heavy painkiller to kick in, and then got to work with the knife. I slit her throat, carved up her body, making the scene as bloody as I could, since that was what Alejandro wanted, the asshole.

When I was done, I placed the Black Cat's queen of clubs on the bed and stabbed it through with the hunting knife, leaving it behind. I'd wiped it free of prints, and I'd bought it secondhand, so it wouldn't be traceable. My gloves were bloody, so I removed them and pulled the extra pair from my other pocket, trading them out. After putting on the spare, I opened the door and closed it behind me, stepped over Miller, and then crouched in the archway between the hallway and kitchen, listening.

Twenty minutes had passed, I noted on the clock on the kitchen wall. I could hear the three men in the living room; they were loud as they watched the game. Scott was with them. I was glad he'd covered himself and wouldn't be causing Alejandro trouble. I'd hate to have to hunt him down and kill him too.

With them occupied, I silently crept through the darkened kitchen to the back door. Opening it, I slipped out, turning the lock before pulling it closed behind me. I picked up my bag and went back the way I came. In the woods once more, I changed out of the Huntington Beach police uniform and returned to my car.

As I drove away, I dialed Alejandro. When he answered, I said, "It's done."

"*Bueno.* No issues with the officers?"

"No."

"Your next targets are Kendrick and then her partner,

Reyes. They know too much. I don't care how you do it; make it look like an accident or a home invasion. Just get it done tonight."

"Are you sure that's a good idea?" I questioned.

"If you aren't going to do what I pay you for, then maybe I need to terminate your contract and you."

"Have I ever not completed a contract you put out on someone?"

"See that you don't this time either because I will make you disappear if you do." He hung up.

"Fuck." I hit the steering wheel. This was getting out of hand, and Alejandro was getting too cocky for my liking. The longer I stayed in LA, and the more assassinations I did, the greater the chance that I would get caught. And this cop, Marcy Kendrick, I'd read up on her. She was good. Not just at her job, but overall a good person. She didn't deserve this.

I could disobey him and fly down to Mexico instead. It wasn't as though he'd ever find me. Maybe I could break my contract without losing my reputation; it was something to think on.

34

A WAKE-UP CALL

MARCY

Frank hadn't been able to come over, so I'd spent the evening binging four episodes of *Reacher* before getting ready for bed. Being alone, I'd taken a quick shower and then put on an old T-shirt with Scooby-Doo on it and a pair of cotton shorts. It had taken me forever to fall asleep as my mind played through all the evidence of the case.

A sound somewhere in the house woke me. I grabbed my Glock—I still hadn't gotten my service weapon back—from the bedside table and pulled the slide back, chambering a round. Listening intently, I swung my legs over the edge of the bed, putting my bare feet on the wooden floor. My bedroom door was open, so I could move into the hallway easily. I kept my back to the wall as I walked through my house. I looked in the exercise room first, then the guest room, clearing them both, then moved into the kitchen.

If Jordan had broken into my house, I would not hesitate to shoot him. The man had lost his marbles, and he was asking for trouble. He'd already beaten Katie, so I wasn't going to let him do the same to me. He had to know I wouldn't be bluffing.

I started toward the back door to check if it was still locked when I heard a creak on the floor behind me. I spun and fired a shot, startling the man standing there as something clattered to the floor. I kept my gun pointed at him as I looked around for the object that he'd dropped. I found it in the sliver of moonlight that shone through the window. A syringe.

I backed up and hit the light switch by the door, flooding my kitchen with light. He was holding his ear as he pulled a gun from his back and pointed it at me.

"This is going to go one of two ways," I said, feeling rather feral as adrenaline flooded me. I recognized him as the man who had followed me while I was jogging the other day. Knowing who he was now sent a chill down my spine at how close I'd come to being another victim of El Vibora.

He arched a brow and stared at me, almost mockingly as if he was asking me to explain my thought.

I wanted to snarl at him and just shoot him anyway, but I didn't. Not yet. "I shoot you in the face and you die, or you drop your weapon, and you live to see another day." My voice was hard.

He didn't move a muscle; his finger was flat against the trigger, not poised to pull it yet as he said, "I didn't want it to come to this." His voice was bland, unemotional.

"It still doesn't have to. Killing me isn't going to stop the wheels of justice. Your boss is going down no matter what. Valerie has already given her video testimony in case something happens to her. And we have Samson's files. Video evidence of El Gato. Alejandro Gómez is going down, and you're going with him."

"I'm not going do—" he started as the glass in my kitchen window to the left of me shattered. His gun hand moved from me to the new target, and he fired two shots toward the window.

I heard a scream from outside that sounded an awful lot like Jordan. I glanced toward the window, but as soon as I turned back to El Vibora, I realized he was gone. I heard the front door slam shut and hoped that he'd left, but I was afraid he was attempting to trick me.

Pissed off, I headed out the back door and around the side of the house to see Jordan on the ground, holding his right shoulder.

"You fucking shot me!" he screamed.

"I did not," I said, squatting down to check his wound. It was a through and through. "Don't move. I'll go call this in and get you an ambulance." I kept my tone calm; however, I was anything but that.

Returning to the house, I cleared it, turning on every light in every room to make sure that bastard wasn't hiding out anywhere. I checked behind curtains, under beds, and in every closet. When I was sure he was gone, I grabbed my cell and called in both the break-in and Jordan's injury, then pocketed the phone as I returned to his side with my gun still in my hand. I wasn't putting it away for anything or anyone.

He was moaning on the grass, his hand on his shoulder, trying to stop the blood. "What the fuck took you so long?" he slurred.

It was then I realized he was drunk. "What the hell were you even doing here, Jordan? Why did you bust my kitchen window? Was my bedroom window not enough? Hell."

"You made Katie leave," he mumbled under his labored breath.

"That was all you, Jordan. Not me." I heard the sirens coming and added, "Just hang in there; the ambulance is almost here."

His eyes were fluttering, and I wondered if he was going to pass out. I wasn't even sure I cared if he did. I didn't think his wound was fatal, but he was losing quite a bit of blood, so I hoped they'd hurry and get here.

"Jordan?" I said, looking at him, reaching a hand down to shake his good shoulder.

The hand he'd been holding his wound with slid from it, and he didn't answer me.

"Damn it," I muttered, setting down my gun on the ground within easy reach, and putting pressure on the wound with both hands. I wasn't going to let him die here in my yard. Lord knew he'd probably come back and haunt me forever if he did.

35

CAUGHT IN THE ACT
MARCY

A s the paramedics arrived, I felt my shoulders relax a little. Patrol officers were right behind them, as three police vehicles, their sirens wailing, came to a halt in front of my house. I was sure my new neighbors were thrilled at being woken at three in the morning by all of this. I was going to have to do something big to apologize to them. I was really glad I didn't live in an HOA neighborhood. They'd probably kick me out for all of this.

Of the six officers who'd arrived, I only recognized two of them, Mendoza and Peters. I gave them a nod as they rushed over.

"What have we got?" Mendoza asked, his weapon drawn.

"I need an immediate search of my house and the neighborhood." I knew it was probably a fruitless endeavor, but I wanted to know if El Vibora was still hanging around. "You're looking for a man with graying brown hair, hazel eyes and a large nose dressed all in black. Be on your guard; he's absolutely lethal."

"Yes, ma'am," Peters replied as he turned to direct the other officers.

"Ma'am, we'll take over," one of the medics said, trying to move me away from Jordan.

I released my hold on his shoulder, wiped my hands on my shirt, and picked up my gun. Moving out of the way, I left them to do their job and went to the front of my house. I heard another siren and turned to see an SUV quickly approaching.

A moment later, Angel was running toward me. "Marce! Are you okay?" He grabbed my forearms and looked me over.

"I'm fine, Angel," I replied, "just a little shaken. Who called you?"

"Robinson."

That made sense. Dispatch would have informed him one of his officers was attacked.

"Where is he? I'll kill him." He was seething as he looked around, his eyes lighting on the paramedics in my side yard. He started toward them, but I grabbed his arm.

"Don't. It wasn't Jordan. Well, it was, but for once, he actually might have just saved my bacon."

"What?"

"El Vibora was here. He was going to kill me. At least I'm pretty sure that was his intention." I wondered if the syringe he'd dropped was still in my kitchen. As I explained what had happened, Angel's face grew pale.

"Stay here. I'm going to check your kitchen and make sure patrol cleared your house."

"Pretty sure he's long gone, but whatever," I said with a nod.

He paused and looked back at me. "Call Frank," he said before heading toward my house.

I pulled my phone from my pocket and hit Frank's number. He answered almost immediately.

"TT? What's wrong? Are you okay?"

"Frank, I need you to be calm."

"What the fuck happened? Who do I need to kill?"

"You sure you want to ask that? I'm a police detective too, you know."

"TT, stop making jokes and please tell me what's going on before I have a heart attack."

"El Vibora was here. In my house," I said, trying to keep my tone calm. "I'm fine. I swear, no injuries. At least not to me."

"You shot him?"

I snorted. "No, might have grazed his ear, but I don't think so. He shot Jordan."

"Jordan? What the hell is going on over there?"

I explained everything that had taken place.

He sighed. "Damn it. I'm taking PTO and heading over to you."

"Frank, I'm okay. You don't have to do that—" I started.

"I know I don't, but I don't like what's going on. If El Vibora is targeting you, I'm going to be there to help protect you. I get that Angel is your partner, and during the day you're covered, but every other second of the day, I'll have your back. I can't lose you, Marcy."

"If you want to be here, I'm not going to send you away. But you know I can take care of myself."

"I know you can, but that doesn't mean I can't make it easier on you."

"Okay. See you soon," I said as my phone buzzed, indicating I had another call. "I need to go."

"I'm already out the door." He hung up.

I clicked to answer the call. "Captain?"

"It's been a busy night, Kendrick. Just got a call from Santa Monica. El Vibora hit the safehouse. Burnett is dead."

I nearly dropped my phone. "How the hell did he manage to get past the detail on her? Did he kill them all?" My heart was racing. He'd killed Valerie and who knew how many others tonight.

"No. He incapacitated one of the officers, but the others were none the wiser until they heard screaming from the officer on Valerie's bedroom door. Valerie wasn't just drugged, she was mutilated."

"Shit." My whole body was shaking. El Vibora had gotten to Valerie. She was dead. He'd come to murder me after killing her. I could have died. I started hyperventilating.

"Kendrick?"

I couldn't answer. I was starting to spiral. I sank to the ground, my legs giving out.

"Kendrick!"

My jaw worked as I tried to stop the panic attack. I took several deep breaths, counting backward from ten in my mind.

"Kendrick!"

"Here, sorry, sir," I finally replied.

"Are you okay?"

I continued breathing deeply and said, "Yes, sir. I just... I had my own encounter with El Vibora tonight. Your news... it hit different."

"He was there? I thought it was Brasswell you called in about. I was told he attacked your house—"

"He did, and El Vibora shot him. Jordan interrupted his attack on me."

I still couldn't believe how lucky I had actually been tonight. First hearing him entering my house, then turning at just the right time to miss being stabbed with that syringe, and then the standoff prior to Jordan breaking the window. It was a miracle I was still alive. I glanced up at the night sky and thanked the Lord for watching over me. I wasn't sure He existed, but things like this made me believe he probably did. I'd err on the side that He did.

"You said Brasswell was shot?"

"They're loading him into the ambulance right now."

"Okay, okay." He paused, and I could almost hear him thinking. A moment later, he said, "Once your house is secured, you and Angel head over to the safehouse in Santa Monica. They've already removed the body, and their CSI team is doing their own investigation, but I know you'll want to see the scene for yourself. I've contacted Captain Stafford, and he's asked CSI to hold the scene for you. I'm also having everything they've found sent over to our CSI team. You'll have the reports by the time you get back later. I'll check in with the hospital on Brasswell and keep you updated."

"Captain, about Jordan. It might be a good idea to put him on a seventy-two-hour psych watch. He's not stable."

"I'll make it happen." He hung up.

I started toward the house as I dialed Frank again. He answered before the first ring was even complete.

"You still good?" he asked, then added, "I'm turning onto Santa Monica Boulevard right now."

"Hey, I'm still good, but stay in Santa Monica. I have to come there. The safehouse was hit, and Burnett is dead."

"Shit, okay, what's the address? I'll meet you there."

"I'll text it to you as soon as Robinson sends it to me. See you in a bit."

"Be safe."

I pocketed my phone and stepped through my front door. "Angel?" I called.

Angel came out of the kitchen with a plastic evidence bag containing the syringe. "What's up?"

"Burnett's dead. El Vibora hit the safehouse."

"Shit." He moved toward me and pulled me into a hug, holding me tight. "I could have lost you tonight." His body was shaking as he held me.

"You didn't."

"But I could have."

I allowed him to take several calming breaths before I pushed at him, and he let me go. "I'm okay. I'm not going anywhere," I assured him. "I'm going to get dressed, and we need to head over to Santa Monica."

He nodded slowly. "I'll have Mendoza take over the scene and get this evidence to Lindsey."

I glanced into my kitchen and saw the broken window. "Can you also have him grab some wood from the shed in the backyard and cover the window?"

"I'll handle it."

"Thanks, Angel." I moved to my bedroom, set my Glock on the dresser, and closed my bedroom door. I changed into my usual work attire and holstered my weapon, grabbed my purse, and returned to the living room.

After giving my house keys to Mendoza, Angel and I headed to Santa Monica. He drove, and I sent Frank the address. We were there within the hour. The SMPD CSI team was still there, as were the officers who'd been on duty watching over Burnett.

I still couldn't figure out how they'd managed to not hear anything. I was livid. El Vibora should never have been able to get to her. I strode over to the four officers, who were seated on the couch in the living room. Frank and Angel flanked me, their arms folded like two badass bodyguards; all they needed were the dark glasses to finish the look. The idea made me smirk internally, but I kept my amusement off my face. It wasn't hard. I was still pissed off these officers had allowed Burnett to be murdered.

"Explain to me how an assassin was able to get past the three of you to incapacitate her"—I nodded toward Officer Miller—"and kill Detective Burnett?" I demanded.

"We've been over this already with SMPD," one of them, Drake, complained.

"Yeah, read our statements," Officer Schueller said, sounding mulish.

My eyes flashed to Miller, who was rubbing her neck and looked haunted. "What about you? How did he manage to get the drop on you?"

"I don't know. I was standing in the hallway outside the bedroom door. I was leaning against the wall, my eyes shut, but I wasn't asleep. I swear I wasn't. I heard a sound and partially opened my eyes, but the only person I saw was Scott. I figured he was checking on Valerie, so I started to say something, and a moment later his hand was on my mouth. Next thing I knew, Scott was stabbing me with a needle—"

"It wasn't me! I was in the living room with them." He pointed at the other two officers, Drake and Castavella. "Wasn't I? Tell them!"

"He ordered pizza, and we were all waiting in the living room for it to arrive," Officer Drake said. "He was out of our line of sight for about two minutes, but we could hear him the whole time as he called in the pizza order."

"Well, it damn well looked like you," Miller insisted. "If it wasn't you, you've got a fucking psycho twin out there!"

I pinched the bridge of my nose. Somehow El Gato hadn't just found out where the safehouse was, he'd known who the officers on duty were and had given El Vibora Officer Schueller's image to mimic. We had another leak. I had to wonder though, since these officers were from Huntington Beach, if the leak had come from their precinct. How many police departments had El Gato infiltrated? We'd need to widen our search. I needed to talk to the DA.

"I want to see the scene," I said, turning to Angel and Frank.

"You sure about that? It's pretty bloody," Officer Castavella said.

I looked over my shoulder and stared blandly at them before returning my gaze to Frank and Angel. "Where's the CSI lead?" I asked, trying to recall his name. "It's Jazz, right?"

Frank nodded. "I thought I saw him outside; want me to get him?"

"Please."

"Should we head on back to the scene?" Angel murmured, looking around.

"Yeah. Frank, meet us back there with Jazz."

"Will do."

We walked around the couch and through the archway into the breakfast nook area, then turned right to get into the hallway. I paused and returned to the archway, looking at the

layout. I glanced at the group seated with their backs to us.
"What were you three doing while you waited for the pizza
to get here?" I called from the opening.

All four turned to look over their shoulders at me, but it
was Schueller who answered. "I was seated over there"—he
pointed to a chair that was out of the kitchen's line of sight—
"Drake and Castavella were on the couch, pretty much
where they are now, and we were watching the game."

"What are you thinking?" Angel asked.

"I'm thinking he came in through this door," I replied,
tilting my head toward the back door in the kitchen.

As I spoke, the front door opened, and Frank and Jazz
started down the hall toward us. "The front door has that
squeak. He wouldn't have come in that way unless one of
them let him in," I murmured, keeping my voice low.

"You think one of them is compromised?" Angel questioned, his voice barely a whisper.

I nodded. "I do, but I still don't think that's how he got
in." I glanced at Jazz and smiled. "Hey, Jazz. Good to see
you."

"You too, Detective Kendrick. You want to see the scene?"

"I do, but first, did you dust this door for prints?"

"We dusted every possible entry point including the
door, and good guess. There's scrapings on the lock, but no
prints. Pretty sure the killer wore gloves," he replied as he
pulled the back door open and showed us the dead bolt
keyhole.

"I just remembered," Miller said, joining us. "The hand
that was over my mouth... I think he was wearing clear latex
gloves or something. I could see the flesh of his hand, so it
was definitely see-through, but I felt the smoothness of the
gloves."

"If you remember anything else, give us a call," Angel said, handing her a card with our direct line.

"I will." She took the card and returned to the living room.

Jazz shut the door and then directed us to the scene. Inside the bedroom I could see the bloody outline of Valerie's body. Jazz explained that they had pictures of everything, but they were already on their way to Lindsey along with all the evidence they'd collected. He showed us where the queen of clubs had been and how it had been stabbed with a hunting knife.

"This isn't his usual MO, is it?" I murmured, looking at Angel.

"Not usually. I'm guessing El Gato wanted to send a message," he replied.

"Don't cross him would be my guess," Frank said. His eyes were haunted as he looked at me.

I watched him clench his fingers into fists, and I was sure he was doing his best not to drag me toward him and wrap me in his arms in an effort to keep me safe. I gave him a slight shake of my head. Now wasn't the time.

His gaze met mine, and after a moment he gave me a nod. "What now?"

"Can you make sure whatever detective was on this scene gets us their statements?" I hadn't seen another detective, so I assumed they'd released the scene to Jazz and his crew.

"I can do that," he replied as we left the bedroom.

"If you don't need me anymore, I'm going to finish up and get out of here," Jazz said.

"We're good. Angel and I are going to head back to LA and get started on going over the reports as they come in." I looked back to Frank. "Are you still going to take PTO?"

"I was planning to," he replied, opening the front door.

"I'll meet you at the car," Angel said, taking off.

I glanced at Angel and then looked back at Frank. I took a step closer, and my fingers found his. "Can you come by the station and pick up my house keys? Mendoza has them because he's making sure my house is locked up."

"Sure." He squeezed my fingers with his. "I'll call the window guy too and get that fixed. Maybe we should go stay at a hotel tonight. I don't like the idea of this guy being who knows where with a hit out on your head. A hotel room might throw him off and give you some added security."

The idea of that had merit, so I nodded. "I'll think about it, but I don't want to give him the satisfaction of knowing he's scared me."

Frank shook his head, but smiled. "You are so stubborn, you know that?"

I grinned. "I do. You love me anyway."

His face grew solemn, and he nodded. "I really do."

It was then I realized what I'd just said. My eyes widened as I understood what he was saying. I swallowed and stepped closer. "Me too," I whispered, my heart racing.

He raised a hand to my cheek, caressing my face, his gaze on mine, and I could see a lifetime of love in his eyes. "Promise?"

"Promise." Not caring who was watching, I pushed up on my toes and kissed him. "I do, Frank," I said, my voice breathy.

"Be safe, please? I can't..." His voice broke as he looked deep into my eyes.

"I know. I will." I hugged him tight. "I have to go," I said, stepping back from him.

"I'll see you later," he promised, and then walked me to the car.

We said our goodbyes, and I got in the car, and Angel and I headed to the station. Angel was quiet for most of the drive, but I didn't mind. I was still reeling from that conversation with Frank. We hadn't exactly said the words, but it was the closest we'd gotten to admitting our feelings.

"You okay?" Angel asked, glancing at me as we pulled up to the station.

"Yeah. I'm good." I smiled.

As we walked into the office, my phone rang. The number wasn't familiar, but something told me not to ignore it. "This is Detective Kendrick," I answered, keeping my voice even, though I was hesitant.

"I'm calling to give you a present, Detective." The male voice had a Hispanic accent to it.

I froze. "Who is this?"

He chuckled, but it was dark and humorless. "You know the answer to that. Do you not want to know the gift I have for you?"

Warily, I replied, "I won't be accepting any gifts from you unless it's you turning yourself in and confessing."

Once again, he chuckled, but then his voice turned to a growl. "I'm going to ignore your impertinence. I suggest you head down to your evidence room. El Vibora should be there as we speak. I've ordered him to destroy the evidence you've got on me. If you hurry, you'll catch him in the act, and you'll have your killer, but you won't be able to touch me. Goodbye, Detective."

"Angel! Captain! El Vibora is in the building!" I shouted.

Angel turned, and Captain Robinson came from his

office. Chaos ensued as everyone began talking, asking questions.

"He's in the evidence room," I said, hurrying to my desk and picking up the desk phone to call down to the evidence room.

The phone rang several times, but no one answered.

"Kendrick, Reyes, Hummel and Vance, go down there and don't let him get away," Robinson ordered. "Call up if you need more backup. I want this guy today!"

We rushed to the elevator, and I pressed the button over and over again, willing it to reach us faster. I knew it didn't work that way, but I didn't care. As soon as the doors opened, I pushed inside and hit the button for the basement. The ride down felt like it took hours, but it was less than a minute.

I pulled my weapon and noticed the others do the same. Rushing down the hallway, I noticed several fallen officers lying prone on the floor. "Hummel, Vance, check for survivors and then call up to the captain and get more backup."

"On it," Hummel murmured.

Angel and I continued forward, passing a couple more injured cops, through the doors into the evidence room. Two of the officers there lay on the ground, bleeding out from gunshot wounds. One who was still lucid pointed toward the aisles of evidence on the left of the room.

I nodded and mouthed, "Hang in there; help is on the way."

I passed through the barrier gate into the evidence area and moved to the end cap of the closest aisle, then peeked around the corner. It was empty, so I quietly moved to the next aisle and did the same. I could see El Vibora standing in the middle of the aisle, digging through one of the evidence boxes. I pulled back and indicated to Angel to go around to the other end, and we'd box him in.

Angel nodded, and I watched until he disappeared around the end, then counted to three. We'd done this before.

On three I moved, aiming my gun at El Vibora, and said, "LAPD, you're under arrest!"

36

HE'S A GHOST

MARCY

"**D**on't move!" I shouted, adrenaline racing through my veins. "If I even think you're going for a weapon, I will shoot you."

El Vibora dropped the hard drive he'd had in his hand into the box. He turned, his hands up, and smiled, but it was a creepy smile. His eyes held amusement, as though this was all a joke to him. "Well played, Detective. I'll come quietly."

Angel rushed from the other end of the aisle and grabbed El Vibora's hand, pulling it behind his back as I read him his Miranda rights. Once he was cuffed, Angel patted him down and found his gun as well as two syringes.

There was a bag leaning against the shelving unit, and I squatted down to look in it. It held what looked like C-4 and some wires. I glanced up at him and backed up. "See if he has a remote on him somewhere. I don't want this going off and taking out half the evidence room."

Angel patted him down again, pulling everything from his pockets, then made him lift his feet so he could take off his shoes and socks to check in them. He found the remote in his left shoe. "Got it."

A moment later, more officers poured into the room, and I said, "Everybody stay back; we've got a potential bomb!"

Angel and I started moving with El Vibora toward the end of the aisle. As we passed through the gate, the captain arrived.

"Sir, we need bomb squad," I said.

We took El Vibora, who was placid and quiet, up to booking. We'd have him in an interview room soon, after he was processed.

I was shocked that it had been so easy to take him down. In fact, I was a little freaked out about it. I kept waiting for something more to happen. For him to escape or disappear like a ghost or spirit.

I couldn't figure out if he'd gotten sloppy or if El Gato was just so stupid that he thought giving us El Vibora would make us lose interest in him.

An hour later, Robinson let us know that the bomb squad had deactivated the bomb, and the evidence on El Gato was still intact. "The problem is we're getting nothing on this guy. He's given us several names, but not one is legit. He's got no fingerprints, looks like he burned them off with acid, and facial recognition is coming up with nothing. It looks as though he's had plastic surgery to change his appearance multiple times. He was actually wearing a false nose and a wig as well."

I sighed and pursed my lips. "We knew he was a master of disguise. It's how he's gotten away with nearly every murder. I want to interview him."

"The DEA and CIA heard we had him in custody, and they want to interview him. They'll be here in a day or two. I think they want to charge him with federal crimes, which would trump ours."

"Sir, please. Let me and Angel have a crack at him."

"Okay, Kendrick, I'll set it up," he acquiesced with a nod.

A wave of relief passed over me. Handing him over to the feds didn't sit right with me. I wanted to be the one to bust him, to break him. He was responsible for numerous murders in my city, and he'd killed a cop. Granted, she was dirty, but she was still a cop who had tried to make amends in the end.

"Marce." Angel nudged me.

"What's—" I turned and realized Frank was here. "Hey." I smiled, greeting him. "Mendoza left my keys on my desk; let me grab them." I crossed the room back to my desk and picked up the set of house keys. I turned, and Frank was right behind me, so I was practically in his embrace.

He smirked, his eyes lighting up before he took a step back, leaving a respectful distance between us. "Careful, Detective," he murmured, "wouldn't want to invite rumors." His voice was husky as he teased me.

"Wouldn't we?" I smirked back as I held out my keys.

He winked and took them from me. "I heard you caught El Vibora."

Nodding, I grew a little more serious. I was, of course, elated that he was in custody, but the cost of getting him in custody had been six injured cops and two in critical condition. "We did. Thankfully."

"So no hotel, then?"

"No, I think we'll be okay at my place now, don't you?"

"El Gato may still have a hit out on you," Frank said, his voice taking on a slightly worried tone.

"Maybe, but I think I'll be okay."

"Okay." His shoulders heaved as he sighed. "I'll head over to your place and get your window taken care of. I already scheduled the appointment. Want me to grab us dinner, or do you want to go out?"

I didn't really care either way as long as I got to be with him. "You choose."

"Okay, see you back at your place." He winked again, juggled my keys in his hand and then headed out.

It was only then that I noticed Angel had disappeared.

37

PERSUADING AN ASSASSIN
MARCY

I looked around the detective pool, wondering where Angel went. Had he gone to talk to the captain in private? My mind drifted back to just before Frank arrived and the look on Angel's face as he'd nudged me to let me know Frank was here. He had looked almost hurt, maybe a little upset. Was that why he'd disappeared?

I decided to look for him and headed to the break room first, thinking maybe he'd gone there to get a snack from the vending machines and to get his head straight. I knew he was struggling with his feelings for me, but he'd been better the last day or so. At least I'd thought he was. Maybe this scare with El Vibora had brought those feelings forward again? I hoped not.

He wasn't in the break room, so I decided to check outside. Maybe he'd gone to the food trucks. In all the excitement I just now realized we hadn't eaten breakfast, and we'd missed lunch as well. It dawned on me that I was starving. On my way back through the detective pool, the captain stopped me and returned my service weapon. I was glad to have it back in my hands. After locking up my secondary weapon, I grabbed my purse and then headed outside. As I was going out, I saw Angel heading in.

"Hey, I was just looking for you," I said, smiling, hoping for the best.

"Didn't think you'd even noticed I left."

My smile fell, and I gave him an uncertain look but then decided to play it off like he was teasing. "Of course I did. Figured your stomach was giving you fits so you went to grab food." I brought my smile back up, trying to lighten things between us.

He looked at me ruefully and grinned. "You guessed it. Couldn't stand the rumbling anymore, so I grabbed a couple of burgers and tore into them."

"Just realized I was starving too, so I'm going to grab something, then you want to go over the game plan for interviewing this guy?"

"Sure, sounds good. Frank leave?" he asked, sounding genuinely curious and not at all upset, so maybe I was worried for nothing.

"He's meeting the window guy at my house. He's going to stay with me tonight."

"That's good of him." He walked with me to the Lobsta truck and waited while I ordered. "I could see he was worried about you."

"Yeah, he was. I think that's the downside of him living and working in Santa Monica."

"There's an upside to living in Santa Monica?" Angel teased.

"You know there is. He's got the beach. Not to mention it's pretty chill over there." I smiled. "And no Jordan to make a pest of himself and break windows."

Angel chuckled. "That's true. Have you been over to the hospital to see him?"

I gave him a look. "Now why would I do that?"

Shrugging, he replied, "Well, technically, he did sort of save you from El Vibora."

"Ugh. Don't remind me. I don't want to be grateful to him. He broke two of my windows, and he hurt Katie. And yeah, I don't even like her, so what does that tell you?" I arched a brow at him while I waited for my food.

"I thought you and Katie were getting along better now that she'd left him."

"Just because she came to me for help to get away doesn't make us BFFs. I helped her the same as I would any abused wife."

"Oh come on, you know she's growing on you," he teased.

I rolled my eyes. "Not at all."

Twenty minutes later we were back on an even keel, sitting at our desks and working together like there had never been anything awkward between us. I was glad about that, it made things easier, and I didn't want to lose him as a friend. I enjoyed our friendship, and I couldn't imagine him not in my life. By the time the interview time rolled around, we were ready to go.

Angel and I walked into the interview room to see a man I didn't recognize handcuffed to the table. I glanced at the officer on the door, and he nodded. I took my seat, and Angel sat down next to me.

The man across from us was actually fairly handsome without his disguises. His dark hair was shaved close to his head, his brown eyes were bright, and he had a nice smile. If I would have passed him on the street, I'd probably think he was very nice. He didn't seem threatening at all. I supposed that was what made him so dangerous.

I clicked the recorder and said, "The time is four twenty-three p.m., commencing interview with suspect known as El Vibora, Detectives Marcy Kendrick and Angel Reyes attending."

"Please state your name for the record," Angel told the man.

He smirked. "You may call me El Vibora if it makes you happy. Or Jack Matthews, or Jose Gonzalez, or Sam White, or Nate Pierce... it does not matter."

I gritted my teeth and narrowed my eyes at him. "Are those all your aliases?"

Again he smirked. "None of them are."

"What is your actual name?" I asked.

"No comment," he replied. His eyes held amusement as though he were here for his own entertainment and not because we'd caught him red-handed.

I bit the inside of my cheek. There were times when I secretly wished I could beat the crap out of a suspect to get the information I needed, or because they were complete scum and deserved it, but of course, I didn't. It wasn't ethical, and it was illegal. It went against the oath I'd taken to uphold the law, and I always kept that in mind. Even when I went up against criminals who had no problem killing me to get away with whatever shit they were doing.

I decided to let that go, since without prints there was no way for me to actually find his true identity. El Vibora would have to do. "Very well, then we'll just continue to call you El Vibora."

"As you wish, Detective."

"You are aware that your boss, Alejandro Gómez, aka El Gato, turned you in, aren't you?"

He shrugged, but there was a twitch of his eyelid that belied his nonchalance. "That doesn't surprise me."

"I suppose he thought giving you to us would eliminate him as a suspect," Angel suggested.

El Vibora's look was bland as he said, "My boss is a fool. You still hold all the evidence you had before, linking him to each of these crimes." He stared at me and added, "El Gato has no loyalty to anyone but himself. He is upset with me for missing an assignment last night. He would not have shed a tear over my death at your hands, and probably hoped that you would kill me when you found me in the evidence room with the C-4 he wanted me to use."

"You could flip on him, give us even more. I'm sure there are things we don't have on your boss," I suggested. "You might even get to be housed in a nicer prison for helping us."

His lips twisted up in a wry smile. "Not going to offer a possible reduced sentence?"

It was my turn to smirk. "No. You've killed a lot of people, including a cop."

"Correct me if I'm wrong, but wasn't the cop dirty?"

"Be that as it may, you still killed her."

"I'm not admitting to that."

"Why not give him up?" Angel asked, sounding curious.

"You know, of all the cops I've come across, I admire the two of you. It's rare to find incorruptible cops who have actual morals."

I ignored his compliment and stared at him. "Why are you refusing to flip on him?"

He leaned back and smiled. "You shouldn't concern yourself with the matter. It will be handled."

The way he said that was like he knew something I didn't, and that had me worried. "What do you mean?"

"I'd like to go to my cell now. I'm done talking."

"But—" I started; however, Angel put a hand on my arm, stopping me with a slight shake of his head.

I huffed, my shoulders heaving. "Fine. Interview ended at four forty p.m." I clicked the end recording button and then stood.

Angel and I walked out as an officer came in to escort El Vibora to his cell. I was frustrated and a little angry that I'd gotten pretty much nothing out of him. I wasn't sure why I had expected him to talk. He'd given no indication that he would.

"There was no use badgering him, Marce, he wasn't giving us anything."

"I know that. I just have an uneasy feeling about him saying it will be handled. We need to bring Alejandro Gómez in as soon as possible. We've got more than enough, don't we?"

"Let's go through everything and talk to the captain about obtaining a warrant for his arrest."

I nodded. I felt as though we needed to hurry before whatever El Vibora was planning took place. I had that tingly feeling of anticipation running over me that had me antsy and anxious. I needed this done right now.

"Let's get on it," I said, heading back to my desk.

38

BRINGING IN THE BLACK CAT
MARCY

Angel and I had spent the rest of yesterday's shift preparing everything to get the warrant set up to bring in Alejandro Gómez for the murders of Ruby Gold, Samson Martinez, Dennis Butler, and Detective Burnett. I'd also set up a detail to keep an eye on Alejandro's movements so we'd know where he was when we were ready to execute our plan. When we had all our ducks in a row, we took it to Captain Robinson, who sent it up the chain to get our warrant signed.

Now it was just a waiting game. I was sitting at my desk, staring into space, actually thinking about Frank, when Angel said, "We got it!"

I looked up to see him rushing toward me, a wide grin on his face. "We've been approved?"

"Yep."

"For both?" I was a little shocked that the judge had signed off on it, given Gómez's status in the community as a wealthy, philanthropic businessman.

"Warrants for his arrest and for searching both his home and G & G Imports/Exports."

"Excellent." I was almost giddy.

"So how do you want to execute this?"

A slow smile spread across my lips. "As publicly as possible. I want this man outed for what he's done. I'm thinking we get the captain to order a press conference as soon as we have him in custody, so they'll all be here for the perp walk... what do you think?"

"I like it. Let me go talk to him," Angel replied, swerving away from my desk and back toward the captain's office.

While I waited, I called down to patrol and set up a detail that would go with us to acquire Mr. Gómez. I wanted at least eight units in case things went sideways, plus the search and seizure team to execute the search warrants. I also called Officers Kim and Desmond, who were part of the detail watching Gómez's movements, and checked on his location. I wanted to be ready to go when we had the all clear.

"Hey, Kim, it's Kendrick," I said. "What's your twenty?"

"Sitting outside G & G Imports/Exports in an unmarked car. Gómez is inside the warehouse."

"How many with him?"

"Counted four, but there could be more in the building."

"Okay, thanks, keep me posted if he makes a move. We'll be heading your way soon."

"Gotcha."

As I hung up, Angel returned, his grin still in place.

"We good to go?" I asked.

"Absolutely."

"I'm thinking we might need vests, just in case," I said, hesitating.

"Good idea. We don't know what kind of firepower this guy might have. Do we have a location on him?"

"His warehouse. Kim's got eyes on him."

"Great, let's go."

Within forty minutes we were at the warehouse. Angel and I moved toward the door, our guns out, with several patrol officers just behind us, ready to break in if they didn't open the door. I looked to make sure everyone was in place before knocking. "LAPD, open up!" I shouted as I pounded on the metal door.

I could hear shouting inside and people running. I nodded to patrol to get the door open, and within a minute officers poured through the door.

El Gato's men bolted toward every available exit, which included several windows. They wouldn't get away though; we had the entire warehouse surrounded. The room was full of crates, and there were tables set up with drug paraphernalia, as though they were inserting the drugs into various crates of art. We'd hit the mother lode here.

The thought that Valerie could have busted this operation years ago, had she not gone dirty, made me sad. She could have saved so many lives if she'd just done her job. If she'd just held strong and not caved when this asshole tempted her with paid-off medical bills and money. She had compromised herself and, in the end, the department with her actions. I was glad that she'd confessed and sought to redeem herself before she was murdered.

"We've got him, Valerie. Rest in peace," I murmured as I scanned the chaos that was taking place in the building.

"See him?" Angel asked, standing at my side.

Patrol was busy arresting anyone who wasn't a cop, but I'd yet to find our main target. I kept my eyes open for the head of this organization, Alejandro Gómez, aka the Black Cat. "Not yet. You?"

"Nope—" Angel started and then nudged my arm and directed my gaze toward Gómez standing in an office doorway.

I noticed him reaching for something inside his jacket, and was afraid it was a weapon. "Alejandro Gómez, you're under arrest!" I called as Angel and I rushed forward, our guns drawn. "Get your hands up!"

He stopped reaching into his jacket and raised his hands as he gave me a black look. "You've no right to arrest me. I'm a law-abiding citizen."

"Save it; this warrant says otherwise," I replied, grabbing his hand and twisting it behind his back to cuff him as I read him his rights. I turned to Angel and said, "Pat him down."

Angel moved forward and began to pat him down; in the jacket he discovered a Taurus GX4, which was semiautomatic and could have done a lot of damage. He also pulled a butterfly knife, which was illegal as well in California, from his pants pocket. Angel bagged both the gun and the knife.

Disgusted, I passed Gómez off to Angel with a push. "Get him in a car."

"You got it," Angel replied, sounding utterly pleased.

"I want my lawyers!"

"You can call them after you've been booked."

I followed Angel and Gómez, watching Angel's back to make sure no attacks came from any direction. Once we had Gómez in the patrol car, Angel and I got in ours and followed it to the precinct. I was thrilled to see the captain on the steps, giving the press a show.

As we pulled up, reporters rushed toward the cars, trying to get video proof of the Black Cat's identity. Questions were shouted at me, Angel, El Gato and even the patrol officers who were opening the door. Alejandro was yanked from the back seat and passed to me and Angel as we walked him in. Cameras flashed, and he did everything he could to hide his face.

"No use hiding now; the whole world now knows you're El Gato, Mr. Gómez."

"You have no proof," he muttered.

"Oh, but I do. Your assassin didn't destroy anything. We caught him before he set off his little C-4 bomb," I murmured.

"I don't know what you're talking about," he blustered, his face getting red.

"I'm sure you don't. You know, he was right."

"What do you mean?" Alejandro looked nervous. "Who was right?"

"El Vibora. He said you had no loyalty to your people."

His face got even redder. "He has no loyalty to me!"

I arched a brow at him. Too bad I hadn't saved that for the interview, I thought.

We got him in the building and took him to processing. It would be a little while before we could conduct our interview, but in the meantime, I was ready to celebrate.

"You seem happy," Angel said, bumping my shoulder.

I grinned. "That would be because I am."

"Should we go celebrate our victory over the infamous Black Cat with lunch?" he asked.

"I thought you'd never ask." I laughed. "Let's go."

39

KILLING THE KINGPIN
EL VIBORA

I had contingency plans in place for situations like I found myself in now. People who were loyal to me, at least loyal enough when I paid them good money. I just needed to wait until things were in place.

When I'd failed to assassinate Detective Kendrick, which I had to admit I wasn't too upset about, I'd known Alejandro would lose his shit. He'd sent me on the stupid task of destroying evidence, which I'd suspected was a setup. I wasn't wrong. Because of that, I'd made plans of my own. I'd purposely been sloppy, took my time in getting into the evidence room. It was regrettable that there had been so many officers down there, but I supposed they'd all survive. Probably some of them would get to retire with full benefits. Good for them.

I knew that Detectives Kendrick and Reyes would be going after Alejandro today, and I was just waiting to hear that he'd been arrested and locked up. That was my only reason for staying in this jail. That and I had to wait for my contact to come on shift this morning.

I sat on the cot in the cell, waiting patiently for him to arrive. There were no other inmates near me. The closest was about six cells farther down the hallway. This was on purpose, of course. My contact had arranged for me to be set apart.

There was no clock in the cell, so I wasn't sure exactly how much time had passed, but I'd had breakfast around seven, and I knew that my contact would come on shift at nine. I was fairly certain it was past that, so now it was only a matter of time.

Approximately ten minutes later, I saw him coming down the cement hallway. His shiny black shoes tapping their way toward my freedom. It was time.

The cell door swung open, and he walked in. "Cameras will be down for about an hour," Officer Davis murmured as he handed me a guard uniform and my bag of tricks. "You should have everything you need to get in and out of there."

"Where is he?" I asked, quickly changing out of the orange jumpsuit and into the guard uniform, which included a badge and a keycard I'd need to get around the jail.

"Cell block two. And here's the cell master key."

"Perfect. If everything goes well, you'll get your bonus."

"I've done everything I can for you. It's up to you now. And my mother thanks you for paying off her mortgage."

"My pleasure."

"Oh, and there's a black Ford Escape SUV parked in the lot for you. Key is in your bag."

"Thank you."

There wasn't a mirror in the cell, which I'd known would be the case, and I'd prepared for it when I packed my bag and left it for Officer Davis to pick up. Opening the bag, I pulled out a spinning makeup mirror.

"Hold this," I handed it to Davis and then reached into my bag again, getting out the blond wig and sealer. I pulled it on and affixed it with the sealer. Once that was in place, I grabbed my contact case from the bag and used the mirror to put in the blue contacts. Then I added false teeth to complete the look. I reached into a different section of my bag to get the syringe I'd mixed up just for this occasion and put it in my pocket. It was a lethal cocktail that would feel like fire running through that traitor's veins.

I didn't bother with gloves this time because wearing them now wouldn't look right since I was trying to blend in with the other guards. It didn't really matter because I couldn't leave prints behind anyway. I'd burned mine off years ago. The gloves were just a precaution and honestly a habit from back in the day before I'd found the acid that destroyed my fingerprints.

I removed the car keys from the bag, closed it up, and handed it to Officer Davis. "Take this out to the SUV, set it just under the driver door." I had another disguise in there for later, since I'd need to dump this one as soon as I got out of here.

"Yes, sir. Good luck to you." He nodded and left.

I made my way to cell block two and used the keycard and my newly acquired badge to gain entry. Cell block two was rowdy, which was good for me. I found Alejandro adorned in a bright orange jumpsuit in a cell about halfway into the block. He was lying down on the cot, trying to ignore everything going on, I assumed. He seemed uncomfortable being in here, which I greatly enjoyed. I wanted him to suffer. I wanted to see him writhe in pain as I injected him with my venomous cocktail. It was rare for me to take it upon myself to assassinate someone, but this death was well deserved.

I put the cell key in the lock and opened the cell door, then closed it behind me. Alejandro looked up, surprise on his face. I supposed he wasn't expecting a visit from any of the guards.

"What do you want?" he questioned without getting up. "Am I being taken somewhere else? Is my lawyer here yet?" He finally sat up, a look of hope on his face.

I smiled. It wasn't a pleasant one, I was sure. He didn't recognize me. "You are a disloyal piece of shit. You tried to jam me up. After everything I've done for you." I uncapped the syringe in my pocket.

Alejandro's eyes widened, and he suddenly looked scared. "What? Who... El Vibora? How did you get out of your cell? Did they let you go?"

I smirked. "It is nice to see you recognize me, amigo. And in a way, yes, I was let go. And now it's time for you to go—"

"I told you I had a weird feeling, Angel, and here we are only to find the cameras are down," a female voice carried down the cement hallway.

"Time to die," I murmured, raising the syringe.

Alejandro screamed, and then in a surprising show of strength, strength I didn't think he had, he knocked the syringe from my hand. There was no time to grab it now and get away. Making a last-minute decision, I punched Alejandro in the throat and chose to save myself rather than kill him. I got out of the cell and was locking it as Detectives Kendrick and Reyes approached.

"Hey! What are you doing?" Kendrick called. "That's our prisoner," she added.

"Sorry, had the wrong cell," I muttered and brushed past them to head to the main hallway.

"What the hell?" Reyes said.

I figured he could see Alejandro with his hands on his throat, trying to regain his voice by now.

"Get this cell open," Kendrick said. "Death is too good for you, Gómez. You deserve to spend your life behind bars, paying for what you've done!"

That gave me pause. Perhaps she was right. He did deserve everything coming to him. I quickened my pace though before they realized I wasn't a guard. It wasn't a moment too soon, either.

"Stop that guard!" Reyes shouted, but by then I had joined up with a couple other guards, and nobody knew exactly what guard he wanted stopped.

I used the confusion to duck into an unused office and pull the wig off. I kept the teeth and the contacts, just until I was out of the building. I slipped out of the office and walked out of the building as nonchalantly as I could, found the SUV and picked up my bag.

I was in my new disguise before I even left the parking lot. Now I just had to make it to the 405 and head south. I wasn't even going to stop at my apartment. There was nothing there I needed anyway. Everything I needed was in Mexico, and that was where I was heading.

At least for now.

40

MEDIA CIRCUS
MARCY

One Week Later

I was headed to the courthouse with Frank at my side. We were meeting Angel there to watch the arraignment of Alejandro Gómez and to make sure he didn't try to escape as El Vibora had, and also to make sure there wasn't a hit out on him. I hadn't put it past El Vibora to disguise himself as a court clerk or a guard so he could take El Gato out.

We weren't there in an official capacity, mainly because Police Chief Warren had dismissed my concerns over Gómez's safety. I figured it was because he actually hoped that El Vibora would come after Gómez and save the taxpayers some money with his death, and we'd somehow be able to nail El Vibora again.

So far, we had no answers about how El Vibora had managed to escape. There was a lot of scrutiny at the jail as they tried to discover who had helped him. I figured I'd be looking into that as well, when we had some downtime. As for the cops Valerie had mentioned who were working for Gómez, they were now under indictment, along with the deputy mayor. I was glad about that. Alvarez though had merely gotten suspended for leaking Valerie's corruption to the press. I figured he'd gotten off easy and probably should have been fired, but then, I wasn't in charge. I wanted every dirty cop, every dirty guard, and politician for that matter, brought to justice. Maybe that did put me in alignment with IA, but I wouldn't be changing jobs any time soon. I still loved HSS and catching serial killers, even though the killer had gotten away in this case.

"What's the matter?" Frank asked, sounding concerned.

"Just realizing that I didn't actually get the killer."

"You mean El Vibora?"

I nodded. "He's the second one who's gotten away."

Frank's brow furrowed. "Who was the first?"

"The woman who helped your brother," I admitted.

Frank was quiet for a moment. "She was an accessory, but Daniel did the killing."

I could hear the pain in his voice speaking about his brother. I laid a hand on his forearm. "No matter what he did, it's not on you. You're a good man, Frank. He made his choices, and they were his, not yours."

He smiled, but his eyes were sad. "I know. It just still stings that I didn't see it and couldn't stop him before he broke. I have a lot of regrets when it comes to him, but I don't blame myself for his choices. It's taken me a bit to get there, but I'm healing. You're helping." He drew me close and kissed my forehead.

"Come on, we're supposed to meet Angel at the doors."

We walked into the courthouse amid the media circus. It

took the reporters half a minute to recognize me, and they began shouting questions.

"Detective Kendrick! How does it feel to take down one of the largest drug kingpins in California history?" Bill Meeks called out.

I hadn't seen him in a while, but I wasn't surprised to find him here now. "No comment."

"Are you going to be switching over to Vice, Detective?" he asked.

This one I could answer easily. I looked right at him and smiled. "Absolutely not. HSS is my home, and I won't be leaving."

"Good to know," he replied.

I caught sight of Angel and waved. "There he is," I murmured to Frank, and we met up with Angel.

Angel smiled at Frank and held out his hand. "Hey, glad you could make it. The more eyes we have on the scene, the better, considering we couldn't get an official detail."

"No problem. Captain Stafford has been allowing me to take my vacation days as I've needed them, but I'm taking a whole week off starting today."

I glanced at him and grinned. "You didn't tell me that."

"Surprise." He chuckled. "Now that Mom is back home and doing better, maybe you and I could take a little weekend trip."

"Sounds like fun. Where to?" I replied. Captain Robinson owed me a full weekend off, and I was going to take it. I needed a break.

"Weekend in Vegas?"

"That sounds amazing," I agreed.

"It does," Angel added, sounding thoughtful.

"Why don't you and Callie join us?" Frank said, looking at Angel.

"I'll talk to her, see if she can get coverage for her salon." I was glad that he seemed to have gotten over his jealousy and we could be easy together again. "Great. I hope she can go."

"Hey, before we go in, I thought you might want to know," Angel started.

"What is it?"

"Jordan's been admitted to Shine View. He confessed that he was the one who followed you to Santa Monica."

"He was driving a van though. Where'd he get it?"

"Rented it."

I sighed. I was glad Jordan was getting help, but that didn't excuse his behavior. "Is he being charged for what he did to me?"

"Yes, once he finishes his time at Shine View, he'll be remanded to county lock up to serve six months for the vandalism and harassment."

"How do you know this? Why wasn't I contacted?" I asked, feeling as though I'd been pushed to the side because I was the victim.

"I was with Robinson when he got word about it. I told him I'd pass it on to you."

I supposed that made sense, so I let my anger about it go. "Okay, well, thanks."

"Shall we?" Frank gestured toward the doors.

"Let's go," I agreed.

We entered the courtroom and found seats on the prosecutor's side. Gómez was brought in, a chain between his ankles, his hands cuffed, and was seated in a chair at the defense table. His lawyers had done everything to get the evidence thrown out, but hadn't been successful, so he was sitting there looking mulish and sullen. It made my heart giddy to see it.

Surprisingly, he accepted the plea deal that the DA offered, so he pled guilty in front of the judge, and his sentence was read out. He'd be in jail for a long time, at a minimum-security prison—which I personally thought was a bad idea—and he'd have a chance for parole in twenty years.

Leaving the courthouse, Frank and I headed for the cemetery. I had flowers I wanted to lay on Valerie's grave. Because of her status in the department, she hadn't been given a big fanfare funeral, which I thought was kind of crappy considering the big productions that had been given to her colleagues months ago. However, I think her mother had been grateful for the small affair. There had only been about a hundred people in attendance and even fewer at the graveside service.

Frank and I walked hand in hand as we approached the woman in the wheelchair at Valerie's grave.

"Mrs. Burnett," I murmured. "How are you holding up?"

She sniffled and gave me a watery smile. "No parent should have to bury their child. It's not natural."

"I know." I let go of Frank's hand and took hers as I laid the bouquet of flowers on Valerie's grave.

"Thank you for those." She glanced at the colorful bouquet. "Valerie would have loved them."

I thought so too when I saw them. They seemed like something she'd choose. "If you ever need anything, you can call me," I offered, handing her my card.

She took the card and looked up at me. "I wish Valerie

had gotten to know you sooner. Maybe you could have saved her from herself."

I doubted that, but I didn't say anything to contradict her. "Take care, Mrs. Burnett." I patted her shoulder, and then, grabbing Frank's hand again, we headed to the car together.

As we drove home, I couldn't stop my thoughts from drifting to the killer who'd gotten away. "Think El Vibora will come after me again?"

Frank grew quiet and thoughtful for a moment. "I don't think so. From what you told me, he didn't want to come after you in the first place."

I nodded. He made a great point. I wasn't sure how I felt about that. On one hand, I wanted to capture him, on the other, I really hoped I never saw him again. He wasn't like any other killer I'd ever chased. For me, I preferred the psycho killers to the cold hitmen who looked at murder as a job. Not that I wanted either to be operating in Los Angeles. However, the psychos nearly always made mistakes, and I was able to catch them.

"I hope you're right," I said eventually.

"Come on, let's go have a fun night. The Angels are playing, and we're meeting Stephen and Yazmine at your place for dinner. We can celebrate you getting that black cat put behind bars." He reached over and took my hand, squeezing it. "I'm proud of you, TT. You and Angel managed to get a lot of drugs off the streets."

I glanced at him and grinned. "Yeah, we did."

THANK YOU FOR READING

Did you enjoy reading *Kill Count*? Please consider leaving a review on Amazon. Your review will help other readers to discover the novel.

ABOUT THE AUTHOR

Theo Baxter has followed in the footsteps of his brother, best-selling suspense author Cole Baxter. He enjoys the twists and turns that readers encounter in his stories.

ALSO BY THEO BAXTER

Psychological Thrillers

The Widow's Secret

The Stepfather

Vanished

It's Your Turn Now

The Scorned Wife

Not My Mother

The Lake House

The Honey Trap

If Only You Knew

The Dream Home

The Detective Marcy Kendrick Thriller Series

Skin Deep - Book #1

Blood Line - Book #2

Dark Duty - Book #3

Kill Count - Book #4

Pay Back - Book #5

Printed in Great Britain
by Amazon